HOPEWELL

C.J. PETIT

D1444394

TABLE OF CONTENTS

HOPEWELL..1
PROLOGUE 4
CHAPTER 1 15
CHAPTER 2 30
CHAPTER 3 44
CHAPTER 4 94
CHAPTER 5 126
CHAPTER 6 145
CHAPTER 7 161
CHAPTER 8 184
CHAPTER 9 217
CHAPTER 10 285
EPILOGUE 312

PROLOGUE

May 17, 1874
Ninety-Four Miles Southwest of Fort Worth, Texas

"Earl, how are we gonna get him outta there?" Ed asked as he stared across the canyon.

"It's not gonna to be easy, that's for sure," replied Earl as he sat with his back against their granite protector.

Ed Crandall leaned back against the rock face, pushed his Stetson back on his head and wiped the sweat from his brow with his shirt sleeve.

"Got any ideas?" Ed asked.

Earl took a peek around the boulder's edge and answered, "It'd take a stick of dynamite to blow him out of that hole."

"As we don't have any around, that ain't helping much, and I'm getting kinda tired of sitting around here just waiting for him to come out."

Earl said, "I'm going to take another look."

Earl scrambled up the canyon wall behind them then quickly hunkered down behind a smaller boulder that had been their observation post and stared at Jack's rock formation one more time. The rocks created a three-walled fort with the only opening to the back. But the natural walls were tall enough to hide his horses, so climbing over the top would be difficult at best. They could wait until dark and try to sneak up on him except for the minor problem of water. They didn't have enough to last the day – not in this Texas heat.

They had cornered Crazy Jack Carson three hours ago and thought they had him, but he had run into this canyon and had holed up behind that massive set of rocks that would have been a geologist's dream but became the lawmen's nightmare.

They couldn't get a good angle on him and he'd shift positions after firing so they couldn't even shoot at his smoke. They had tried ricocheting a few rounds into his hideaway, but the bullets always deflected upward and then the ringing echo of their bouncing lead would soon be followed by Crazy Jack's cackling laugh as a reminder of their futility.

To make matters worse, he could keep them at bay and wait them out because he had a pack horse and they didn't.

They didn't know how much ammunition he had left, but Earl knew their Winchesters were going to be starving pretty soon if they didn't come up with some way of getting him out of those rocks. Ed was right. It was a tough nut to crack.

But the thought of using dynamite kept bouncing around in his head. Dynamite would be the answer, but even if they had a stick, getting it across ninety yards of open ground would be hard to do.

He levered in a fresh cartridge into his Winchester '73, fired uselessly at Jack's barricade to keep his head down and quickly slid back down to their big rock.

Once safely behind their shield, Earl said, "You know, Ed, I think I may have a way to get him out of there."

"How do you figure on doing that?"

"We scare him out."

Ed looked at his partner, snickered and shook his head.

"They don't call him Crazy Jack for nothing. He ain't afraid of anything short of a rattlesnake in his pants, and I ain't sure of that. How can you scare him out?"

"Just watch."

Earl stood behind their own rock fortress, stepped back to their patiently waiting horses, reached into his saddlebag, then rummaged for a few seconds before he pulled out some pigging strings. He searched the ground for a few minutes, then duck walked twenty feet back toward the mouth of the canyon, picked up an old branch and quickly made his way back,

After he was safely hidden from Crazy Jack's bullets, he dropped to his heels, took out his knife and set to working on the branch.

Ed watched curiously as he cut a ten-inch-long section out of the old branch, then began sanding the ends on the nearby boulder, until each was flat, making a nine-inch-long rod. Then he stripped off the bark, leaving an off-white tube, stuck the tip of the knife into one end and began drilling until he made a half-inch deep hole. He picked up one of the pigging strings and rammed it into the end and held it up for Ed's inspection.

Finally, Ed could see where Earl was going but asked, "You don't think he'll fall for that, do you? I mean it kinda looks like a stick of dynamite, but that pigging string doesn't look much like fuse cord."

"He's not going to notice the color. Now, hand me your powder flask."

Ed looked at his partner curiously but picked up his nearby powder flask and handed it to Earl.

Earl spread some powder on a flat rock, put some more into the hole at the end of the stick and handed the flask back to Ed. Then he took his canteen and splashed a small amount of their scarce water on the rock and ran the pigging string through the water, letting the leather absorb the moisture.

As he worked, he explained what he was doing by saying, "That'll slow down the burn. I don't want it just flashing."

Then he rolled the pigging string around in the gunpowder until it was covered before shaking it to remove most of the powder.

"I need to see how long this fuse burns. I don't want it going too fast," Earl said as he pulled out a match.

Ed watched closely as Earl set the end on fire, then counted the seconds mentally as the cord popped and smoked like a real fuse.

When it finally fizzled out, Earl leaned back and smiled at Ed.

"Twelve seconds. That's perfect. Now, I'll make another one and wedge it into the stick as tight as it can be by making a knot on the end. Hopefully, we'll spook old Crazy Jack into running out of there and then we'll have him. Now I'm going to throw this thing after warning him that it's coming, so you need to be ready to draw down with your Winchester."

"Earl, how the hell are you gonna get that thing into his hole? That's almost a hundred yards of open ground," Ed asked incredulously.

"I'm going to give him an open shot at me when I get onto the open ground. I'll make it hard on him by zigzagging but he'll be firing as fast as he can, but I want you to give me some cover. When he sees what I've got in my hand, he might be panicking a bit, too. At least I hope so."

Ed shook his head, "Earl, that's crazy. You can't do it."

"Sure, I can, Ed. Now, I'm going to leave my rifle here along with my hat. When I rush out of here, I'll go around the right side of the rocks. As soon as he fires his first shot, you take your Winchester around the left side. He won't pay any attention to you because he'll be focused on me and my smoking stick. Get in position and lob a few rounds in there to keep him occupied, then when he makes his break, shoot him."

Ed tried once more to talk Earl out of this insane idea, but Earl was convinced they could pull it off and Ed knew better than to argue with his fellow U.S. Deputy Marshal when he was set in a plan.

"Ready, Ed?" Earl asked.

Ed sighed and replied, "As ready as I'll ever be."

Earl removed his hat, laid it beside his Winchester, then snuck to the right edge of their covering rock.

Once he was ready to sprint, he shouted, "Jack, this is U.S. Deputy Marshal Earl Crawford! Now, you'd better come out of there soon. We've been playing it easy so far, but my partner, old Ed here, is getting on my nerves. So, he told me to use the heavy stuff. I didn't want to bring you back in pieces, so I'm asking you really nice to come out with your hands up."

Crazy Jack's reply was as expected when he yelled, "You two tin badges are lyin' bastards. You ain't got nothin' that can get me outta here. You may as well get on your horses and leave."

Earl shouted back, "That's too bad, Jack. I reckoned you were smarter than that. I guess you really are crazy after all. Don't say you weren't warned. But when this is over, we're not going to bother finding all of your pieces. We'll let the critters enjoy the feast."

Earl readied himself, struck a match against the rock and touched it to the end of his pigging string fuse, then sprinted around the outside of the rock and veered to his left toward Crazy Jack's sanctuary.

Crazy Jack was still contemplating what the marshal meant by 'heavy stuff' and was stunned when he saw Earl bolt from behind their rocks and run straight at him with something in his hand…and it was smoking! *Dynamite! That bastard was going to blow him up!*

He quickly levered in a new round into his Winchester, hurriedly took aim at the rapidly approaching lawman and fired, knowing he had just seconds to kill him.

Earl ran straight for just three or four seconds before planting his right foot and cutting to his left quickly.

Jack was panicking as he began to rapidly fire at the onrushing deputy marshal, trying not to imagine his body in chunks scattered around the canyon as suppertime for vultures, coyotes and all sorts of other slimy creatures.

Earl knew it only took two seconds to cycle the Winchester's lever and reacquire the target, so every other step, he'd alter his course as he began to pull back the smoking stick, preparing to make his throw.

Ed made his break around the left side of the rocks after Jack's first shot, cut right and jogged down to the flat ground, took a knee fifty yards from Jack's fortress, then began to fire at his smoke to throw off Jack's aim. Neither of them would ever realize that it was just a waste of ammunition as Jack was barely able to see his own front sight as his fear dominated his mind.

Earl was only twenty yards out and knew that his fake fuse was nearing the end of its life, so he lobbed the stick into the air and hit the dirt, sending a final message to Crazy Jack that a massive explosion was imminent. The smoking contrail arced through the air toward the space occupied by Crazy Jack and Earl hoped he hadn't left it short.

Jack saw the smoke and flying stick of dynamite and then watched as Earl threw himself to the ground, his hands covering his head He spent just a fraction of a second staring at Death as it reached its smoking zenith before it began its descent to where he was standing.

"Jesus Christ Almighty!" he screamed before he raced out of the back of what had just been his refuge but was now a death trap. He didn't care about his horses as he shot past them, pivoted around the left side, and raced away hoping that the rock walls that had protected him from the lawmen's .44s would still keep him safe.

As he passed the last rock formation, he spotted the other marshal aiming his Winchester at him and swore as he huffed to catch his breath. Jack's rifle was already cocked, so he shuddered to a stop, swung it toward Ed and hurriedly fired as he prepared to hit the dirt, sending his rushed shot eight feet to Ed's left.

Ed saw him bring up his rifle and fired just as Crazy Jack pulled his trigger. Ed's shot didn't miss, as his .44 caliber missile punched into the left side of Jack's chest, ripped through his lung after pulverizing a rib, then, because of the angle Jack had been standing, shattered his sixth thoracic vertebrae. Jack tumbled awkwardly to the ground and rolled for another fifteen feet before coming to a dust-clouded stop. His right foot twitched twice, but they were the last movements Crazy Jack would ever make. He died wondering why the dynamite hadn't gone off.

Earl popped to his feet, jogged over to Jack's body and gave him a hard kick to make sure he was dead, and wasn't surprised by the lack of a response.

As his partner approached, Earl said, "Good shooting, Ed," then reached down and picked up Jack's pistol, which had fallen from his holster.

"Damn! This hombre was well-armed. This is the first one of the new Colts that I've seen. Do you remember whose turn it is?" he asked as he turned and grinned at Ed.

Ed was miffed but didn't want to show it, as he replied, "Well, I ain't got any of the cartridges for that gun anyway. Is it a .45?"

Earl popped out a cartridge and replied, "Nope, it's a .44 rimfire like all those Winchester cartridges that fit my Russian."

Ed's face could no longer mask his jealousy and displeasure.

While Ed sulked, a still grinning Earl undid Jack's gunbelt and noticed that he had been wearing a two-gun rig. It irritated him because he hadn't noticed it and that information wasn't on the wanted posters or in his briefing for the mission, but it didn't matter now.

"Wait a minute, Ed. You may have some luck, yet. Let's head back to his little fortress and see if he lost his second pistol somewhere."

Ed perked up as they began to backtrack toward Jack's hiding hole. and he was almost giddy when they found a second Colt model 1873 lying on the ground.

"So, do you get both pistols, seeing as how it's your turn?" Ed asked, pretending that Earl had a choice.

"Nah. Our rule was one gun per bad guy. That's yours. Did you want this fancy rig, too? I don't need it."

"Sure. I might start wearing two and keep my New Army as a backup."

Earl tossed him the empty belt and watched a grinning Ed catch it in mid-air.

Earl then said, "You'd look kind of goofy with two different pistols. You take both of these Colts. I'm kind of partial to Smith & Wesson anyway."

Ed replied, "Are you sure, Earl? I mean, it's your turn."

"I'm good. Now, let's bury Jack and then head back to the office."

Before burying the outlaw, they went through his pockets to see if he had anything to identify him. He didn't, and only had a total of $27.40 on him. They split up the cash and put him in the ground, then rounded up his horses and searched his saddlebags. There was nothing worthwhile inside; just some food and other basics along with four boxes of .44 cartridges. They quickly went through the panniers on the pack horse and found even more ammunition.

Earl looked over at Ed and said, "We were worse off than we thought we were. He could have held us off until the second coming."

Ed then picked up the white stick with its ragged and burnt end and asked, "Mind if I keep this so the boys won't think we're lying? Did you even hear that pop when your fuse hit the end and touched off the powder you packed in there?"

"I was busy, Ed, and I reckon you were, too."

Ed slid the stick into his pants pocket, then replied, "That crazy plan of yours worked pretty good, Earl."

Earl laughed, then said, "Maybe I should be called Crazy Earl. I hear that that name is available now."

Ed was laughing as the two lawmen headed for Crazy Jack's horses to start their way back to the office.

They finally left the canyon and headed back to Ft. Worth, trailing Jack's horses. It would be a three-day ride, but this was Texas, so it seemed like three-day rides were the minimum.

They had just buried Jack in the canyon as the nearest town was a day's ride away and by then, all sorts of bad things would happen to the body in the heat. Besides, whether he was buried by some mortician in a town where nobody knew him wasn't any different than being buried in the place where he died.

CHAPTER 1

South of Hopewell in East Texas

Claude was angry. It seemed to Eva that Claude was always angry about something, and this was a bad one as he stood in front of her with fire in his eyes and closed fists.

"Damn it, woman! I told you we was goin'. So, you get off your butt and get dressed proper!"

"Claude, I don't feel very good. You hurt me too much last night. I've been feeling bad all day now."

"You're just making excuses, Eva. Me and Elmer aim to have a good time tonight and you're comin' with me. He wants me to bring you along. I don't know why, but he seems to like you. Are you comin' or are you gonna' force me to make you?"

Eva slowly stood. She was hurting and it was much worse than usual. When Claude had returned from drinking with his friends last night, he had wanted her to provide wifely duties, but she was already cramping and told him so. He didn't care and hit her hard to the stomach to 'help her with her female problems' and then he had her anyway. She hadn't gotten better all day, functioning at a minimum just to keep from being hurt again. If David hadn't helped her with her chores, then he would probably have been worse.

After the first few months of their marriage, he'd revealed his true nature and she wished that she had never married Claude.

The only good thing to come out of the marriage was their six-year-old son, David, who was the focus of her life. Now she had to face Claude again, and he was getting angrier, but her pain was already too powerful to ignore. She'd try to convince him that she couldn't go but was certain that her words would be futile.

She was practically begging as she said, "Claude, I just can't. I've been trying all day to feel better, but it's just getting worse. Maybe I'll be all right in an hour or so."

"That ain't good enough, Eva. You're comin'! Even if I have to drag you there!"

Before Eva could make another plea, Claude grabbed her by the left arm and yanked hard as she was trying to turn away. She felt the arm snap and was horrified to see a bone sticking out of her forearm with blood pouring out of the wound and screamed when the pain slammed into her brain.

David had been hiding in his room, listening to the heated exchange between his beloved mama and his hated father. He wished he was bigger, so he could protect her, but when she screamed, his size didn't matter, and he raced from his room.

Claude suddenly realized that he had gone too far and this is one injury she couldn't disguise, so he released Eva to the floor, her blonde hair cascading around her head as she crumpled to the wooden planks.

But once she was free of his grasp, her loud sobs and crying made Claude even angrier.

"Shut up, Eva! It ain't so bad. Just shut up!" he shouted as he stood over her, staring at her pained face so he didn't have to see the ugly fractured arm.

But even Claude knew it was bad and was on the verge of panicking when he heard feet running toward him, looked to his right and saw David rushing at him.

As he charged his father, he shouted, "Leave mama alone!"

David then launched himself at his father, struck his father's side, then staggered back two feet and began to pummel his big stomach with his small fists.

Claude reached down and grabbed David by the belt with his right hand and screamed, "You little son of a bitch! I'm tired of your whining, too!"

Claude then grabbed the back of David's collar with his left hand, swung him once in a circle and released him, sending him flying face first toward the fireplace. David didn't have time to protect himself, and with both arms flailing wildly, his forehead smashed into the rock face. He was already dead as his small body crumpled onto the stones along the base.

Despite her own pain, Eva was devastated watching what had just happened to her son.

She screamed, "You, bastard!", and kicked Claude from the floor, her small foot catching Claude's ankle.

Claude whipped his eyes from his murdered son's body to glare at his angry, wounded wife and unloosed his own kick which struck home on the side of her chest. As she screamed in more pain, he stomped his heel onto her stomach and was satisfied when she finally stopped screaming and just moaned and began to cry.

He knew that he had just murdered his son and probably his wife, so he took the coward's way out. He turned, ran across the room, threw open the door and raced from the house.

After exiting the small house, he turned right toward the main ranch house. His father was in town, so only his mother was home, which would make it easier. After just fifteen seconds, he flew across the porch, yanked open the door and saw his mother sitting in a chair darning a pair of socks.

She looked up at her older son and saw wildness in his eyes. *What had he done?*

She had grown to despise her older son. He had always been a bully and had only gotten worse since he married Eva. His sudden, panicking appearance made her instantly suspect that it had something to do with Eva or her grandson.

"What do you want, Claude?" she asked tersely.

"I need something," he hastily replied as he quickly walked past her and down the hallway.

She set aside her darning, stood, and trailed him into the kitchen, wondering what he had done.

Claude reached up to the top shelf, then took down and opened the pickle jar containing their household money. He quickly emptied the jar and rammed the money into his pocket.

"Claude, you put that money back right now! It's not yours!" his mother shouted as she pointed at him.

Claude turned and snarled, "It is now. Now, go back to your knittin' or whatever."

Lydia approached Claude, believing that even he wouldn't dare hit his own mother. But even she didn't understand just how far down he had sunk into depravity. If she had known what he had done in the small house she and her husband had built for him and Eva, she never would have even followed him.

"What have you done, Claude? What did you do to Eva? How bad did you hurt her this time?" she snapped as she glared at him.

Without answering and with no hesitation, Claude shoved his mother out of the way to make his escape.

Lydia's was shocked as she stumbled aside, then struck her head against the table and slumped to the floor, unconscious.

Claude looked down at his mother without pity or remorse and wasn't even sure if she was alive but didn't even bother to check. He just left her on the floor as he hurriedly exited the kitchen.

He ran back outside and into the barn, where he saddled his horse and mounted quickly, still in a state of panic. Once in the saddle, he raced from the barn, down the access road and turned north toward Hopewell, leaving dust, pain and death in his wake.

As he galloped down the dirt road, he spotted a rider coming his way and recognized her immediately, even before he thundered past. She was Eva's younger sister, Jessie, and he momentarily thought of stopping her from going to the ranch, but she had passed him before he came to a decision.

He glanced back at his sister-in-law and realized that they soon would know what he had done, and he had to get away. He wasn't worried about the law in Hopewell, it was the other county sheriffs that worried him, but he'd find refuge with his friends.

————

Jessie had watched Claude as he shot past her. Even in the waning light, she could see the maniacal look in his eyes. She moved her horse, Butter, to a faster pace, fearing for her sister. Claude had hurt her and their son so often that it had almost become routine, which, in itself, was horrible. Yet everyone seemed to accept that it was just his right as a husband and father to discipline his wife and son.

Five minutes later, before her mare had even come to a complete stop, she was stepping down in front of the small house. She just dropped her reins as she felt her worries building, trotted up to the door and without knocking, threw the door open and ran inside.

It only took a few seconds of witnessing the carnage to understand why Claude had run. She rushed over to where the unmoving David was lying and felt his chest. There was nothing she could do for her small nephew, so she turned to help her sister, who was laying on the floor with blood still leaking from her broken arm, but Jessie could see her chest moving, so she was still alive.

Jessie was breathing rapidly to hold back the combination of anger and stark horror from what her eyes were telling her. When she saw her sister's bone sticking out of her left arm, she felt her stomach lurch and had to swallow to avoid vomiting. She could see dirt on her dress in the shape of a boot before she knelt by her sister and put her hand under Eva's head. She had to control her emotions and couldn't afford to cry or let anger take her. She needed to help Eva.

She leaned closer to Eva's pained face and asked, "Eva! It's Jessie. Can you hear me?"

Eva's eyes opened slowly and saw an angelic face with big, compassionate eyes looking at her. For just a brief moment, she thought that she might have died, and she was looking into the eyes of an angel and hearing her holy voice whispering to her and welcoming her into heaven. Her vision quickly evaporated as the omni-present pain put a lie to the hope.

After her eyes focused and she recognized that those compassionate eyes belonged to her sister, Eva spoke weakly, her breathing already shallow.

"Jessie, it was Claude. He was mad at me because I was too sick to go to the social. He…he began hitting me and then when David tried to stop him, he…picked him up by his britches and, oh, my God! He threw him into the fireplace! He just threw him as if he was trash! Jessie, he killed David! He killed my son! And now…now, he killed me, too."

Eva's growing anger had demanded too much of her waning strength, so as tears continued to slide down the sides of her face, she coughed lightly, and bubbles of blood formed on her lips as she struggled to tell her sister her last words.

She managed a weak, bloody smile as her glazed eyes stared into her sister's before she wheezed, "I never...tell Earl…"

Then Eva simply died with her blue eyes still open as if she was looking for an answer to why this had happened to her and her son.

Eva's pain was gone, but Jessie's was not. She began to sob and shake, her tears falling on her dead sister's face even as a deep rage focused on Claude filled her, momentarily pushing aside her grief.

There was a sound at the door and Jessie jerked her head around, momentarily terrified, thinking that Claude had returned, but it was Lydia, Claude's mother.

Lydia surveyed the room with wide eyes and with a disbelieving face as she slowly approached Jessie.

"My God!" she exclaimed, *"What has that monster done?"*

Jessie wiped her tears away and looked up at Eva's mother-in-law.

She replied with a shaking voice, "He murdered Eva and David, Mrs. Crawford. I need to get my parents to come and help, so I'll go and get them and have them bring a wagon. We'll notify the sheriff, so he can send a posse after Claude. He can't get away with this. He just can't! He should burn in hell for this!"

"Yes, he cannot escape justice any longer," said Lydia, her eyes still staring at the carnage left by her older son, then whispered, "I should have stopped him a long time ago."

———

Three days and some odd hours later the two lawmen rode to the offices of the United States Marshal service in Fort Worth. As they usually looked after an extended chase, each of them was dusty and in dire need of a shave and a bath.

Ed and Earl stepped down and swung their horses' reins around the hitching rail, then took a few seconds to try to remove most of the dust from their clothes by swatting their britches and shirts with their hats, but it didn't help much. Ed opened the door and they entered the large outer office.

Andy Kenworth had the desk and said, "Welcome back, gentlemen. So, how did your little romp through central Texas go?"

"We got him, Andy. When you read the report, you'll be impressed how we did it, too," Ed replied.

Andy looked at Earl and said, "Before you get started writing, Earl, the boss wants to see you."

Earl nodded and stepped into the back office where U.S. Marshal Dan Grant awaited. Earl wasn't a small man by any standards, standing just over six feet and a solid two hundred pounds, but when he stood next to Dan, he looked like a dwarf. Dan was five inches taller and outweighed him by fifty pounds. Earl, and just about all the other Deputy U.S. Marshals liked and respected Dan.

"Afternoon, boss," said Earl as he entered the office.

"Welcome back, Earl," answered Dan, standing from behind the desk to shake Earl's hand.

"C'mon in and close the door, will ya?"

As he closed the door, Earl knew that closing the door was never good news and was already trying to think of what he might have screwed up badly enough to come to the boss's attention.

"Have a seat, Earl."

Now Earl was concerned with both a closed door *and* a sit-down session and wondered if he'd broken one of the bigger rules. The gun recovery deal was the norm, as was the removal of any small amounts of cash. The big cash and the horses came back for proper disposal.

Earl sat down and noticed a concerned look on the marshal's face.

"Earl, I'm gonna give it to you straight. I have a tough assignment for you, but if you don't want it, I'll understand. Even the Rangers passed on this one because they think the perpetrator might be headed to the Indian Nations."

"What have you got, Dan?"

Dan blew out his breath, then asked, "You're from Hopewell, aren't you, Earl?"

"Thereabouts. I grew up just outside of town on the family ranch, the Star C. Why?"

"There's been a double murder there. A man killed his wife and son then went on the run."

"There's a bastard that deserves a rope."

"The problem for me is that the murderer is named Claude Crawford. Am I wrong in thinking that he's a relative?"

Earl didn't answer for a few seconds. Finally, he slowly replied, "He's my brother, Dan."

"So, I gather then that you'd rather me send someone else?"

Earl already had his answer immediately after hearing that it had been Claude who had committed the heinous crime. He knew his victims and it was even more difficult to hold back his seething anger. But he managed to remain calm as he shook his head.

"Absolutely not. I'm the best choice to head over there. I know all his haunts and saddle buddies. I'll bring him in one way or the other."

Dan was mildly surprised and quite impressed that Earl hadn't shown much emotion and that he'd agreed to go on the assignment.

So, he asked, "Earl, maybe you'd better fill me in on why you're so anxious to take this job. I didn't even know you had a brother."

Earl sighed before replying, "I don't talk about him because I know what he is and it's more than just embarrassing. My brother and I were the only living children of our parents. They ran the ranch and we were pretty much the only cowhands on the place once we hit ten years old. It wasn't a big outfit.

"Claude was always a bully when we were growing up and not just to me, either. He'd beat any kid in school that he knew he could lick. He stopped trying to take me on when I was twelve and he was fourteen. He was taller than I was, but I was a lot beefier. That's because he didn't like working. So, I'll take the assignment, Dan. It'll take some time, though. I have a feeling that he's gonna run hard."

"Okay, Earl. You go ahead to Hopewell and start from there. Do you want someone to come with you?"

Earl thought about it for a moment before answering, "No, I don't think so. I don't want to leave you undermanned for that length of time. I'll keep you abreast of what's going on with telegrams. I'll need a packhorse for this one, though."

"That's fine, Earl. See Andy. And Earl, take these."

Dan reached in his drawer and pulled out three sheets of paper and two temporary U.S. Deputy Marshal badges.

"These John Doe warrants should help. If you need any local help, give them one of these."

Earl nodded and shook Dan's hand, then rose, left Dan's office and told Andy he'd need a pack horse loaded with the essentials for a long trip. Then he went into the same office that Ed was using to write his report, sat across from him and took a paper and pencil.

Ed stopped writing, sat back, and asked, "So, what little nasty thing did you do to get the boss riled?"

Earl looked at his partner and said, "I need to head back to East Texas to my hometown. It seems my brother killed his wife and son then lit out. I'm gonna either find him and arrest him, or I'm going to send him to hell."

Ed was startled but quickly asked, "Am I coming along, Earl?"

"No, Ed, if I know my brother, this is going to be a long one. I'm going alone."

"Wasn't he married to a girl you visited when you were a kid?"

"He was, and she was one of his victims. Her name was Eva and she was a really pretty girl. I never could figure out why she married Claude, though."

Ed nodded, then they finished writing their reports in silence.

Despite starting well after Ed, Earl finished first. Ed tended to add too many details that Dan didn't even care about.

Earl set his report aside, stood, then shook Ed's hand and said, "I'll see you when I get back, partner. Stay alive till then."

It was their standard gallows humor sendoff, and this time, Ed hoped that it would hold true.

Earl left the office, mounted his horse and rode back to the boarding house where he stayed. They had a small barn in back that he boarded Target when he was in town. The horse received that tag for two reasons: he had a six-inch white spot on his otherwise black hide, and Earl had been riding the horse when he had been shot for the first time since the war.

He went to his room and began packing. He didn't have a lot, just a few spare shirts, two pairs of pants, some underpants and socks, and a spare vest. Earl always wore a vest, so he could keep his badge on his shirt and show it quickly if he needed to, and at the same time, not advertise it to any potential adversaries.

He put his clothes in a spare set of saddlebags and left them on his bed, then went to the washroom at the end of the hallway. There was no point in taking a bath because he'd be dirty again tomorrow when he headed out, but he washed up as best he could and shaved. He was reasonably presentable when he went back downstairs.

He found the landlady in the kitchen, preparing dinner. There were six guests staying at the house, four were single men and there was one young couple.

"Mrs. Albertson, could I talk to you for a minute?"

"Sure, Earl, come on in," she replied as she wiped her hands on her apron.

Mrs. Albertson was a widow about forty years old. She was still pleasant to the eyes and had a kind soul.

"Mrs. Albertson, I'll be leaving tomorrow on an extended job. I may be gone for up to a month, so I'll be checking out. I hope this doesn't leave you in the lurch."

"Nothing bad, I hope."

Earl took a breath, then replied, "Well, to be honest, it is. It seems that my older brother killed his wife and son. I'm going to track him down and bring him to justice, one way or the other."

Mrs. Albertson was stunned, and it showed on her face.

"That must have been a terrible shock for you."

"No, ma'am, it really wasn't. My brother was always a bully. He was mean to almost everyone, including me. I just wish he hadn't taken it out on his own innocent family. It was only terrible for them."

"Well, you're a good man, Earl. Maybe the best I've ever known, and that includes my late husband."

"Thank you, ma'am. Coming from you that's high praise."

"Now, you're paid up through the end of the month, so I'll owe you some money."

"Not at all, Mrs. Albertson. You've been such a gracious host and friend, and I'd rather you keep the money, Go buy yourself something that you may have wanted but put off."

She smiled at Earl, stepped forward, hugged him and kissed him on his cheek.

"God bless you, Earl Crawford. You stay safe."

"I will. I'll still be here for dinner, but I'll be sneaking out very early in the morning, so don't be worried if you hear someone out there in the wee hours."

"I won't worry."

Earl tipped his hat and returned to his room, stretched out on his bed and reminisced about those last few years in Hopewell. He still had a clear vision of Eva, and that was twelve years ago when he had gone off to war. She was just sixteen then and he hadn't seen her since.

Once he discovered that she had married Claude, he hadn't returned to Hopewell, not once. He would send and receive letters from his mother, and knew he was being unfair to his parents by staying away. It wasn't their fault. He would have visited them if Claude and Eva weren't living in a small house that his parents had built on the ranch. It still burned him that Claude, even though he had Eva and a son to support, still did almost nothing around the ranch. But now he'd be going back; going back for the worst possible reason – to kill his brother.

CHAPTER 2

In the dark hours before the predawn, Earl quietly stepped down the stairs, opened the front door and gently closed it behind him. He was a little less stealthy after he had crossed the porch and stepped down the stairs.

Twenty minutes later, he was riding Target into the streets then trotted the horse to the marshal's office's official livery stable, where he found a fully loaded pack horse with a note attached to the saddle.

He pulled it off and had to move toward the street to get enough light to be able to read the handwriting, which he quickly recognized.

Left you a present in the pack. Thought you might need some extra help. Ed

Earl smiled. Good old Ed. He guessed what it was but would wait to find out if he was right when he stopped for the night.

By dawn, he had left Fort Worth far behind and was following the regular stage route. He'd have to pass through Dallas around noon, but after that, it was pretty easy riding. As he rode in the warming Texas sun, he started thinking about where Claude would be headed. It seemed as if he always had some other thuggish friends around him, so Earl wondered if he was running with a gang or just a loose bunch. He doubted if Claude was alone because it would require too much work, and Claude hated work.

Two hours later, Earl was almost drifting when he glanced to the right of the road maybe two hundred yards ahead and instantly became alert. *Now, what was that jasper doing?* He stopped Target for a few seconds, then pulled both horses off the road and walked them behind some old oaks where he sat and simply watched.

The man he had spotted was on a flat rock about thirty feet to the south of the road. He had a repeater, either a Henry or a Winchester '66 lying on the rock next to him, identifying the gun by its brass side plate.

Earl doubted if he was alone, so he scanned the opposite side of the road, and it took a few minutes to spot his accomplice, but he found him. The other man was behind a larger rock formation and Earl only spotted him because one of the two horses he was holding must have gotten antsy and had bolted a few feet from behind the rock before he could regain control. He wondered why the second man wasn't acting as a lookout for eastbound traffic. He was so buried in those rocks that he couldn't see a thing while his partner was concentrating so hard looking east that they wouldn't have spotted a column of infantry marching down the road from the west. They must be either really confident or really stupid, but probably both.

Normally, this had all the earmarks of a stage holdup, but the morning stage had already passed Earl on the way to Fort Worth an hour earlier. They were waiting for someone else. Earl pulled his Winchester and cocked the hammer, then he released the pack horse from Target and tied the loaded gelding to one of the oak's branches.

Ten minutes later, the man on the rock whistled, so Earl walked Target from the oaks and kept his eyes on the two men as he quietly approached.

31

In the distance, he heard the sound of multiple hooves and the crack of a whip. Suddenly the one on the rock stood and pointed his repeater down the road as a fancy black carriage with a coat of arms painted on the door approached.

The man yelled, "Hold it, right there!"

The carriage driver brought the vehicle to a rapid halt and threw up his hands. The carriage was still rocking as the second man rounded the rocks and trotted over to the carriage. Earl noticed that he hadn't been holding two horses, he had three. Now Earl understood their criminal intentions. It was a kidnapping, not a robbery.

The man with the rifle jumped down from the rock and walked around to join his partner, surprisingly not even noticing the approaching lawman on his big horse.

As the two men began moving toward the carriage, Earl knew he had to move fast now. Once they opened the carriage doors, it was likely there would be a hostage situation. He was about fifty yards away now, and it was time to announce his presence as he raised his Winchester level and aimed at the man with the rifle.

He shouted, "Put your hands in the air! I'm U.S. Deputy Marshal Earl Crawford. Drop your weapons and lie on the ground face down. If you fail to comply, I will shoot you, and if I see a weapon pointing in my direction, the one pointing it will die!"

Both suspected kidnappers whirled to see Earl's Winchester pointed in their direction. Even though they knew it could only be aimed at one of them, each believed it was meant for him. They had to decide which option to take, and only a moment to make it.

They chose poorly. The armed man made the first move and began to swing his weapon to face the new threat.

As soon as Earl saw that muzzle move in his direction he pulled his trigger. His Winchester bucked, spewed a large cloud of gunsmoke and a twelve-hundred foot per minute, .44 caliber bullet. The spinning bullet crossed the hundred and thirty feet of space in a small fraction of a second, drilling into the upper center part of his chest and severing several vital arteries.

As he dropped to the ground, the horse holder, who had drawn and cocked his pistol, turned and brought it to bear on Earl. But he was in a rush and never let his sights settle before firing and sending his shot wide by more than three feet. Earl's second shot hit his throat and exited the back of his neck. The bullet still had enough power to ricochet off the rock behind him and chip off a chunk of granite, as the man wavered, grabbed for his neck that was spraying blood across the Texas ground, then fell to his knees before collapsing face first into the dirt.

Earl then walked Target toward the carriage as he slid the Winchester back into its scabbard and drew his pistol. When he and his horse reached the carriage, Earl stepped down, never taking his eyes from the two on the ground. He had to be sure that they were dead and not playing possum. There were too many stories of criminals pretending to be dead and then miraculously resurrecting themselves in time to plug some careless lawman. Earl was never careless.

He walked to each man and kicked him once – hard. They weren't playing possum or any other marsupial. He hadn't even looked at the carriage driver yet, but finally turned and looked up to the carriage as he slid his pistol into its holster and pulled the trigger loop in place without thinking. The driver was Mexican and well-dressed.

"Amigo, do you know either of these men?"

"No, senor. They are both strangers."

Earl stepped over to the three horses, moved them off the road then returned and slid the first body, the one with his neck half ripped away, off the road as well. As he was moving the second, the carriage door finally opened, and a very beautiful young woman stepped down. She was dark-skinned but didn't have brown eyes, a combination which Earl had never seen before.

He dropped the shooter's body next to the horse holder's body, then looked back at her.

"Ma'am," he asked, "do you know either of these men?"

She looked down at them, shook her head and replied, "I have no idea."

"Why would they try to kidnap you?"

She looked at him with a startled expression and asked, "*Kidnap me? How do you know that?*"

"Ma'am, they were waiting here with three horses. There were only two of them, so they must have wanted to take someone with them. I'm assuming that would be you."

She shuddered and replied, "I don't understand. Why would someone want to kidnap me?"

"Judging by your carriage, I'd say that they intended to hold you for ransom."

Her eyes grew wide as she put her hand over her mouth and for a second, Earl thought she might faint, but he was too far away to do any good if she did.

"Ma'am, if I may ask, what's your name and where are you from?"

She regained her composure and replied, "I'm sorry. My name is Teresa O'Toole and I live in Dallas. I was going to Fort Worth to visit a friend."

"Well, Miss O'Toole, unless it's urgent for you to go to Fort Worth, I'd suggest that we all head back to Dallas. I'll bring these two along and I'll follow your carriage. You'll have to drive more slowly though."

"Yes, I think that's safer. I never did thank you. What's your name?" she asked as she threw a dazzling smile his way.

Earl was very impressed with Miss O'Toole, smiled and answered, "I'm United States Deputy Marshal Earl Crawford, miss. If you'll give me a few minutes, I'm going to load these two on their horses. You may as well wait in your carriage."

"Would you like my driver to help?"

"No, ma'am. I've done this a few times before."

Earl noticed that she didn't return to her carriage, but just stood and watched as he positioned a horse and threw the first body over a horse then tied it down with leather strings.

Teresa was impressed with the display of strength to do such a task so effortlessly, but it was far from the only thing about the deputy marshal that had impressed her. He was a tall, handsome man that exuded masculinity. The fact that he'd probably saved her from something that might have been worse than kidnapping only added to her fascination.

After the second body was lashed down, Earl went through their pockets looking for identification, but finding nothing. He hooked both dead men's holsters and pistols around their horses' saddle horns and put the repeater, which turned out to be a Henry, into its scabbard. It was in good condition, and he would see if he could appropriate it after talking to the county sheriff. Neither handgun was a cartridge weapon, so Earl didn't care what happened to them.

When he had finished, Teresa O'Toole smiled at him again, then with an appropriate amount of grace, entered her carriage. The driver turned the carriage back toward Dallas and began a slow drive following Earl.

Earl was sure that Miss O'Toole was aware of the impact that her smiles would have on men, and he had been no different in that respect. But with Earl, it was different because he had been getting them all his life. Even when he was a youngster, his good looks would have all the girls trying to get his attention. He almost wished someone would break his nose to stop the looks that also had the added negative of making the other boys dislike him. He had more caps set for him in the past ten years than he could count. After the Eva debacle, he wanted to be sure the next one was the right one, and it surely wasn't going to be Miss O'Toole. He had a job to do.

They arrived in Dallas just after noon and Earl directed them to the county sheriff's office. He knew the sheriff and thought he was a good man. When they reached the office, Earl told the driver to wait outside for a few minutes while he cleared their departure with the sheriff.

Earl stepped down and tied Target to the hitching post along with the pack horse and the other three, two with bodies draped over their saddles.

He went inside the office, saw an older deputy at the desk and asked, "Is the sheriff in?"

"And who are you?" he asked in a surprisingly rude tone.

Before he could answer, the sheriff walked into the front office from the back hall and said, "Frank, you had better mind your manners. That's U.S. Deputy Marshal Earl Crawford you're talking down to. I've warned you about your attitude before, so knock it off."

The deputy didn't seem to care what his boss thought, as the condescending look stayed plastered on his face.

The sheriff glared at his deputy for a couple of seconds before turning to his fellow lawman and asking, "What can I do for you, Earl?"

"I've got a couple of bodies outside, Jim. It looked like they were set to kidnap a young lady named Teresa O'Toole. She's outside in her carriage if you need to talk to her or her driver. I was riding in from the west and saw what they were planning to do, and those idiots never even saw me, even as they were ready to close their trap. I rode up behind them as they halted the carriage, had them under my Winchester, shouted my identification and told them to drop their weapons. Even though I had them dead to rights, they decided to see if they could get lucky, but it didn't work out very well for them. The lady and the driver say they're both unknown to them. Want to go outside?"

"Hell, yes! Let's go."

The two lawmen walked outside, and the sheriff stepped to the carriage, looked inside with a big smile and asked, "Are you all right, Miss O'Toole?"

She smiled back and replied, "Yes, I'm fine, Sheriff, thanks to that exceptional law officer."

"He is that, ma'am. I know where I can find you when we investigate this incident. You can go along now."

Before the carriage left, Teresa swung the carriage door wide, looked and found Earl standing behind the sheriff, and with one more display of feminine charm, smiled broadly and said, "Thank you once again, Marshal Crawford. You are an amazing man and I'd be happy to entertain you at my home."

Earl smiled and tipped his hat as he replied, "I've got an assignment, ma'am, but I appreciate the offer."

She then gave him one last impressive smile before saying loudly, "We can go home now, Pedro," then she waved, closed the door and the carriage began to roll across the cobbled roadway.

After watching the carriage leave, the sheriff turned and looked at Earl as he asked, "You gonna pursue that, Earl? She's the most eligible woman in the county, if not all of Texas. She's got lots of money, too."

"No, Jim. I'm off on a mission. Besides, she's not my type."

"Not your type! *What are you, dead or just blind*?"

Earl laughed, and answered, "No, just choosy. Say, Jim, do you care if I abscond with that boy's rifle? It's a nice Henry. I don't have one of those yet."

"Sure, go ahead. The county will probably just chuck it out anyway. How about the pistols?"

"You can have them and their horses and tack, too. They're not cartridge guns and that's my preference after buying my Smith & Wesson. Well, I've got to be going, Jim. Do you need me to write a report?"

"No, I'll get the information from Miss O'Toole. She may not be your type, but I won't mind spending some time with her."

Earl snatched the Henry, smiled at the sheriff and said, "Good luck with that, Jim. I'm off to East Texas."

"Hope it's an easy job, Earl."

Earl was mounting his gelding as he said, "I don't think so, Jim. I've got to track down my older brother. He murdered his wife and son."

The startled sheriff had no response as Earl turned Target and his pack horse eastward and rode away.

———

Earl finally made camp about fifteen miles east of Dallas after finding a perfect location near a good-sized pond surrounded by oak and cottonwoods. He stripped Target and let him drink as he unloaded the pack horse. Once that was done, he let the pack horse join Target, who was now munching on a nearby patch of thick grass. He hobbled both horses and returned to his camp to start a fire. He was far enough off the road and hidden by the trees, so he wasn't concerned about anyone sneaking up on him. Besides, he had an early warning device in Target. He'd been with Earl long enough to know that acting as a lookout was part of his job.

After he started his fire, he was going to go to his pack to start cooking dinner, when he remembered Ed's note. It was easy to spot the extraneous parcel and pulled the leather pouch from the tie down and opened the bag. He was not surprised to find the Colt Peacemakers and the two-gun rig inside along with another note.

Figured you could use these more than me. Ed

Earl smiled. He and Ed got along well. They'd been on over fifteen missions together that had ranged over a good part of Texas. He'd saved Ed's life once, or so Ed had claimed. They'd been chasing three outlaws who knocked off a small bank in Plano and absconded with a total of less than two hundred dollars. For that small amount of cash, they had killed a clerk and a woman customer.

When they finally caught up with them, the three decided to make a fight of it, knowing that they faced the noose. Earl had taken out the first two, and Ed was about to put the third one down, but his old Colt had misfired. The remaining bad man smiled and was ready to fire at Ed before Ed could get cock his hammer to bring the next cylinder into line. But before the outlaw could fire, Earl had put a round through the killer's right arm and into his chest. He never pulled the trigger on Ed, who was so mad at the pistol, that he threw it into a small ravine. Earl let him have all three of the miscreants' weapons to make up for the unfaithful Colt.

After returning the two nice Colts and their gunbelt to the pack, he checked out the Henry. It was the first repeater that really worked and was the father of the Winchester '66 known as the Yellowboy because it shared the Henry's brass sides. Earl wasn't sure that he would use the older rifle because it did have some serious design flaws and wasn't as good as his Winchester '73, but he just wanted it because he didn't have one. It was in excellent condition, and didn't need a cleaning, so he put his newest acquisition aside and made himself a boring dinner. After he had cleaned up, he removed his boots and crawled into his bedroll.

———

Claude sat at a table with Charlie, Weasel, Joe and Elmer. The last couple of days, they had been living off Claude's take from his parents' house, but now, they needed to get some more cash. They had been in White Oak for a day now, had scoped out the bank and knew it would be an easy snatch-and-grab.

"Where will we go after the job?" Weasel asked.

Charlie replied, "We head east for a while until we make sure we don't have a posse on our tail. As long as we don't shoot nobody, they usually don't care. They'll send a telegram whining about it, but they ain't gonna risk their hides for a few hundred bucks."

"Who's gonna stay outside and watch?"

"Claude and Elmer. They haven't been seen in White Oak before, so this should be an easy job."

They planned on hitting the bank in the afternoon, just before closing.

———

Earl was up with the sun, which was normal when he was on the road. After he ate a breakfast that was even more boring than his dinner the night before, he loaded the pack horse and then saddled Target. He was on the road, riding into the sun and thought he'd make Quitman before nightfall, then have a nice meal at the café before passing through and camping outside of the town. It was close enough to Hopewell that he should be able to make it to the ranch by early afternoon tomorrow.

As it turned out, he arrived in Quitman before five o'clock, and enjoyed that full dinner at a nice eatery before heading out. He knew that if he had wanted to, he could have made Hopewell before midnight, but he just pressed on until he found a decent location and set up his camp.

After stripping the animals, he sat back and thought about tomorrow and his arrival in Hopewell. He would see his parents for the first time in almost twelve years, and he'd have to interview them as witnesses more than his parents, and then he'd have to see the Mitchells as well as part of his investigation.

He would be in town no more than a day or two and by then Claude would have been gone for about a week or so, depending on when the crime had been committed. He hadn't gotten the details from Dan before he left because he thought he'd rather have it from those on the scene anyway.

He wondered what their reaction would be to his return. *Would they be angry or cold? Would his mother welcome him back like the prodigal son?* He suspected that she would be very happy to see him, but he was most curious about how his father would react when they met.

When they had been growing up, his father had taken Claude's defense after every altercation simply because he was the firstborn. He was his real son and Earl had been that other boy. It had hurt at times and if it hadn't been for his mother's support, then he wasn't sure how he would have turned out.

He hoped that his father had finally recognized the evil that lurked in his older son and realize that it was his second son who had grown into the man who could make a father proud.

He also was curious about the welcome he'd receive from the Mitchells. When he had been visiting with Eva, they had treated him like the son they never had, but his brother had murdered their daughter and their grandson. *Would they put some of the blame on him being Claude's brother?*

These questions were running through his mind as he drifted off to sleep.

CHAPTER 3

Earl intentionally took his time making breakfast and readying the horses to depart. He washed and shaved in a nearby stream, making sure he looked every bit the part of a United States Deputy Marshal. When he was done, he felt ready to face his parents, but was more nervous than he had ever been when he had been facing down desperate outlaws.

He mounted Target and began the final leg of his journey to the place of his childhood.

Three hours later, he was approaching from the south, so he would find his parents' ranch before the town, then he'd go and see the local law after he had met his parents and the Mitchells.

There was little or no traffic on the road as he saw the ranch entrance road on his left about a mile distant. A few minutes later, he took a deep breath and turned Target down the access road toward the ranch house.

Why should he feel such dread for simply meeting his parents? Was it even dread, or was it guilt?

As he approached the house, he noticed some activity off to the right and saw his mother pumping water into the trough. He could see how hard the years had been on her and felt remorse creeping into his thoughts knowing that he should have been here to help her.

Lydia heard the clopping of two horses approaching from the access road, then turned and put her hand over her eyes to block out the Texas sun as Earl waved. She was unsure who he might be for a few seconds until recognition began to sink in. Suddenly, the hand that was shading her eyes dropped to cover her mouth and she began to run as tears rolled down her face.

Earl stopped the horses and stepped down to welcome his mother into his arms. Her eyes were pouring tears as she threw herself into his arms and sobbed as her son held her tightly with her feet four inches above the ground.

"Hello, Mama," he said.

"Earl! Earl! You've come home at last!"

"Yes, Mama. I'm here."

Finally, he set her down. She was such a small woman when he had gone, and now, she was past fifty and he didn't know if he had gotten even bigger or she had grown smaller. Maybe he was remembering her through a ten-year-old's eyes, but she was still his mama.

She wiped the tears from her face and eyes and stepped back.

"Let me look at you. You've gotten so big! But you're still the most handsome boy in Texas," she said as she smiled warmly.

"And you're the prettiest lady I've ever seen, Mama," he replied.

Lydia blushed at the compliment, knowing it was heartfelt.

"Are you here to visit or are you here as a marshal?" she asked.

"Both, Mama. I've been assigned this case because I know the area and I know the people involved."

She sighed and said, "Then you know what Claude did."

"Yes, but not the details."

"You'd get those best from Jessie."

"Jessie Mitchell?" Earl asked in surprise, "Is she still here? I thought she was married and moved out. I don't even know her new name."

"Yes, she's here. She's the one who found Eva and little David," she said as she began to cry again.

"I'm sorry she had to find that, Mama, but I'll need to talk to her today. Where is she staying?"

"She's back at her parents' farm again. I'll let her tell you why."

Earl nodded, thinking that it must be an interesting story, then asked, "Where's Papa?"

"He's in town talking to the sheriff," she answered, then paused before adding, "He's trying to convince the sheriff that some stranger killed Eva and David."

"Is there any doubt, Mama? The word I received from my office was that it was pretty definite."

"No, there was no doubt whatsoever. Jessie found Eva still alive and told her what had happened before she died. All of us knew, but your father refused to accept it. But you know how he was all the time you two were growing up. Nothing bad that your brother did was ever Claude's fault. I wondered then and I am sure now, that his fawning over Claude allowed him to become the lazy monster that he has become. I feel like such a poor mother for allowing that."

Earl's hope that his father had recognized his older brother's true nature dissolved as he looked at his mother's sad eyes, finding it hard to believe that she could even think of blaming herself.

"Mama, that's nonsense. You were a perfect mother. Claude just didn't listen to you at all because papa would always give him an easier path. Now, look at me, Mama. I'm your son, too. I'm a lawman and I protect the innocent. I believe in right and wrong, and never lie, cheat or steal. Those are all the values I got from you, Mama."

Lydia smiled at her son and asked, "Do you have a wife, Earl? You never said in your letters."

"No, Mama. No wife and no girlfriends, either. It's not like I haven't had chances. Women seem to like me, but they just don't match up to my favorite girl, and I'm talking to her right now. One day, Mama, I'll find her. I'm always looking for the one, and you'll be the first to know when I find her. Okay?"

Lydia Crawford smiled at her son; now her only son as far as she was concerned. But if the truth were told, Earl had always been her only son while Claude had belonged almost exclusively to her husband.

"Bring your horses into the barn and come into the house and let me fix you something to eat. I know how poorly you must eat when you go out on one of your trips."

He complied with her request and as she returned to the house, he led the two animals into the barn and stripped them of their gear. Then he brushed them down and led them to the trough to sate their thirst before releasing them to the corral and returning to the house.

His mother had almost finished making his large lunch and had a steak frying with onions on the cookstove as she warmed some biscuits and had some beans in a pot on the side hot plate.

"Mama, that's a feast. I haven't eaten that much in years."

"Then it's time you had something good in your stomach. I don't know how you can keep that much weight without eating good food," she said.

Earl sat down and asked, "So, how are you feeling, Mama?"

"I'm doing well, especially for an old lady."

"Mama, you'll never grow old. You have too much life in your soul."

"Earl, are you still going to stay away now?" she asked plaintively.

"No, Mama. I'll come and visit as often as I can. I just couldn't face seeing Claude with Eva. I know that I had only visited with Eva for a year or so, but I just couldn't put up with his gloating."

"I know," she said as she placed the finished steak and beans on a plate with two of her biscuits then set them in front of him with some coffee before she sat down at his left side with her own cup of coffee.

"Earl, I know that you thought you were in love with Eva, but she was never really right for you."

"I know, Mama. After I received your letter telling me that they had married, I went through a whole range of moods. I was angry and disappointed at the same time. More than anything, I suppose, I was confused because it made no sense that she had chosen Claude when Eva could have had any man in the county. But after a while, I realized it was probably just an infatuation on my part at least. I got over it, but it was still too difficult for me to see her with Claude. Now I can come home to see you more often, Mama."

"Then at least something good has come from this tragedy," his mother said before she took a sip of her coffee.

As Earl was finishing his steak, which was cooked rare, as he always liked it, the front door slammed, and his father walked into the house.

As he walked down the short hallway to the kitchen, he asked, "Lydia, why are you cooking…"

Then he stopped in his tracks as he spotted Earl at the table.

"Hello, Papa," smiled Earl, as he stood and offered his hand.

His father just stood there, looking at him not even taking Earl's hand.

Instead, he glared at Earl and harshly asked, "What are you doing here after all these years? I'll bet I know. You're going to join the lynch mob that's hunting down Claude. You think that badge you're wearing will give you a license to kill him. Don't you, boy?"

Earl was stunned by his father's reaction which was even worse than he had anticipated. He stared down at his father who was a good five inches shorter than him. His hair had gone mostly gray, and his face had become tired, but there was fire in his eyes, as there always had been when he defended Claude.

"No, Father, my badge doesn't give me a license to kill. In fact, it's just the opposite. It gives other men a reason to kill me just because I wear it. I have to wait until someone has either shot at me or is aiming at me before I can even reach for a gun.

"So, don't use that as an excuse for hating me. I'm just her to do my job. I've been assigned the mission to investigate the murders and, if Claude was responsible, to bring him to trial. If he resists and tries to kill me, then yes, I will defend myself, but only then. I'm good at what I do, and I've brought in a higher percentage of my targets in alive than anyone else in the United States Marshal Service. So, you'll have to pick another reason to defend Claude this time."

He didn't wait for a response, but turned to his mother, and said, "Mama, I'll be back later today after I go to talk to the Mitchells and the sheriff. I also need to send a telegram to my boss."

He took one long stride, bent over, kissed his mother on the forehead, then snatched his black Stetson from the peg on the wall and turned to his father, saying, "We'll continue this conversation when I return, Father."

His father watched him leave, and Earl noted that the fire in his eyes had been dampened somewhat. His mother had noted the change in her husband as well and wondered if it had as much to do with Earl's words themselves as his change from the familiar 'Papa' to the more formal 'Father'. She'd see what impact it had when Earl returned. She knew her husband wouldn't talk to her about it, as he would never speak with her when the subject was Claude, but she was so very proud of the man her only real son had become.

Earl stepped out to the barn to saddle Target. He wasn't angry because he had expected some form of denial or verbal defense of Claude, but it still hurt to have his father fail to recognize that his older son wasn't the one he should respect. His father's violent refusal to believe the obvious fact that his older son had murdered his daughter-in-law and his only grandson did shock him. *How can any sane person deny reality?*

Ten minutes later, he'd finished saddling Target but left his packs on the barn floor as he led his gelding out of the barn.

He mounted and as he turned to ride down the access road, he glanced back toward the house and spotted his mother standing on the porch and waving. He smiled as he waved back to her then soon left the ranch and turned north to head for the Mitchells to see Jessie.

He wondered what Jessie looked like now. When he'd been visiting Eva, she was a pre-teen girl, but now she was a full-grown woman who had been married. He remembered the pleasant hours he'd spent with her while waiting for Eva. There were many times that he had actually been disappointed when Eva finally bounced out of the house which would end the chats with Jessie.

He hoped that her cheerful demeanor hadn't changed over the years but suspected that her marriage might have darkened her personality. His mother's reply when he'd asked why she had returned to live on the family farm had seemed to indicate that it wasn't just a matter of widowhood. He'd find out soon enough.

The Mitchell farm was less than two miles down the road and was within sight of the town itself, which made transport of their primary crop easier. They raised vegetables for resale as well, but the money crop was the hundreds of acres of hay. They had contracts with surrounding ranches, the town livery and others. Each season, they would have a team of reapers come in and scythe the acres of hay and tie them into bundles. The livery and ranchers would come and pick up their orders, but they would store about a third of the crop for later delivery.

Ten minutes after leaving his family ranch, Earl turned into the Mitchell farm. There was no long entrance road and the house was easily reached from the road as Earl pulled up to the hitching rail in less than a minute.

He stepped down and walked up to the front door, removed his hat and knocked. It was less than a minute later before the door opened, and Ada Mitchell, Eva and Jessie's mother stood before him.

She looked at him curiously for a few seconds before tilting her head and asking, "Earl, is that you?"

Earl smiled and replied, "Yes, ma'am. How are you, Mrs. Mitchell?"

"I'm all right, I guess. Come in, won't you?"

Earl nodded and stepped inside, finding the main room to be almost exactly as he remembered it from twelve years earlier when he was visiting with Eva. There were a few changes in some of the furniture and decorations, but it was basically the same.

"Can I get you something to drink, Earl?" she asked.

"No, I'm fine."

"You look as handsome as ever, Earl. You've gotten bigger, too, I see."

"Just finished growing, ma'am," he said as he smiled.

"Have a seat. Tom is in town and Jessie is out tending the vegetable patch on the east side. So, what brings you back, although I have a good notion."

"As you've probably already guessed, I've been assigned the mission to find and arrest Claude. I need to do some preliminary investigation first, so I really need to talk to Jessie. My mother told me that she was first on the scene and I need to see her as soon as possible."

"I'm glad it's you who's going after him, Earl. I don't think any of us would feel that justice would had been served if some unknown lawman did what needs to be done. Do you think you can shoot him if he puts up a fight?"

"Without a doubt in my mind, Mrs. Mitchell. I've known what he was longer than anyone else, even my parents. But even I was stunned to hear what he did because it was well beyond what I thought he was capable of doing. I can only imagine that it's because he's gotten meaner over the years. My boss told me to take as long as I need to get the job done, and I'll find him. I also promise you this, Mrs. Mitchell, I will succeed. He will pay the ultimate penalty for what he did to Eva and your grandson."

Ada's eyes filled with tears as she simply replied, "Thank you, Earl."

Earl was uncomfortable seeing her tears, despite knowing that she'd probably shed many more in the days before his arrival.

He said, "Well, I'll go find Jessie, Mrs. Mitchell. We'll probably come back here to talk and maybe your husband will be back by then."

"He went to talk to the sheriff because your father had been talking to him about looking for a different killer."

"My mother told me what he'd been doing and even I found it difficult to believe. My father and I had a short and unpleasant talk before I came here, but I don't think he'll change his mind. He's spent his entire life defending Claude, but now it doesn't matter what he believes, I'm going to find him."

He then stood, walked back out onto the porch, then stepped onto the hard dirt, leaving Target at the rail as he began walking east to the vegetable garden. It was a good four hundred yards from the house as the location had been chosen because of its proximity to a natural spring. He began his long, smooth strides toward the garden already spotting Jessie in the distance.

Jessie was weeding the rows and had worked up a sweat as she pounded the hoe into the hard ground. Water just seemed to be sucked down into the dirt no matter how much she poured, so the ground was almost always difficult to break up. Those damned weeds seemed to like it anyway. She was wearing her old bib overalls and a beat-up, wide-brimmed hat and looked every bit the picture of a farmer's daughter.

Jessie set down her hoe, leaned back to stretch her back, and saw a man walking towards her three hundred yards away.

"My God!" she thought, "It's him! Earl's come back and here I am looking like a scarecrow!"

Jessie Mitchell recognized Earl's unique walk even though she hadn't seen him for a dozen years. She was only twelve when he went off to war and had been in love with him since she was ten. At first, it was because he was the best-looking boy in the school by far. All the girls had a crush on Earl at one time or another, but for Jessie, it was much deeper than that.

She had the opportunity to spend more time with him when he started visiting her older sister two years later. She found out that unlike other handsome boys, Earl didn't seem to care about his pleasing appearance. To him it was just there, like his light brown hair or his blue eyes. He didn't strut or brag, and in fact, he was quite shy. When he began spending even more time at the house, she found even more to admire. He was honest and kind and ever so thoughtful. They had spent long times together just talking as he waited for Eva to dress and primp. All those times when she was just a twelve-year-old girl talking and laughing with Earl had only deepened her feelings for him, even knowing that he would be marrying her older sister.

She knew that he was comfortable talking to her and after he had gone off to fight in that war, she vowed to wait for his return because Eva had already moved on.

She was sixteen by then and blossoming into a handsome young woman in her own right, but not as spectacularly pretty as Eva. She had several boys who wanted to call on her, but she turned them all down, waiting for Earl to come home. Even after he didn't return to Hopewell after the war because of Eva's decision to marry Claude, she held out. Her parents were exasperated, and she finally gave in and married when she was twenty-one, but it was always Earl. And now, he was only a hundred yards away and moving in that cat-like grace that marked him so well.

He smiled and waved when he saw her looking his way, so she returned both the wave and the smile as she melted inside.

Then she heard him shout, "Jessie!" and she melted a little more.

Finally, he was in front of her as his blue eyes sparkled at her. If anything, he was even more handsome than she remembered and that made her attire seem almost clownish. She knew that she must appear to be almost a tramp with her light coating of dirt and sweat. Her hair was tied with a strip of leather, which at least kept it from looking as frightful as the rest of her.

Earl had been studying Jessie since he'd spotted her, and the closer he was, the more impressed with the incredible changes she'd undergone in the past twelve years, but he wasn't surprised. She had been a pretty twelve-year-old when he'd left, and she was still pretty, just more so as her face had rounded out as nicely as the rest of her.

Earl smiled at her and asked, "How are you, Jessie? I thought I was going to say that I could hardly recognize you, but that wouldn't be true. I would always recognize you, Jessie, because of your eyes. I've never known anyone with eyes like yours, but you've certainly grown up."

Jessie was surprised at what he'd said because no one had ever commented on her eyes being different. She was doubly surprised that Earl had noticed them at all as no one looked at her when Eva was around. But still, those few words sent a flush of heat rushing through her.

"I'm so happy to see you, Earl," she said as she stepped to him and gave him a hug.

She had waited twelve years for this moment and was gratified that Earl hugged her back.

After she begrudgingly let him go, she asked, "Are you back permanently now?"

"No, I'm afraid not. I'm on a mission to find Claude and arrest him."

"I'm sorry it took this to bring you back, Earl. I've missed you."

"I heard that you were a married woman, Jessie. Has that changed?"

"Yes. I'll talk about it later. I'm sure you want to talk about that night."

"I'd rather talk about anything else with you, Jessie, but I do have to learn what you saw and heard. Then I need to go to talk to the sheriff and send a telegram to my boss. So, why don't we start walking back to the house and you can tell me as we go."

Jessie brushed off some grass and dirt from her overall's knees before she and Earl began walking.

"This all happened eight days ago. I was supposed to go and mind David that evening so Eva and Claude could go to some social in town. You would have liked David, Earl. He was a thoughtful, smart little boy and I loved spending time with him. He reminded me of you in many ways. Anyway, as I was riding to the house, I saw Claude go racing past me without even acknowledging me. His horse was already lathered, and it was only a mile to the ranch. His eyes were wild, and I was scared just seeing him like that, so I nudged Butter to a canter to put some distance between us. I arrived at the ranch just a few minutes later and rode directly to the house that your parents had built for them rather than stopping in and seeing your mother as I usually do."

She blew out her breath and continued, saying, "I didn't even bother looping the reins before I jumped from Butter, ran to the door, and just went in without knocking. I was absolutely terrified of what I was going to find before I threw that door open, and it was worse than I had imagined, Earl. Can I sit down, please?"

"Of course, Jessie."

Jessie exhaled sharply, sat on the ground and hugged her knees before taking a deep breath.

Earl sat in front of her, knowing how hard it would be for her to relive what must have been unimaginable for her to have discovered.

"I opened the door and it was totally quiet inside. There was no sound at all. I walked in and saw David first. He was lying on his back near the fireplace his face was smashed and bloody and there was blood on the fireplace off to the right. I ran to David and felt his chest, but I knew it didn't matter. I began to cry as I looked at Eva and saw that she was still breathing. I went to her, knelt by her side and put my hand under her head."

Jessie began to sob quietly so Earl slid beside her and put his arm around her shoulder before Jessie wiped her eyes and continued.

"I slowly lifted her head and told her I was here. She was a mess. You could see boot marks on her dress where she had been kicked and she even had a whole boot print on the front.

Her left arm had been broken and you could see the bone sticking out. She opened her eyes and she said…she said."

Jessie took another deep breath and Earl could feel her shaking.

"She said, 'Jessie, it was Claude. He was mad at me because I was too sick to go to the social. He began hitting me and then when David tried to stop him. He picked him up by his britches and threw him into the fireplace. Jessie, he killed David! And now, he killed me, too.' Those words will never leave me, Earl. They'll haunt me until the day I die."

When she finished speaking, she was shaking much worse and Earl knew there was nothing he could do, so he just let her pour out her grief as she finished.

"Then she said, 'I never', then she paused. Her last words were, 'tell Earl', then she just died."

She paused, looked at him and said, "Earl, Eva and I didn't get along as well as two sisters should, but she was still my sister. Seeing her like that made me want to kill Claude. Poor David died trying to protect his mother and paid the price for his love. What kind of monster would do this?"

She was shuddering as Earl felt enormous compassion for Jessie, knowing that her eyes had witnessed something that was usually reserved for war, but it had been her sister and nephew who had been violently killed.

Earl wished he could do more for her, but replied, "Jessie, as I just told your mother, Claude was always a bully and a thug, but even I was surprised to hear he had reached this level of depravity. I'll find the bastard, Jessie. Depend on it."

Her shaking subsided somewhat as she finally realized that he was holding her, and said, "I know, Earl. Thank you."

He removed his arm from her shoulder and asked, "Can you walk now?"

She nodded and replied, "I think so. I'm sorry for blubbering like that. I'm usually a lot stronger."

"I understand, Jessie. I don't think I could have done any better having seen that kind of horror inflicted on someone I loved."

Jessie knew he had spent four years in the war and then another eight years in law enforcement, first as a deputy sheriff and then as a U.S. Deputy Marshal and had probably seen worse. But she was deeply grateful for his sincere understanding.

She walked back to the ranch house hanging onto his arm, and when they entered, Earl was glad to see that Tom Mitchell had returned and was sitting in the main room with his wife, awaiting their return from the garden.

Tom saw his daughter's red eyes and knew that she had just finished telling Earl the events of that fateful day, so he stood and offered his hand to Earl, who took it.

Earl was relieved that both Mitchells didn't seem to attach any blame or guilt to him for what his brother had done.

"Well, Earl," he said, "can I assume you won't be taking your father's viewpoint on this?"

"No, sir. I never took his viewpoint on anything that involved Claude. When I was first notified of the assignment, I was given the option to turn it down, which we never get. But I knew that it was most likely true, and I would be the best choice to find him because I knew Claude better than anyone else. I knew he was a bully, but even I was surprised at this level of violence. This is well beyond normal human behavior. There is no place in hell hot enough for my brother. I'll find him and try to arrest him, but deep down, I want him to resist. I want to send him to hell, Mister Mitchell, and I will."

"I couldn't ask for more, Earl. I always knew Eva was making the wrong decision to marry him, but she was stubborn. At least she was an adult and could do something to defend herself. What he did to little David was beyond just murder."

"I completely agree with you. Now, what I need to know while I have you all here, is where do you think he might go, and who he has been hanging around with these past few years?"

Jessie replied, "I know who he considered his drinking partners. My ex-husband, Elmer Jackson was one. He and Claude used to go off to Cleland's Saloon and come home drunk every few days. Neither was very pleasant when they finally dragged themselves home, either. When they were there, they sometimes met with another man named Overton, but I never met him."

Earl's eyebrows arched as he asked, "Overton? That wouldn't be Charlie Overton, would it?"

"Yes, I think that was his name. Why?"

"We have a warrant out for him in Fort Worth. He's wanted for bank robbery and assault. We had word that he was forming a gang with Weasel Holland and Joe Atherton. Both are known to us as well, but they have no warrants. Holland was suspected in two killings but there wasn't enough evidence, and Atherton was just one of those guys that always seemed to be with the wrong crowd. I'll ask the sheriff about it when I go to town in a little bit. Who's the sheriff these days?"

Tom Mitchell replied, "A worthless pile of cow manure named Hank Burton. He never leaves his office and has a deputy that's even worse. After the crime was reported, he didn't even ride out to the ranch, but just dispatched the undertaker and sent some telegrams."

Earl's eyes widened as he exclaimed, "You're kidding me! *The man never investigated a double homicide? Did he send out a posse to chase after Claude?*"

"No. Not at all."

Earl shook his head in disbelief, then said, "Maybe I'll remove him from office. He's got no right to be wearing a badge."

"You can do that?" asked Ada.

"If I find a lawman who I judge to be incompetent or corrupt, I can remove him from his office until they run an investigation. But in this case, with a bad deputy, I don't think it would make a difference, at least not now. I'd have to find someone else to take his place and I don't have the time. When I finish my mission, I'll take care of the sheriff."

"Earl, you'd be the most popular man in Hopewell if you did," said Tom.

"I need to go into Hopewell and send a telegram and meet your poor excuse for a lawman," he said, then turned to Jessie and asked, "Did you want to come along, Jessie? I want you there when I interrogate the sheriff as to his malfeasance in failing to properly investigate a double homicide in his jurisdiction."

"I'd love to come and watch him squirm," she replied.

"Good. Did you want me to saddle your horse?"

"No, I'll do it. I'm used to it," she answered and left the room, heading to her bedroom to change for her ride to town.

"Earl, would you care to join us for dinner?" Ada asked.

"I'd enjoy that immensely, Mrs. Mitchell, and I'm sure it would be more enjoyable than the one I'll have this evening. I left my father with some things to ponder when I left, and I need to go back to continue that conversation, so I'll have to sadly turn down your offer. He needs to understand the reality of who Claude is and what he's done, but I'm not sure he ever will."

"That must have been some greeting you received when he first saw you," said Tom.

"He accused me of coming here to head up that lynch mob that was going after his innocent son."

"You've got to be kidding!"

"Nope. After all these years, I thought even he would finally recognize what Claude was after having this terrible murder occur on his own ranch, but it didn't have any impact on him at all. I found that incomprehensible."

Just three minutes later, Jessie stepped out of her room looking very unlike the farm girl she was. Instead, she looked like a Texan princess wearing a riding skirt, a white blouse, a dark brown Stetson and nice Western boots.

63

Her mother raised her eyebrows a bit as she knew Jessie rarely wore her best riding outfit for local rides, but she also knew that Jessie had always admired Earl. Yet until she walked into the room, she had no idea just how deep her feelings for Earl were.

"I'll go and saddle Butter, Earl. Are you coming?" she asked from the front door.

Earl stood and said, "I'm right behind you, Jessie."

As they exited, Ada looked at Tom and gave him the '*did you notice that*' look.

Earl had been impressed with Jessie's change in attire. Jessie had always been cute, rather than beautiful, and if anyone had ever taken the time to ask, he always preferred cute. She was even cuter now than when she was twelve, and he thought that maybe he should have come back sooner just to see Jessie again.

As Earl took Target's reins and they began to walk, Jessie glanced at his gelding and asked, "What's your horse's name?"

"Target," Earl answered as he caught up to her.

"I assume it's because of that white circle on his rump?"

"That and on my first mission with him I was shot."

His reply stopped Jessie in her tracks before she quickly asked, "You've been shot?"

"A few times. Most were just pass-throughs or grazes, though."

She looked at him with her brown eyes wide and asked, "How many is '*a few times*'?"

"Seven altogether. Four during the war and three since."

"You've been shot seven times? You don't seem worse for the damage."

"That's because the scars are all hidden. One is on my left shoulder. Two are on my chest, one on the right and one is on the left. Another one is the left side of my belly, then there's one is in my left thigh and one on the calf on the left."

"That's six. Where's the seventh?"

"I'd rather not say but suffice it to say I wasn't riding for a couple of months."

She laughed then they began walking again, heading to the barn. Earl realized that he had never heard Jessie laugh as an adult. She was usually a little more serious when she was younger, although they had shared laughs together even then.

Jessie was the anti-Eva, with darker hair and those bewitching brown eyes with purple streaks. He'd never seen anyone with eyes like that, which is why he knew that he'd always be able to identify her. She had a cute nose that accented her rounded cheeks and full lips and almost looked cherubic, except in the paintings the cherubs all seemed to have Eva's hair and eyes, which was too bad. The artists had missed the real angel.

Earl stood holding Target as he watched Jessie saddle her mare, and was pleased that she did it so well, but was more impressed with how much Jessie had changed.

Ten minutes later, they were mounted, had left the farm and turned north to Hopewell.

"Are you going to send your telegram first or visit the sheriff?" she asked.

"I'll visit the sheriff first. I'll probably want to include the discussion with him in the telegram. The boss needs to know if we run into a local law enforcement issue."

"What else did you need to tell your boss?"

"What you told me about that night and where I'll be going. I also need to tell him about an incident that happened between Fort Worth and Dallas. I should have notified him when I got to Dallas, but I needed to hit the road. He'll be irritated, but he'll get over it by the time I get back."

"When will you be getting back?"

"I have no idea. This could take me weeks to track Claude down, especially if he has hooked up with Overton and that crowd. I have to take my time if there are five or six of them."

Jessie was horrified by the thought of Earl taking on a half-dozen bad men on his own, and exclaimed, "You can't do that, Earl! You can't go after that many by yourself!"

Earl looked across at her, then replied, "I've done it before, Jessie. Usually, there'd be at least two of us, but I can deputize at least two more temporary deputy marshals if I need to. I'll figure that out when I get closer to them. The way I usually approach having more than three is to wait until they separate, then pick them off one at a time. You know, if they go for supplies or something. I've even arrested one group as they began filtering out of their hideout to use the privy outside their cabin. It was cold enough that I'd grab one as he was leaving and then a second. That left only three in the cabin and I smoked out the rest. I'll handle it, Jessie, don't worry. Claude won't get away."

"I wasn't worried about Claude getting away, Earl. I was worried about you getting killed."

He looked over at her and smiled. "It hasn't happened yet, Jessie."

Jessie was astounded by his cavalier attitude toward death and wondered what made him like that. He hadn't been that way before he left. *Was it the war or something else?* Maybe it was something she didn't even know about. She knew that it wasn't an act to impress her with his bravery because she already knew he had courage. It was just that he didn't seem to dwell on his own mortality.

They entered Hopewell and the two riders turned left and found the sheriff's office's door open. It was going to be a hot late spring day, and the men in the office wanted as much slightly cooler air in the jail as possible.

They stopped in front, stepped down, and looped their horses' reins over the hitching rail. Earl walked in first and saw the deputy with his feet on the desk admiring his pistol, as he spun the cylinder.

"Deputy, is the sheriff in?" asked Earl loudly.

The deputy was so startled, he dropped his gun to the floor and jerked his feet off the desk, almost falling over backwards. He picked up the pistol and returned it to his holster, then as he looked up, he recognized Jessie, of course, *but who was this big galoot who was with her?* He then made the poor decision to try to impress her in front of her escort.

"And just who the hell do you think you are barging in here like that?" he asked in a snarl.

"Deputy, I just asked a simple question. I didn't barge in, nor does my question deserve a response like yours. Now, I'll ask you again. Is the sheriff in?"

"No, he ain't. So why don't you just mosey on outta here and come back when he's here?"

Earl was getting annoyed, and asked again, "Deputy, you're not making a good impression. Now, where is the sheriff?"

"If you must know, he's havin' his lunch, and he don't like to be disturbed when he's eatin'."

"Well, I think Miss Mitchell and I will go and have lunch as well and see if the sheriff won't mind talking to me. And deputy? One more thing; you don't want to have that Colt loaded with all six cylinders. You just dropped it and were lucky it didn't fire and blow your ass off."

Jessie giggled as they turned and left the office.

The deputy was flummoxed as he pulled out his pistol and checked it. *How did that guy know he had all six cylinders loaded?* One wasn't even visible.

Jessie wondered the same thing as she took his arm crossing the street to the café and asked, "How did you know all of the cylinders were loaded?"

"He was rolling the cylinder just as we stepped onto the boardwalk. I heard the sound and looked for the source. The light was right, so I could see the rounds go by and there wasn't a hole. That man is an idiot."

"He is. His name is Clarence Willoughby and he's the mayor's son. He tried calling on me a few times and was slow figuring out I was not in the least bit interested."

"Why am I not surprised?" Earl asked rhetorically as she laughed.

They entered the café, and the smell of steaks on the grill set Earl's mouth watering, which was a surprise as he had eaten a steak only a few hours earlier.

Jessie needlessly pointed out the sheriff because Earl had identified him without even seeing the badge. He just looked like a man who watched out for himself first.

Earl turned and headed in his direction with Jessie at his side, then when they reached his table, he pulled out a chair across from the sheriff for Jessie, and after she was seated, he sat down next to her.

The sheriff stopped eating, his fork in mid-air as he began to say something, but Earl spoke before he did.

"Sheriff Burton, I'm United States Deputy Marshal Earl Crawford and I'm sure you know Miss Mitchell. I've been sent here by my boss to assist you in your investigation into the murder of Eva and David Crawford eight days ago. What have you discovered so far?"

Hank Burton was torn between being angry for having his lunch disturbed and just plain annoyed at having someone poking their nose into his business.

"That's none of your concern, Deputy. I got it handled."

"Really? Have you investigated the crime scene?"

"There was no need for me to go out there. They were dead, so I sent out some telegrams."

"Have you initiated a posse to go after the suspected murderer?"

"He was already out of my jurisdiction when I was notified," he replied, then suddenly asked, "Wait a minute! Did you say your last name was Crawford?"

"I did. The murderer was my brother."

"So, that's it. You're here to make sure it stays quiet. Well, more power to you, then," the sheriff replied before he shoveled in a large helping of mashed potatoes and gravy into his mouth.

"Sheriff, if you had even half a brain, you'd notice that I was sitting here with the victim's sister. Now, would I be here to keep this quiet if she was sitting at the same table? I am here to arrest my brother and have him stand trial, which is something you should have done. By not acting quickly, you've made my job both necessary and more difficult.

"You are disgrace to every real lawman in this country, and if your deputy was halfway competent, I'd pull that badge off your chest right now. As it is, I need to go out on my mission. When I return, you can count on being unemployed and your useless deputy can follow you out the door."

Earl's strong voice made his last words have the sound of an official statement of pending action. There were eight other diners in the café who plainly heard the marshal's announcement and Earl knew that the word would get out.

The sheriff's eyes were bulging as he chewed, but didn't reply.

Earl stood and said to Jessie, "Jessie, I'll send that telegram to Fort Worth now. We can come back for lunch in a little while."

She smiled at Earl, then stood and said, "Enjoy your lunch, Sheriff Burton."

Then she turned, took Earl's arm and they crossed the café's floor heading for the door leaving smiling faces on the other diners who wondered if Earl really remove the sheriff and his deputy from office.

Earl and Jessie stepped outside, then stopped as Earl scanned the street.

"Where is the telegraph office, Jessie? It wasn't here when I left."

"Just down the street about a half a block. You can see the wire over there," she replied as she pointed at the obvious cable hanging from poles on the other side of the street.

He looked at Jessie, smiled, and said, "Some detective I am."

Jessie laughed as they stepped away from the café.

They walked to the telegraph office, leaving their horses at the sheriff's office, with Jessie still holding onto Earl's arm, which he didn't mind at all.

When they entered the small office, Earl spotted the telegrapher sitting at his equipment tapping out a message. He was a small man with a sharp nose and receding hairline, which was almost a caricature of what one would expect a telegrapher to look like, but seemed proficient at the job. As Earl listened, he was impressed with his speed and efficiency with the key. He, like most deputy marshals could read and send Morse code. It was a critical skill to have when your life could depend on what the operator was keying.

He took a sheet and wrote:

US MARSHAL DAN GRANT FORT WORTH TEXAS

ARRIVED HOPEWELL
SHERIFF NEVER INVESTIGATED MURDER
RECOMMEND REMOVAL FOR INCOMPETENCE
DEPUTY AS WELL
WILL SEARCH FOR CLAUDE CRAWFORD
BELIEVED WITH CHARLIE OVERTON AND THREE OTHERS
STOPPED ATTEMPTED KIDNAPPING ON WAY TO DALLAS
KILLED BOTH MEN AFTER REFUSING TO SURRENDER
LEFT BODIES WITH DALLAS COUNTY SHERIFF
SORRY FOR LATE NOTIFICATION

US DEPUTY MARSHAL CRAWFORD HOPEWELL TEXAS

He handed it to the telegrapher who had stopped sending his message and asked, "Can you get this off right away and mark it urgent? I'll be back in an hour for a reply. The marshal is very good at responding."

The operator looked at the message and the corners of his mouth twitched ever so slightly upward when he read about their sheriff's imminent departure.

"Of course, sir. That'll be sixty cents."

Earl gave the man the money and nodded before he and Jessie left to return to the café.

"Do you think we ought to move the horses to the other side of the street?" she asked.

"That may be wise," he answered as he grinned at her.

They moved the horses from the front of the jail, and soon re-entered the sheriff-less eatery. No sooner had they sat down than an eager waitress arrived at their table. She was a little younger than Jessie and had almost white blonde hair. She wasn't unpleasant to look at, but Earl noticed the wedding ring on her finger, not that he was interested anyway. He just liked to keep his observation skills sharp.

She smiled broadly at Earl as Jessie said, "Hello, Helen."

"Hi, Jessie. Who's your friend?" she asked continuing to smile at Earl and never even glanced at Jessie.

"Helen, I'd like you to meet United States Deputy Marshal Earl Crawford. He's my brother-in-law."

Earl was momentarily startled. He had forgotten that he was legally related to Jessie.

"Oh!" said Helen, "You're Claude's brother. Are you here to go after him?"

Earl smiled at her bluntness and replied, "Yes, I am."

"Good luck to you. He deserves to hang for what he did."

"At least that, Helen. Can we order some lunch?"

"Oh, I'm sorry. Of course, you can."

Jessie ordered a ham sandwich and coffee and Earl had the same. Helen smiled once more at Earl before turning and walking away with a noticeable sway in her motion.

"I would have thought you'd order more food than that, Earl. You're not exactly a small man," said Jessie.

"I don't eat as much as you might think. The rule on the trail is to eat when you can because you never know when you'll get your next meal. When I'm not actively in pursuit, I just don't eat much. Besides, my mother fed me a big breakfast."

"How is your mother? I haven't seen her since the funeral five days ago."

"She's fine. She looks a bit tired, though. I don't think it's because of her age or the amount of work she does, either. I think my father's constant defense of Claude had put a lot of pressure on her over the years. I wish my father wasn't the way he is, but I don't believe that I could have changed him. If anything, if I'd returned after the war, I'd probably have made him even more defensive. He's not a bad man, but he just let Claude get away with too much for too long. I hate to do it, but I'm going to need to really lay into him tonight before I leave in the morning."

"When are you leaving?"

"I'll probably hit the road around sunrise and head east after reaching Hopewell. I know the tendencies of bad men. They stay away from big towns because they're more likely to run into decent lawmen."

"How do you track them down? They've been gone for eight days."

"Whenever I arrive in a town, I'll ask a lot of folks if they've seen them passing through. Generally, after their initial post crime run, the outlaws slow down if they don't see anyone following, so I make up time that way. Then they usually stop at bars and saloons and sometimes will spend a day or two relaxing. But the difference here is that no money was involved. Claude is on the run but didn't profit financially by it, so they need to get some cash."

"Didn't your mother tell you?"

"Tell me what?"

"After he murdered Eva and David, he went into the house and walked right past your mother and into their kitchen where they had their household money. He stole almost a hundred dollars and even knocked your mother aside knocking her unconscious."

Earl sat back, and felt his anger return in spades, but took a few seconds to let it pass, then shook his head and replied, "I guess I shouldn't have been surprised that he hurt my mother. Thanks for telling me about it, though. She never mentioned it, most likely because it would be a ticklish subject in front of my father because it would make Claude look bad. So, now he has money as well. That is more money than they usually get from a stage robbery and some bank holdups."

Helen brought their sandwiches and coffee, smiled at Earl again and left with the same impressive sway.

Jessie noticed and looked at Earl, who apparently hadn't as he was already taking a bite of his sandwich.

She was annoyed after seeing Helen's obvious flirtation as she asked, "Does that happen to you often?"

Earl swallowed before he replied with his own question, "Does what happen often?"

"Women smiling at you like that, and then emphasizing her interest with that display when she walked away."

Earl couldn't help smiling at her obvious annoyance and glanced back toward Helen who was clearing another table.

When he returned his eyes to Jessie, he replied, "It happens more than I'd like to admit, and Helen was married, too. It's really annoying, to tell the truth."

"You're not flattered by it? And how did you know she was married? You don't even know her, do you?" she asked with raised eyebrows.

"No, I never met her before, but I did notice the wedding band on her finger. It's just a lawman's habit to notice details even when they may not be important, so we can keep our wits sharp. Now, about your other question about whether or not I was flattered by what she just did. Would it surprise you if I said that it had just the opposite effect? It's kind of demeaning, really. It's no different than when a man looks at a woman and leers at her. I know that women don't like it and neither do I. Most of the women who make eyes at me don't even know who I am."

"But I smiled at you."

"Ah, but, Jessie, you know me better than most people, even my parents and you saw me at my most foolish."

"You weren't foolish, Earl. You were in love with Eva."

76

"I'll talk about it some time when we have the time to do that subject justice, Jessie. Let's have our lunch and then we'll head over to the telegraph office to see if Dan's sent a reply."

They finished their sandwiches and Earl left a silver dollar on the table for the twenty-cent bill and hoped Helen didn't get any ideas about the enormous tip as it would probably make her husband jealous.

As they walked into the telegraph office, the operator didn't look up from his bench as he was in the middle of writing down an incoming message. Earl caught the last few words: Fort Worth Texas. His timing was good and even he was impressed by his boss's rapid reply.

The telegrapher finished writing and handed the response to him.

DEPUTY MARSHAL CRAWFORD HOPEWELL TEXAS

TAKE ACTIONS AS NECESSARY PER SHERIFF AND DEPUTY
PROCEED WITH CAUTION ON OVERTON
GOOD JOB ON KIDNAPPING ATTEMPT
MUST HAVE MADE IMPRESSION ON OTOOLE
THREE TELEGRAMS ON YOUR WHEREABOUTS
NOTIFY HER ON YOUR RETURN
GOOD LUCK

US MARSHAL GRANT FORT WORTH TEXAS

He thanked the operator and began to put the telegram in his pocket when he saw Jessie's curious eyes looking at him.

"What did he say?" she asked.

He handed her the telegram, which she quickly read, then asked, "That's great news about the sheriff, but what's this about a kidnapping? And who's O'Toole? Is it someone you know?"

"No, ma'am, but I'll tell you on the ride back. It's a short story, anyway."

They walked back to the horses, mounted and as soon as they turned back toward the farm, Jessie asked, "Well? What's the story?"

"After I left Fort Worth, I came upon these two yokels setting up to do something illegal, so I stopped and watched, and they never even saw me. It turned out they were waiting on a carriage, and when I saw they had an extra saddled horse with them, I knew it was probably going to be a kidnapping. So, I called out for them to surrender and they decided to shoot it out instead. I shot them both and returned them and the carriage to Dallas. Like I said, it's not a big story."

"So, who is O'Toole and why is she trying to find you so badly?"

"She said her name was Teresa O'Toole and she was the one those boys were going to kidnap, but I have no idea why she's looking for me. She must have felt grateful for preventing her from being a victim of their plot."

Jessie stopped Butter and looked at him as she asked, "Did you say Teresa O'Toole?"

Earl pulled Target to a halt beside Jessie and answered, "That's the name she gave me. All I know about her is what the Dallas sheriff told me. He said she was rich, which was obvious by her fancy carriage, and that she was the most sought-after young woman in the state."

"He's right about that. She's supposed to be the most eligible woman in the area, if not the state. Is she as beautiful as everyone says she is?"

"I suppose I'd agree with that assessment. She did have an odd combination of Mexican and Irish, with her dark hair and blue eyes, but they worked well together."

"Weren't you impressed? It sounds like she was. Here comes this dashing, handsome lawman to her rescue and now she's trying to find you."

"I'll admit to being impressed with her, but I wasn't really interested, especially seeing how I'll be on the trail for a while. The sheriff seemed eager to interview her at her house, though."

"You mean to tell me you're not the least bit interested?"

"Nope. Sorry to disappoint you."

Jessie was far from disappointed, but she was amazed. At the same time, she knew that if a woman like Teresa O'Toole with all of her money and handsome features hadn't been able to make him notice, her chances were non-existent.

Earl noticed that she had lost some of her lively bounce and didn't have the slightest idea why before he nudged Target into a slow trot and waited for Jessie to catch up.

They rode the short distance to the farm and Jessie was surprised when Earl turned into the short access road with her rather than going to his parents' ranch.

"I thought you weren't staying for dinner?" she asked.

"I'm not. It's only three o'clock or so. I wanted to bring your parents up to date on things. I owe them at least that."

Jessie nodded, again feeling disappointment that he wasn't staying. In a few hours, she would lose Earl again; maybe forever this time if he runs afoul of the Overton gang. That and the news about Teresa O'Toole plunged her deeper into despair.

They reined in before the house, dismounted and went inside. The Mitchells were in the kitchen discussing Earl's return and the obvious impact that he had on Jessie when they heard Earl and Jessie enter and smiled as they entered the kitchen.

"How did it go with our esteemed lawman?" asked Tom.

"I'll have to wait until I return from finding Claude, but my boss gave me clearance to remove your sheriff and deputy. The pair are a menace to the town and the community. The man who has the effrontery to wear that badge never even investigated a double homicide in his jurisdiction. That alone should get him fired."

"Good. Anything else?"

"Not really. Do you have anything else to ask before I head back to the ranch?"

"No. We appreciate you're taking care of this, Earl. Are you sure you can't use any help?"

"No, sir. I'll be fine. It's not the kind of thing that most folks can deal with anyway. I'll be mostly on the road for up to two or three weeks, maybe longer. Food and sleep happen when you

80

can get them. I've gotten accustomed to it and I don't have anyone fretting over me as would most folks, including most of my fellow deputy marshals. I'll do what needs to be done."

Tom shook his hand and Ada gave him a hug, but Jessie just stood back. Earl looked at her and saw the hurt in her eyes and tried to think of what he possibly could have done to cause it.

He smiled at Jessie and said, "Thank you for your help, Jessie. I know it's been hard for you, but you've turned out to be quite a woman, Jessie. And for that reason, above all others, I'm glad I came back."

He gave her another smile, then turned, and left the house through the front door as Tom Mitchell followed him to go to the barn.

Jessie stood in the kitchen, unsure of how to take Earl's parting remark. Her mother looked at her face and read her daughter perfectly.

"It hurts, doesn't it, sweetheart?"

"What does?" she asked, pretended not to understand her mother's question.

"Earl returning after all these years and now he's leaving again."

She finally had to admit to the truth, then sighed and quietly replied, "Yes."

"You really love him, don't you, Jessie?"

"Since I was just a girl, Mama. Even before he was courting Eva. She saw a handsome face, but I saw him as a man and not just a handsome face. I knew his good heart and fine mind. He was always kind to me, even though I was just the little sister. He'd make me laugh and tell me that I was cute, and I knew he meant it. He's all I've ever wanted, Mama. Now he may be gone, and I'll never see him again. I don't even know if he could ever love me.

"Did you know that on the way here he saved Teresa O'Toole from being kidnapped? Since then, she's been sending telegrams to his office asking where he is and having them let her know when he'll be back so she can see him. I asked him about it and he really wasn't the least bit interested in her. Can you believe that? How can he not be interested in the most sought-after woman in the state and find me attractive?"

Her mother smiled softly at her and took her hands before replying, "Jessie, my daughter, don't underestimate yourself. To a man like Earl, beauty itself is secondary. Since we've known Earl, he's had every girl in the area setting her cap for him at one time or another. We'd see it at socials and in even in church, but it didn't matter to him. I still never understood why he visited with Eva, because she wasn't the right match for him. But he was young, and all young people make mistakes.

"When he left to go to war, she didn't even see him off. It took her marriage to Claude for him to understand Eva. Now, he's even more immune to having women throw themselves at him. I think if you spent any time with him at all, and just stayed true to yourself, he'd discover just how special you are."

"But he's leaving in the morning, Mama. I won't even know where he is."

Ada hug her, then whispered in her ear, "You have a horse, don't you?"

Then she released Jessie and winked before she turned to go back to the main room, leaving Jessie in awe of her mother as she quickly began to make plans for an early morning ride.

———

Earl walked Target down the access road to the ranch ten minutes later. It was time to talk to his father. He led his horse into the barn where his pack horse stood munching some hay, dismounted, then stripped off Target's saddle and the rest of his tack and rubbed his equine friend down before putting him in a stall.

He took a deep breath, exhaled sharply, then walked to the house.

He entered through the back door into the kitchen where his mother was already preparing dinner.

"Welcome home, son," she said as she smiled across the room.

"Hello, Mama, how is everything?" he asked, which was code-speak for how his father was reacting to his presence.

"I'm fine, but your father is still upset. He's awfully mixed up, Earl. What you told him caused him to think for a little while."

Earl hung his hat, then said, "I hope it made him more willing to accept the truth. I'll talk to him some more at dinner, and I hope I don't make him too angry."

"Earl, he's needed someone to tell him the truth for a while. Someone that he may have some level of respect for. You know, he was actually quite proud when you became a U.S.

Deputy Marshal. He knows that it's a hard job and they don't take just anyone."

"Well, that's news to me."

"Do they pay you enough, Earl?"

"More than enough, Mama. I don't even spend half of the money they've paid me over the years. In fact, if you need any money, let me know. I can help."

"No, we're fine. Despite the household money that Claude stole. I'm sure you've heard about that by now."

"Yes, Jessie mentioned it."

"So, what did you think of our Jessie?"

"She's grown up to be an amazing woman, Mama. If I didn't have to go out on this mission, I'd really like to spend more time with her."

Then, after a short pause, he said, "You know, Mama, ever since I was a boy, I've had girls make eyes at me or worse, but it never worked. Not because I didn't like pretty girls, it's just that I knew that all they saw was what was on the outside. They didn't care who I really was. But Jessie never did that. Granted, she was only twelve when I left, but when I talked to her while I was visiting Eva, she talked to me like I was me. I actually enjoyed talking to Jessie more than I did talking to Eva. Now, she's a grown woman, and a very cute woman, I might add, and she's still enjoyable to talk to. And you always knew my fondness for cute over beautiful, didn't you, Mama?"

"That's why I'm glad you went and saw Jessie. I wish you both could spend time together, too."

"Well, we'll see when I get back."

He kissed his mother on the forehead and asked, "Where is papa, anyway?"

"Out in the fields checking on the new calves. I think that here are fifteen so far, but there might be more already. We're going to have to add another ranch hand, I think."

"I think I'll head out there. Is he on foot or horse?"

"On foot."

"I'll see you in a little while to chow down on one of your scrumptious meals."

Earl then waved as he exited from the back door and walked out to the pastures, and as soon as he cleared the house, he spotted his father about three hundred yards away and lengthened his stride.

Ray Crawford saw his son approaching and wasn't sure how to react. After being read the riot act about his mission earlier, he had spent a long time in self-examination and didn't like what he had found.

"Hi, Papa," Earl shouted when he got within fifty yards, "How are the calves doing this year?"

"Good. We're up to seventeen healthy calves so far with four more due any day."

"Good. That'll help the herd. Mama said you'll have to hire another ranch hand."

"I think so. That'll give us five," his father replied.

Earl was within normal speaking distance now and said, "Papa, I want to apologize for getting so angry with you earlier. It was disrespectful, and I should have held my tongue."

"No, that's alright. I deserved it. I was out of line."

Earl stepped closer to his father and put his arm over his shoulder.

"No, Papa, you weren't out of line at all. You were right in line with what you've been doing since I've known you. You've been defending Claude despite all the evidence to the contrary, and I understand, Papa. I always have, even when I was eight and heard you defend Claude after he had given me another beating.

"He was your first-born son and meant everything to you. For two years before I arrived, he was the focus of your future. You probably saw him running the ranch after you retired or maybe even becoming governor or a senator. All real fathers do that. They project greatness on their sons, even if it's not there. You saw his fighting as signs of strength, Papa, but it wasn't. He was only fighting those he knew couldn't match him in size or strength. He was weak, not strong."

Earl paused to see if his father wanted to say anything, but when he didn't, he continued.

"Do you know who was strong, Papa? You and mama were strong, and still are. You took this land and turned it into a ranch. You fought off Indians and bandits to keep us safe. You raised two sons in this garden of Eden that you and mama created for us, and just like Adam and Eve, you had one son who turned out bad. It wasn't your fault, it just was.

"I never resented Claude for getting all your attention, Papa. I understood that. I only wished that you could see what a bully he was. All the other children in school knew what he was. It only stopped when I grew big enough to stop him from hurting the other kids and me. I love you, Papa. You have to understand that. Now, I talked to Jessie a little while ago and she told me what Eva's dying words were. There is no doubt that Claude killed her and little David. You need to accept that and realize that I'll do my job within the law."

Earl had watched his father while he spoke, seeing his head sink lower and lower until tears began dropping straight from his eyes and splashing onto the hard earth below.

Ray Crawford had finally admitted to himself what he had known for years but refused to acknowledge; that his older son was nothing more than a lazy, vicious man. He felt so guilty for not saying or doing anything when he had seen the bruises on Eva that she had tried so hard to hide. More than anything, he regretted not disciplining the boy when he was young. He could have stopped all this. It was his job. He was Claude's father, and instead of making him a man, he had helped mold him into a monster.

"I'm so sorry, Earl. This is all my fault," he croaked as he kept his head down and the tears dripping.

"No, Papa. It's Claude's fault. He's an adult. He made those decisions, not you."

"I should have stopped him when I saw Eva's bruises."

Earl said nothing when he heard his father's damning statement. There was no denying the accuracy of his confession and Earl knew there were no words he could say to deny it. He never lied and wasn't about to start, especially now.

Finally, he said, "Papa, there's nothing we can do about that now. All we can do is provide justice and continue our lives hoping that nothing like that ever happens again. Let's go home."

He walked with his almost stumbling father who had stopped weeping but still kept his eyes on the ground. He had his arm around his shoulders as he guided his mentally and emotionally exhausted father back toward the house.

Lydia watched from the kitchen window with her face wet with tears at the sight. She was so happy that her son had brought her husband back to her in more ways than just one. She had been so afraid that he was going to drift into madness with his fight against reality and might even try to end his own life rather than face the truth.

After entering the kitchen, Earl transferred his still disconsolate father to his mother, who took him into her arms and rested her head on his shoulder.

He held onto his wife tightly as Earl left the kitchen and went to the main room to give them time.

While he was sitting in a rocking chair waiting for his parents, there was a knock on the front door. Earl rose, strode to the screen door and saw a boy bordering on being a young man holding a telegram in his hand.

He swung the door open, stepped out onto the porch and the youngster asked, "Are you U.S. Deputy Marshal Earl Crawford?"

"Yes," he replied before the boy handed him the telegram.

Earl handed the boy a dime, double his normal tip, and took the telegram from the departing, smiling messenger. He opened it and read:

US DEPUTY MARSHAL CRAWFORD HOPEWELL TEXAS

**BANK ROBBERY IN WHITE OAK YESTERDAY
STOLE FOUR FIFTY
ROBBERS IDENTIFIED POSITIVELY AS OVERTON AND
HOLLAND ATHERTON
TWO OTHER UNIDENTIFIED WITH GROUP
SOUNDS LIKE YOUR TARGET
GOOD LUCK**

US MARSHAL GRANT FORT WORTH TEXAS

White Oak was only about thirty miles north, and it had happened just a day earlier, so it wasn't going to be nearly the long, arduous tracking job he had anticipated and was glad he hadn't gone east. He re-entered the house with the telegram in hand and found his parents in the main room.

His father seemed to have recovered, and Earl smiled knowing that his mother had a way to heal all sorts of hurts.

"What was it, Son?" Ray asked.

Earl noticed that he had called him 'son' for the first time he could recall.

"I just got a telegram from my boss. There was a bank robbery in White Oak yesterday and the robbers were positively identified as the Overton gang."

"That means Claude will probably be with them," he said without hesitation.

"I think so."

"Does that mean you're leaving right now?" asked his mother.

"No, I'll leave as planned in the morning. There's no need to push this because nothing is ever gained by going too fast. It's always dangerous to rush into anything."

"Are they going to send more marshals?" asked his father.

"No. They're really shorthanded. I'll take care of it. I've done it before. Once with a gang of seven and I know this area probably better than they do. I'll be fine."

"I can come with you, Son."

"No, you're needed here, Papa. Besides, mama would beat me with her wooden spoon if I let you come," he said as he smiled.

"Thank God for his mother," he thought.

She knew Earl didn't want his father along and soon backed up his response to his father's offer.

"You're darn right, young man. And don't think I've forgotten how to use it."

He smiled at his mother then said, "If it's okay with you, before I go, I need to go and check out the crime scene. I've been hesitant to do that, but I needed to get all the background information for my report before I go, so I'll head over there. I'll be back in a few minutes."

"Come back soon, Earl. I'll have dinner ready in twenty minutes," his mother said.

"No problem, Mama."

He waved, walked out of the house and crossed the wide front yard to the smaller house two hundred yards away, then stepped onto the porch and blew out his breath. This was where Eva died with her son, and he already began to imagine the scene when Jessie had walked through that door.

He opened the door and the smell of the blood and death was still there. It was an odor he knew well, and it still made his stomach recoil no matter how many times he'd encountered it. It wasn't because of the smell itself, but for what it represented – misery and death. And for some families, grief from which they may never recover.

He noticed that the room itself wasn't in too much disarray as he walked to the fireplace where he could see a bloody spot about four feet above the floor. Some of the blood had dripped down across the stones. There was surprisingly little blood on the floor. The young boy must have died almost instantly from the blow and the thought of his nephew being thrown to his death made him shudder.

Then he walked to the area where it was obvious that Eva had died. There was blood from the broken arm that had soaked into the unvarnished floor. The thought of her lying there with her arm shattered and the internal injuries that caused her death was almost overpowering. He had come to see Eva as she really was, but that didn't mean that she deserved this. No one deserved to die that way. There were other smells as well from the release of muscular control at death.

Earl walked into the kitchen where he pumped water into a bucket. He then began shaving lye soap into the water, then took a nearby towel and plunged it into the water several times until there were bubbles frothing at the surface. He took the bucket into the main room and began cleaning. He couldn't get all the stains out, but he did a good enough job that he knew the smells would be gone in a week and his mother wouldn't have to go through what he'd just experienced.

He finally emptied the bucket over the spot where Eva took her last breath, letting the soapy water soak into the wood, then set the bucket down and walked through the house opening windows and the back door before leaving the house with the front door open. It needed to be aired out.

Earl walked back to the house firmly embedding the scene in his mind for the moment when he would meet Claude.

When he entered the house, he walked straight back to the kitchen and found his father seated at the table and his mother as she was preparing to serve dinner.

"Just in time, Earl," she said, "Get everything you need?"

"Yes. By the way, I also cleaned up in there, Mama, so you won't have to. I left the windows and doors open, so it'll be back to normal in a few days."

"Thank you for that, Earl. I was dreading going in there."

"Maybe we should burn that place down," said his father, his eyes focused on the table in front of him.

"No, don't do that. It looks like a good house. Besides, it'll give me a place to stay when I come and visit."

"You'd stay in that place, knowing what happened there?" he asked, his eyes now looking at Earl.

"Sure. It's just a house. It didn't do anything."

They ate dinner making small talk and Earl was glad to see this father returning to at least a semblance of normalcy.

"Where will you sleep, Earl?" asked his mother.

"Where do you want me to sleep? Is my old room still a bedroom?"

"Yes, but the bed might be too short for you now."

"That's fine, I'm used to it."

After spending an hour or so talking about what Earl had been doing for the past twelve years, Earl told them he had to get some sleep because of his early start tomorrow and needed time in the morning to pack everything where he needed it.

He stood and kissed his mother on the forehead, then turned and shook his father's hand before going to his old room and undressing. He crawled into bed with his feet hanging over the end and lay there for three hours running through possible paths the outlaws and his brother might take, but finally fell asleep around midnight.

CHAPTER 4

Earl's internal clock woke him a little before five o'clock, then he slid his feet to the floor, stretched and then stood and walked to where he's folded his clothes. He dressed quickly before nature's call went unanswered, then trotted out the back door to the privy. After relieving himself, he returned to the kitchen and found his mother still in her nightdress, fixing his breakfast.

"You didn't think I'd let you go on an empty stomach, did you?" she asked as she smiled.

"I'd be surprised if you did, Mama."

He went into the washroom to scrub himself down and shave, and when he exited, the enticing smell of bacon and hot coffee filled the air.

He found his father also awake, sitting at the table and Earl was pleased to see him smiling.

"Good morning, Son."

"Good morning, Papa. I didn't mean to get everyone up this early in the morning."

"This is a working ranch and we always wake up with the sun. You just beat us by a few minutes."

"Then I don't feel so guilty," he replied with a grin.

Earl had a stomach-filling breakfast of four eggs, bacon, biscuits and coffee and suspected that it was the best breakfast he'd get in a long time, but he had to go.

He stood and said, "Thank you both for everything you've given me over the years. I promise to be a more frequent visitor, but I've got to leave."

His father stood and gave him a warm embrace and said quietly, "Thank you, Son. Now go and do what you do best."

His mother's eyes were damp as she hugged him and kissed him on his smooth cheek. She ran her fingers over his face and said, "Come back soon, Earl."

"As soon as I can."

With his final promise, Earl stepped out the back door and walked to the barn. It was another half hour before he was satisfied with his packing job, but now he knew where everything was, especially his guns and ammunition.

The sun had only been above the horizon for an hour or so when he waved to his parents, mounted, and walked Target out of the yard then down the entrance road, or in his case, the exit road.

He turned north toward Hopewell and had Target moving at a medium trot, expecting to be in White Oak by one o'clock that afternoon.

Earl had almost reached the Mitchell farm when he saw a rider sitting by the side of the road with a pack horse. It looked like a small rider, but in the blinding morning light, he wasn't so sure. He loosened his hammer loop out of reflex, but after another fifty feet, he replaced it after recognizing the rider. It was Jessie.

He sidled Target next to Jessie and asked the obvious, "Jessie, where do you think you're going?"

"With you."

"Jessie, that's insane. You know where I'm going. It's dangerous and no place for a woman."

"That's too bad."

"Jessie, I've got to be in White Oak as quickly as possible. I received a telegram yesterday that Overton and his gang, probably including Claude, robbed the bank there. It's a real break because I can trail them from there and I won't be as far behind as I had originally expected. I don't need to have you slow me down."

"I won't slow you down. Besides, even if you don't want me with you, I'm going to follow, so you might as well have me along for conversation."

Earl knew that this would be a long argument and he really didn't want to waste the time.

"Well, come along and I'll talk you out of it as we ride. I can't spend too much time sitting and trying to get you to change your mind."

Jessie was surprised it had been this easy. She almost thought he'd pull his gun to force her to go back.

They set their horses to a medium trot and Earl began outlining his arguments for her to just turn around and go back to the farm.

"Jessie, I'd really enjoy coming back and spending time talking to you when I'm finished, but not where I'm going now. I've known strong men who give up chasing after three days and this could be much longer. Besides, what would your parents think, knowing that you were out here on the road alone with me and no chaperone?"

Jessie laughed, then said, "Who do you think gave me the idea? It was my mother. Besides, I'm an adult woman and have even been married before."

Earl exclaimed, "*Your mother told you to do this insane thing? Has the whole Mitchell family gone off their rockers in one night?*"

"Maybe we were born this way," she replied with a smile.

Earl rolled his eyes. This wasn't getting any better.

Ten minutes later after none of his arguments had any impact at all, they entered Hopewell, and just a few minutes later, exited Hopewell.

Earl decided he'd try a different tactic. He had seen her rifle's butt above the scabbard and knew it was a sad, small caliber weapon.

"Jessie, can you shoot?"

"Of course, I can. I've been shooting since I was eight."

97

"I mean, can you shoot a real gun? What do you have with you right now?"

"My rifle."

"Let me see it."

The horses kept plodding along as Jessie pulled out her rifle and handed it to Earl.

"Jessie, this is a single shot .22 caliber rifle that's only fit for squirrels and the like. If you brought this into a gun fight, they'd laugh so hard they might miss."

"It's all I have, Earl, but I'm still not leaving."

"Why, Jessie? I always thought you were a very smart girl with a good practical head on your shoulders. This doesn't make any sense at all."

Jessie didn't dare tell him the real reason, but replied, "Eva was my sister, Earl. For all her faults, she was still my sister. Wouldn't you do the same if someone had murdered your brother? Never mind, that was a bad example, but do you understand?"

"Yes, I know what you mean, but there's a big difference. I'm going after Claude because it's my job. It's not vengeance. It's my job."

"Did you go into the house where they were murdered?"

Earl knew she had him as he answered, "Yes, I did. I went their yesterday afternoon and even cleaned it before I left."

"And you were able to look at the blood on the fireplace and floor, knowing how it got there and yet still claim that this is just your job?"

"No. I'll admit that I wanted Claude to roast in the depths of hell, but it's still my job, Jessie."

"Well, at least you admitted that. If you hadn't, I'd have been very disappointed in you, Earl."

Earl stayed silent for a few minutes as he couldn't see a way out. Even if he left her behind, she'd follow and then he'd be more worried than if she was right next to him. At least if she was close, he could protect her.

"Alright. Stop right here," he said in his command voice.

Jessie pulled back Butter's reins and looked at his stern face. *What was he planning on doing to prevent her coming?*

Earl turned and locked his eyes on Jessie's.

"Raise your right hand," he said.

She did, still wondering what he was going to do.

"Repeat after me: I, Jessie Mitchell, do solemnly swear…."

When she finished, he reached into his pocket, pulled out a temporary U.S. Deputy Marshal's badge, and handed it to her.

"Put this in your pocket for now. I'll explain what it entails and how I expect this arrangement to work. It also means that you must follow everything I tell you to do without question. Is that understood?"

"Is that the plan? To give me this and order me to go back?"

Earl hadn't even thought of that as a solution, but it was too late now.

"No. I'm talking about if we get into an engagement with bad sorts. If I tell you to duck, you duck. If I tell you to wait in one spot and cover me, you will do exactly that. I promise you one thing, Jessie Mitchell, before we need to engage these men, I want you trained as well as I can make you. I'll give you a crash course in shooting, caring for your weapons, and even some hand-to-hand techniques you can use. I'll tell you about tactical situations and how to take advantage of terrain. In short, Miss Mitchell, I'm going to make you earn the right to carry that badge. Can you live with those conditions?"

"Yes, sir. I can."

"Good. Now, let's pick up the pace."

Inside, Jessie was beaming. She knew it was going to be hard, but it was a small price to pay. To Jessie, her life had just taken a very hopeful turn.

Once the horses began moving at a faster trot, Jessie asked, "Do you have more guns you can let me use?"

"Jessie, I have more weapons back there than some small armies. I'd imagine almost half the weight on that packhorse are guns and ammunition. That doesn't include the Winchester and Smith & Wesson that I'm wearing. More than likely, you'll be wearing my pistol outfit later. I have a two-gun setup back there with two Colt Model 1873s. I'll use them because the pistols are the same weight. The Russian weighs a few ounces less than the Colt and is much faster to load."

"Russian?"

"Smith and Wesson sold a lot of their Model 3s to the Russian government, so we refer to the gun as the Russian. Which is kind of funny, really. The Russians took the gun, had their engineers make copies of it and now they're selling it all over Europe and even here in the United States. They even canceled the order and refused to pay for the guns that Smith & Wesson already delivered. I only call it the Russian because it's a lot easier to say than a Smith and Wesson Model 3. Another version is called the Schofield and it has a longer barrel, but it's heavier and doesn't have the balance of this version or the Colt '73."

"Oh. What other guns could I use?"

"I have a nice Henry back there. All of my guns shoot the same cartridge, so we can swap ammunition if we ever get that to that point. The Henry works like the Winchester but loads differently. It also has a different sound. I have no idea why, but you can always tell a Henry from a Winchester. Do you have a knife?"

"Yes," replied Jessie, as she pulled a folding knife out of her pocket with a three-inch blade.

"I mean a real knife, like this," Earl said as he pulled out his heavy knife from its sheath on his gun belt.

"No, and I'm not sure that I want one."

"They're not just used for stabbing people. They're incredibly useful on the trail. I'll buy you one in White Oak or Mount Pleasant. As for personal self-defense, I have nice derringer back there you can have. I want you to always keep it in your pocket. It may save your life. We'll talk about other things you may need in White Oak when we get there and have lunch. One of the unwritten rules is that if you're near a town, get a good meal, and sleep in a bed if you can. That's something else we need to talk about up front."

"What's that?"

"I'm not sure you're aware, Miss Mitchell, but you are a very attractive young woman. Now, when we get to these towns, I may have to introduce you to folks. If they don't know I'm a lawman on the trail of some outlaws, it's easy. I'll introduce you as Jessie Crawford, my wife. Is that okay?"

Jessie's stomach flipped when he said that name and replied, "Yes, it's fine."

"The problem is when we're in a town like White Oak. Most of the time, I'll just have you go to the dry goods store and buy some supplies while I go and talk to the local lawman. Sooner or later, it'll come out that I'm on the trail of some bad men, have a cute woman with me, and I may have to improvise."

"How come you said 'cute' that time?" she asked.

"Because that's what you are, Jessie. You've always been cute and probably always will be, as opposed to beautiful like Miss O'Toole."

"You don't think I'll ever be beautiful?"

"I hope not, Jessie, at least not on the outside. I've always had a weakness for cute."

Now *that* lifted her spirits and Jessie decided it wasn't bad to be cute.

They reached White Oak closer two o'clock that afternoon and Jessie turned toward the store with both pack horses while Earl rode down the street to the sheriff's office.

Earl stepped down and entered the office, finding the sheriff talking to two men in the corner of the office, but all of them turned to see who had walked in.

"Can I help you?" asked the sheriff.

Earl flipped open his vest revealing his badge and replied, "United States Deputy Marshal Earl Crawford out of Fort Worth. I hear you had a bank robbery two days ago."

"That was fast. I didn't expect any help for at least another three days."

"I was down in Hopewell investigating a double homicide. I think the murderer is with the bunch that held up the bank."

"Come on over, Marshal," said the sheriff, "This is Herb Winston, the mayor and John Henderson, the bank president. We were just discussing the robbery."

Earl crossed the room and shook each of their hands as he asked, "What can you tell me about the robbery?"

The bank president replied, "It was late in the afternoon, and the bank was getting ready to close. Three men walked in, and they didn't even wear masks. They had their pistols drawn and ordered everyone to go to the floor. One of them then ran around the end of the cashier's window and began pulling out cash drawers. He stuffed the bills into a bag, and they all ran out front. There were two men outside on horseback waiting for them. No one was hurt, but the bank lost four hundred and thirty-five dollars."

"This may sound trivial to you, but did you notice what kinds of guns they used?"

"Strangely enough, one of the customers did. He said they all had Colt New Army pistols. Is that important?"

"Very. If I get into a shootout with these miscreants, I'll know that after six shots, it'll take them longer to reload than if they had a cartridge weapon. They told me you identified the three as Charlie Overton, Weasel Holland, and Joe Atherton. Is that correct?"

"Yes, three of the customers and the cashier identified them. The other two men we hadn't seen before."

"Was one of them about my height, maybe a little shorter, with dark black hair and a weighing about a hundred and eighty pounds but with a bit of a belly?"

"Yes, that sounds very accurate. Do you know his name?"

"Yes, he's my brother."

His answer shocked them, then the mayor asked, "And you're going after them?"

"Yes, sir. I'll find them all, don't worry about it."

"What did he do down in Hopewell?"

"He beat his wife to death and then threw his six-year-old son across the room into the fireplace rocks, killing him. I want him and the others brought to justice."

"Marshal, do you need any help?" asked the sheriff.

"I appreciate the offer, but I'll be able to handle it. I'm good at this and I'm confident that I'll get them all. Which way did they leave town?"

The sheriff looked into his eyes and didn't doubt for a minute that he'd do exactly as he said. He was relieved, too, because he really didn't want to go. He felt it was necessary to keep his standing with the mayor.

"They left on the eastbound road."

"Thanks. I think I'll get something to eat and head out. I don't want to waste daylight."

He waved to the men and left the office, untied Target and walked him back across the street to the general store where he saw Jessie waiting by the horses.

"Did you buy anything?"

"No. I didn't bring any money. That was stupid."

"Not at all, Jessie. You probably thought I'd either get you to turn around, so you wouldn't need any or you'd get to come along at the expense of the government, which is true. Let's go inside."

He wrapped Target's reins around the rail and walked with Jessie into the store.

He walked to a counter where he saw some knives and found a nice model with a leather handle and a six-inch blade. He motioned to the storekeeper and told him he wanted the knife and he'd be back shortly.

Earl wandered to where Jessie was standing and asked, "Jessie, do you have a rain slicker?"

"No."

"How about a bedroll and a spare blanket?"

"No."

"What do you have for extra clothes?"

"Two more riding skirts, two shirts and some underwear."

"Add two more of each. I'll get the slicker, the bedroll and a blankets."

"Are you sure, Earl?"

"You'll need them, Jessie."

"Okay."

Earl stepped over to the other side of the store and bought the slicker, bedroll and blankets. Then he walked to another section and bought four bars of white soap and two of lilac-scented soap for Jessie, knowing she probably didn't bring any. He picked up two toothbrushes, more tooth powder, another tin plate, fork and spoon, and another tin cup.

He returned to the front where the proprietor had the knife sitting on the counter, and as Earl set his items nearby, the man kept a running total as he placed the items into a cloth bag. Jessie arrived and laid her purchases on the counter, and the store owner added the items up to the total and gave the bill to Earl as he placed Jessie's order in another bag. Earl gave him a twenty-dollar gold piece and took back his change, then thanked the man and they returned to the horses.

Jessie asked, "Earl, I thought you said the government will pay for that?"

"I submit an expense sheet at the end of a mission."

"Oh. And I suppose all of my underwear will be on that sheet?" she asked with a grin.

He smiled back at her and replied, "Probably not. I'd turn too red to write it down and wouldn't want to see the expression on the marshal's face when he read it, either. Let's go and enjoy a hot meal before we head east. That's the direction they took."

Jessie felt sort of guilty, but glad she had more clothes. She hadn't packed any dresses because she knew she wouldn't be wearing any.

They ate a good dinner at the café and were soon headed east. As they walked the horses, Earl was scanning the ground, looking for tracks.

"Earl, can you really find tracks after almost two days?"

"Sometimes. It depends on traffic and weather. It's been dry, so they wouldn't have washed out. The traffic has been light and I'm only looking for outbound travelers and they're in a group of five. I've been keeping an eye on this one set of tracks for over a mile now. I think it's our boys. Oh, and I forgot to mention, one of the holdup witnesses confirmed that Claude was with them."

"Well, I'm glad we're not on a wild goose chase."

"Jessie, I want you to keep an eye out for a good camp location. Look for good cover with plenty of trees or rocks, then look for water nearby. I'll glance up every now and then, but I want to track these jaspers as long as I can before we lose the light."

"Okay."

They rode for another ninety minutes miles before the light had diminished enough for Earl to stop bothering looking at the road.

"Will that work?" Jessie asked, pointing to the right.

"Perfect. I'll make a deputy marshal out of you yet, Jessie," he said as he smiled at her.

Earl angled toward the site she had found. It was a combination of rocks and trees that bordered a small creek about two hundred yards off the road, making it almost ideal

After they dismounted, Earl began unloading the pack horses, while Jessie unsaddled both riding horses and led them to the stream. Earl found a nice hidden spot for the campfire that couldn't be seen from the road. It was a small fire because they didn't have to eat, but Earl needed coffee desperately. Jessie had thrown his whole normal scheme of tracking criminals into turmoil.

After they were settled, Jessie and Earl sat by the fire having coffee.

"Jessie, tonight I'd like to postpone any training and just talk to fill in the gaps. Okay?"

"That sounds good. Can I ask you something, Earl?"

"Anything."

"Why didn't you come back?"

"That's the big one, isn't it? After I received my mother's letter telling me that Eva had married Claude, I was disappointed, to put it mildly. Before I left, I had a pretty good idea that Eva would only wait around six months when she didn't even show up to see me off. That was a hint, I suppose. I also suspected that it wasn't going to be a short war like most of the others believed. When I found out that she had married Claude though, that made the decision for me. I couldn't go back. Now, if they had moved to Hopewell, or some other town, I would have returned. But they were living right there on the ranch, so I couldn't go home again."

"Was it because you couldn't bear to see her with someone else?"

"Not exactly. It wasn't so much that Eva married someone else, it was that she had married Claude. If she had married someone else, I could live with that without a problem, but she married Claude. If I had gone back and seen him with her, I'll tell you without a question in my mind, he would have started kissing her and grabbing her in front of me just to try to show that he was a better man. He wouldn't have cared one bit if it embarrassed or shamed Eva, and I couldn't let him do that. Now, I realize maybe I had come back, I could have stopped him from doing what he did. I don't know, Jessie."

"Earl, I think we all feel that way. I know I felt I should have told someone that Eva was being beaten by Claude, but I didn't. Maybe if I had, she'd still be alive and David, too. No one else knew, but I should have spoken up. I didn't even tell my parents."

After Jessie's confession, Earl could see that she had her own feelings of guilt that she had for not preventing Eva and David's deaths.

"You're wrong, Jessie. My father knew she was being abused by Claude, too, and he did nothing."

"He told you that?"

"Yes, he did. I had a long talk with him out in the pastures and explained to him how wrong he had been for defending Claude for all those years. I had known for all of my life what a bully he was and told him about it, but he'd never listen before. It took this tragedy before he finally realized what he had done, but even then, he refused to believe it until I forced it out of him.

"After he admitted that he has been wrong about Claude, he then confessed that he should have stopped him from beating Eva. He'd seen her bruises and done nothing to stop him. He knew that he was probably the only person who could have done it. He could have moved Evan and David into the big house, too. Unlike my father, you had no power over Claude at all, Jessie.

"But after he made that confession and I didn't even attempt to forgive him for his biggest sin, he almost collapsed. He was an emotional wreck and I had to help him back to the house and left him in the kitchen with my mother where she held him like a lost child. I think he's better now. I forgave him for everything he had done over the years to protect Claude, except not doing anything to stop what he was doing to Eva. He understood that as well. He even called me son for the first time in my life."

"He never called you son before? What did he call you?"

"Usually, it was just my name. He always called me Earl, but always called Claude 'son' or 'my son' or 'my boy', but I was always Earl."

"Didn't that hurt when you were a boy?"

"Not as much as you might think because I knew my place. Claude was his dream and his hope for the future. That's why he looked the other way for so long. It never really bothered me. Besides, my mother liked me."

Jessie sat back against the rock. She couldn't fathom not having both of her parents care about her.

"So, tell me, Jessie, why did you wait so long to marry and then marry Elmer Jenkins of all people. I got that letter from my mother and it made me feel worse than the one she sent me about Claude marrying Eva."

"It did? Why?"

"You were a much better person than Eva. I'm just being honest and not following the tradition of not talking badly about the dead. She wasn't a bad person and could have made a good life for herself if she'd married someone who understood her behavior and let it go. She could have turned into a wonderful person once she got past the girl stage.

"But you were always more mature than she was, even when you were twelve. You had a softer soul. That's why I was so stunned that you married that oaf. Now, remember, I still saw you as your twelve-year old self, not the twenty-one-year-old woman that was married. But talking to you now, I know that your personality hasn't changed at all, yet you still haven't answered the question."

"I didn't want to marry him. But after I was well beyond the age that most girls married, my parents said I needed to start my own family. Eva brought Elmer to the house and asked me to marry him, and I really didn't care. She said it would be fun, because Elmer and Claude got along so well. She thought we'd all be good pals together. I didn't really know him that well, so I didn't have much expectations.

"After we were married, he and Claude would go off drinking two or three times a week. Eva told me that was when the beatings started. Elmer got tired of me for a number of reasons, and eighteen months later, he just left. I filed for a divorce after he had been gone for a year and it was granted. So, I became Jessie Mitchell again."

"Did he beat you, Jessie?"

"Not like Claude hit Eva. He would slap me hard sometimes, and he hurt me other ways I'd rather not talk about, but he didn't beat me as often as Claude beat Eva."

Earl took a deep breath and said, "Jessie, I should have come home. I could have helped you and could have helped Eva, too. Now all I can do is clean up the mess. It was a lousy, selfish decision I made back then."

Jessie fumed and snapped, "Earl, stop it right now! You made that decision not knowing what was happening. Who knows what would have happened if you had come home? Maybe you would have married me instead of Elmer."

Earl smiled at her and said, "I can see where that would have been possible, if not likely."

Jessie couldn't believe she let that slip out, but with Earl's answer, she was glad it had.

"Okay, Jessie. Enough deep talk tonight. Now, before we turn in, I need to know what you need for personal hygiene. You know, soap and those things."

"I forgot soap! And I didn't bring my toothbrush, either."

"Do you use white soap?"

"Yes. Do you have some?"

"I picked up six more bars at the store before we left. I was down to one."

"You didn't happen to pick up a toothbrush, did you?"

"No, sorry. I do have one in my saddlebags, though. Let me get it."

Jessie watched him leave and thought about his offer. She hated to go without cleaning her teeth, but sharing a toothbrush was well, different, and she'd have to really think about it.

Earl returned with his saddlebag. He had transferred the lilac soap and toothbrushes and powder while she stared into the dark, thinking about sharing a toothbrush.

"Okay, Jessie, let's see what I have here."

She turned her eyes back to him as he sat down, dropped his saddlebags on the ground, then flipped the leather flap open, then reached in and took out a toothbrush that was still in its paper packaging.

"Well, what do you know. How did that get in there?" he asked as he held it out it to her.

She laughed with relief and said, "Mister Crawford, you lied to me!"

"No, I was very accurate in my statement. You asked if I happened to buy a toothbrush, and I truthfully replied that I did not. I bought two because mine was getting ready for replacement. I also picked up some more tooth powder. Now, the tooth powder we can share, if it's okay with you."

"I can live with that," Jessie replied as she accepted her new toothbrush.

"And as you prefer white soap, what do you want me to do with these? I can throw them in the creek over there."

He handed her a bar of lilac soap and she asked, "Earl, why on earth did you buy these?"

"I thought you might like them. Was I wrong?"

"Absolutely not. I love this smell. I can't wait to try it."

"That's another thing we need to talk about. Now, when I'm on the road, I bathe whenever I can. I just strip off my clothes and dive into whatever water is available, but with you here, that poses a problem."

"Why?" she asked as she grinned at him.

"You know why, young woman. For the same reason that you have when you want to bathe. Unless you do it fully clothed."

"There's always the honor system."

"If you trust me, then I'll trust you. Is it a deal?"

"Of course, it is. No peeking."

"Okay. I'll also keep an eye out, so no one will intrude on your private time. Oh, speaking of private time, I always pack a couple of boxes of privacy paper."

"This trip is sounding like a luxury tour. New toothbrush, tooth powder, lilac soap and now privacy papers. Do you serve breakfast as well?"

"Yes, ma'am, but sometimes it's indistinguishable from other meals or even snacks on the trail," he replied before saying, "Well, as much as I enjoy talking with you, Jessie, it's time we turned in. We have a lot of riding tomorrow, so I'll set up the bedrolls. We shouldn't need extra blankets tonight. Just go ahead and use the trees over there if you need the privacy. The privacy papers I left on top of the pack.

"So, when you're ready for sleep, just kick off your boots and slide into the bedroll. Oh, and before I forget. There's one serious rule when camping under the Texas sky. Because your boots are warm when you take them off, some unpleasant critters may have crawled in there overnight. So, when you get up in the morning, shake out your boots before you put them on."

"Have you ever found anything in your boots?"

"Lots of times."

"Earl, can I ask a favor?"

"Sure."

"Can you shake out my boots in the morning?"

Earl laughed and replied, "Of course, I will."

Earl cleaned up, then took a canteen and brushed his teeth with his new toothbrush, then handed the canteen and tooth powder to Jessie, who took them gratefully and after she finished, she handed them back to Earl.

They crawled into their bedrolls and Jessie fell asleep quickly. Earl stayed awake for a couple of hours trying to figure out how he could adapt his original plan for running down the five outlaws to account for Jessie. He'd have to get her armed and teach her how to use the firearms quickly, and even then, he wasn't sure that she would be able to defend herself. It took a serious amount of conviction to shoot a man, and as much as he admired her spirit, he wasn't sure she'd be capable of doing it. As much as he enjoyed having Jessie around, having her on this extended camping trip presented a whole realm of other difficulties, so he tried to think of any way he could have dissuaded her from coming but couldn't.

Earl looked at her sleeping angelic face and smiled. She sure was special. He finally closed his eyes and managed to get some sleep.

———

He woke up with the pre-dawn, and quickly scanned his surrounding as was his normal practice on the trail, finding everything peaceful.

Earl slid out from his bedroll, shook his boots, and no creatures, hideous or otherwise tumbled out. After pulling on his boots, he hopped to his feet and trotted behind the trees to answer nature's call, then washed quickly in the stream and brushed his teeth.

When he finished, he stepped back to where Jessie was sleeping, picked up her boots, stepped away from her quietly and turned them upside down. A scorpion tumbled to the ground and before it could make its escape, Earl rammed it with his heel. He hated the damned things.

He restarted the fire and put the grate on top, and as he was cutting bacon, he glanced over at Jessie's bedroll and saw those brown eyes with purple streaks looking at him.

She smiled and asked, "Did you find any nasties in my boots, Deputy Crawford?"

"Yes, ma'am. There was a scorpion in your right boot, and I squashed the little bugger with my boot heel. I hate those little bastards."

"You're joking. Aren't you?" Jessie asked with wide eyes, hoping he was.

"Jessie, I never joke about scorpions or spiders. I'll joke about rattlers, but never those crawly things. I really do hate them."

"Are my boots empty now?"

"Yup. I've had them on my bedroll since clearing them out."

He reached over, picked up her scorpion-free boots and carried them to her. Jessie slipped out of the bedroll and hurriedly put them on before she scurried behind the trees as Earl began to cook breakfast. Earl had never been around a woman preparing to begin her day which made him a true rarity at his age, so it was a new experience. He was used watching men start their mornings, whether it was in the army or as a deputy marshal. They'd be out of the bedroll, take care of essentials, and back for a quick breakfast in three minutes.

117

He had already fried the bacon and there was still no Jessie. The coffee was done and the eggs he had picked up in White Oak were being dropped onto the plates when Jessie finally reappeared. Earl had been getting worried, but then thought it was just his own ignorance of what she had to do each morning.

"Breakfast already?" she asked.

"I was beginning to get worried about you. I've never been around a woman when she wakes up in the morning."

"Really? You've got to be joking! You're making fun of me for taking so long, aren't you?"

"No, Jessie, I'm not. It's a revelation, to be honest."

"You've never spent a night with a woman?"

"No. If you're going to make a point about it, I've never been with a woman…period."

Jessie was speechless – for three seconds.

"I'm sorry. I didn't mean it as a criticism, Earl. But as many women that throw themselves at you, I found it hard to believe."

He handed her the plate and had already begun to fork his eggs into his mouth.

After he swallowed, he said, "Maybe that was part of the reason. The unattached women that were really interested in getting together, worried me because if they weren't the one who I really wanted to be with, and I didn't want them to get too attached because it wouldn't be fair to them. The looser women that just wanted a roll in the hay just didn't concern me at all. The married ones were, well, married.

"Besides, I've been pretty busy chasing bad guys around the territory to worry about it. But all that time, I was always keeping an eye out for the one – the one who mattered. The one that would mean everything to me, just like I would mean everything to her. It sounds awfully stupid and a bit insipid, but I didn't want to cheat on a woman that I didn't even know existed."

Jessie stared at him as she softly replied, "No, it's not stupid or insipid, Earl. I think it's very romantic."

"Well, you're entitled to your opinion, Jessie. You go ahead and eat your breakfast. We won't have any more eggs for a while."

Earl had finished his breakfast and was sipping his coffee as Jessie ate.

"Jessie, I gave it some thought last night, and I think from here on out, we'll just be a pair of newlyweds on our way to the next big town. I won't be talking to any lawmen because we're on the trail. Okay?"

"Okay," she answered nonchalantly – although the thought made 'nonchalant' difficult.

"The only problem will come if we bump into either Claude or Elmer because they can identify you."

Jessie dropped her plate and stared wild-eyed at Earl, then hurriedly asked, "Elmer? What has Elmer got to do with this?"

"Elmer is obviously the fifth member of the gang. I thought you knew that all along."

"No, I never thought of that. I thought he was in Mexico or somewhere else far away."

"Is this a problem, Jessie?"

She began wringing her hands as she answered, "Earl, I can't see him again. I just can't. I've got to go back. I'm sorry. I'll just go back, so you can get on with your job."

Earl could see the terror in her eyes and felt his anger begin to rise. *What in blue blazes did he do to her?* It sure wasn't just a few slaps.

She stood, then walked toward the horses with her head down, obviously still very shaken by Earl's revelation.

Earl put down his coffee and walked behind her, when he reached her, he turned her around and hugged her close as she began to shake. Earl wished there was something more he could do to ease her pain and worry. She had been willing to learn to shoot bad guys until she found her ex-husband was one of them, and now she's frightened to death. *What had he done to her?*

"Jessie, it'll be okay," he said softly.

She had calmed to just a shiver as she felt his arms around her.

Earl put his right hand gently on the back of her head and said softly, "Sweetheart, everything will be all right. Trust me."

After another minute or so of the enormous, soothing feeling of being so close to him and hearing his comforting voice, her fear finally evaporated.

"I'm okay, Earl, but I've still got to go back. I'm sorry. I just can't see him again."

Earl kissed her on the forehead. Something she would have paid close attention to five minutes ago, but now it barely registered.

"That's fine, Jessie. You won't have to see him ever again. I'll take care of him for you."

She looked up at Earl and smiled weakly before saying, "I'm sorry, Earl."

"Don't you worry about it. I've got to rearrange the packs before we break camp. Can you clean up the breakfast gear?"

She nodded, then after he released her, she headed toward the fire. Earl knew he had to get her back to a routine, all the while wondering what could have precipitated such a violent reaction. Elmer Jackson had just moved up to number two on the list of people he'd like to shoot. Then, looking at Jessie's pained face again, he moved him up to the top slot.

He looked at the pack horses and decided to drop the added weight and just travel light and fast. Now that he knew he was close, he didn't need that much in the way of supplies. He'd keep the Winchester, the two-gun rig with both Colts, four boxes of cartridges, some food, coffee and the coffeepot. The rest he'd leave with Jessie until he returned. He took out the derringer, loaded it and put it in his pocket, then saddled the horses and finished his packing. Jessie had cleaned and put the cooking gear into their bags which finished their preparations for departure.

As they were preparing to mount, Earl reached into his pocket, pulled out the Remington derringer and turned to Jessie.

"Jessie, I want you to keep this with you at all times until I get back. It's .41 caliber derringer and fires two shots. It's a close in pistol, and it's a perfect defensive weapon for you. Okay?"

She took the gun and slid it into her pocket, saying, "Thank you, Earl."

"You're welcome, Jessie," he replied with a warm smile to make her feel a little better.

They soon mounted, then turned back to White Oak, which surprised Jessie.

"I thought you were going after them?"

"I will, but only after I'm sure that you've reached your home safely."

"I'll be all right."

"Probably, but I want to make sure that nothing bad befalls you on the ride back. You're an attractive young woman and some boys may try to take advantage of you if you're riding alone."

"Then thank you again."

Earl nodded and smiled, even though he knew he was losing valuable time by escorting her back to the farm.

By nine, they were past the town and headed south toward Hopewell. They rode in silence until Jessie finally spoke.

She had been thinking about telling Earl why she was so frightened of Elmer since he had told her that Elmer was with the gang but had found it beyond difficult. It was hard to tell her mother, and this would be much worse. But she felt he needed to know for other reasons that had nothing to do with shootouts or chases. She wanted to see his reaction and wondered if it would be enough to send him away. She couldn't bear getting even closer to him and letting him find out about it when it might be too late.

"Earl," she said as she looked across at him, "I want to tell you something that only my parents know. It's about Elmer and it's why I can't see him again."

She paused, realizing that it was going to be even more difficult than she had expected.

Earl looked at the pain in her face, again wondering what he could have done to her, but didn't reply. It was her decision to tell him and if she changed her mind, he didn't want to force it from her.

Jessie turned her eyes forward, unable to look into his eyes despite her need to watch his reaction. She'd have to wait for what he said after he learned her secret.

With her focus straight ahead, she said, "When he took me to bed, he did bad things to me, Earl. He hurt me. He got angrier and angrier when I wouldn't do the things he wanted. I just can't see him ever again. He didn't really leave voluntarily, either. My father made him leave at the point of a shotgun. I'm sorry, Earl."

As she turned her eyes back to Earl, he replied, "Never say you're sorry, Jessie. You did nothing wrong and have nothing to be ashamed of. That bastard who married you is the only one who should be sorry, but his sort never feel remorse for anything they do, which is why he and Claude were friends.

"I'll take care of Elmer when I catch up with him, so you won't have to worry ever again, Jessie. I'm sorry it had to be that way. It's not supposed to be."

"I know it's not. I had talked to my mother about it before I got married. She told me how it was supposed to be, and it sounded so wonderful and then Elmer turned it into a nightmare. She was who I told what he had done to me and she told my father."

"Your nightmare is over now, sweetheart. We'll get you home and you'll be safe. But before we change the subject, can you give me a good description of the man?"

"Oh, of course. He's about three inches shorter than you are. He has dark hair with a white streak above his right ear. He wears a beard and mustache. He's not fat, but he's not in good shape, either. He looks dumpy."

"Thank you, Jessie. That will help."

Six hours later, having skipped lunch, the outline of Hopewell was in sight and Earl pulled them to a stop.

He turned to her and said, "Jessie, I'm sure you'll be all right from here on in. It's only a mile to Hopewell and another mile to your farm. But before I head out, I'm going to ask something of you."

"Anything, Earl."

"First, hang onto my packhorse and gear for me till I return. Second, I don't want you to let any of those young men to come calling for you, because when I get back, if it's alright with you, I'd like to court you, because I'm finally sure of one thing, Jessie."

She was almost lost as she whispered, "What is that?"

He looked into those brown and purple-flecked eyes, and said, "You're the one."

Before she could reply, he leaned over and kissed her softly, then wheeled Target around and set him off at a fast trot back to White Oak, leaving a stunned Jessie sitting on Butter with her fingers pressed to her lips and not moving.

After a minute or so, she turned and looked at the receding figure and asked herself if that really had happened. Earl had told her he was going to call on her and even kissed her. More importantly, he had told her that she was the one he had been waiting for and after he'd told her how long he'd been searching for the one woman to share his life, it meant more than any possible phrase she'd ever heard.

She'd heard, 'I love you', and 'please marry me' from many men, but 'you're the one', was much more meaningful.

She continued to watch him until he was a dot on the horizon and then disappeared. She felt terrible and elated at the same time. She hadn't stayed with him, but now she knew he'd be coming back to her. Deep down, she knew that she had been a drag on his quest from the start and he'd be better off with her back home, but it didn't take away the shame she felt for quitting. Then she thought of Elmer and what he had done to her and shuddered.

She got the animals moving again and made it safely home less than an hour later.

CHAPTER 5

Earl made up the lost time quickly and by mid-morning the following day, he was passing their campsite from the previous evening. He picked up the still-present trail and moved along at a good pace. He'd be doing cold camps until he found the Overton gang.

He'd moved his Russian to his saddlebags and was still getting adjusted to the two-gun setup with the Colts. The added weight on the left side felt awkward at first, but he'd passed that stage already. When he stopped for camp, he'd practice some dry runs with both weapons to see what worked. He felt comfortable with the new pistols quickly and most of all, he felt better having a dozen shots available without reloading.

He had pressed Target hard yesterday when they had returned to the starting point, so he made an early camp to let him rest. Without the pack horse to slow them down, Earl had estimated that they had traveled almost fifty miles since dropping off Jessie.

After having some cold beans and jerky, he washed and began to practice with the two Colts. He was surprised that after a relatively short time, he was able to smoothly draw and cock the hammer and fire with his left hand. He had always thought of his left hand as a useless appendage and used to joke that all it was good for was counting past five. He found that the trick wasn't in the hand at all, but in his shoulder. Once the pistol was cleanly out of the holster, the rest came instinctively. He had practiced shooting with his right hand so much, the basics of draw, hammer and trigger were natural now with his left.

The next morning before he left camp, he thought he'd try some live target practice with his left hand. He picked out a knot on an old oak about fifty feet away; a reasonable target size and distance with his right hand. His first shot was noticeably slower than his right, but the bullet struck only two inches above the knot. After he had emptied the pistol, he took the full pistol from his right side. He was getting ready to fire when he thought about it for a second and drew out the empty pistol, shucked the empty brass into his pocket and reloaded. The thought of being with no effective weapons even for a minute after he emptied the second Colt gave him goosebumps.

He had to pick a second target as the oak had endured enough damage and selected a downed cottonwood about sixty feet away and picked a broken branch as a target. He'd aim for the base of the branch to see if he could cut it free. He readied himself and pulled the Colt smoothly and fired, then rapidly fired all five remaining rounds into the tree. All six shots had hit within nine inches of the base of the branch.

There was one more thing he wanted to try, then he'd move on. He reloaded all of the cylinders on both Colts and picked out a different spot on the cottonwood. He put his mind into shooting mode and drew both weapons simultaneously and began firing. It was a withering display of firepower as the gunsmoke almost filled the entire glen. He noticed that Target hadn't budged, even with that much noise.

He smiled and walked to the cottonwood, emptying and filling the guns as he went. It was impossible to tell how many hits he had made as that portion of the dead tree was obliterated. He doubted if he'd ever fire that many shots at anything ever again except in practice. He was pleased, though. He'd continue to practice over the coming days until it was as natural as the single gun that he had grown so accustomed to using.

He spent a few minutes cleaning the guns after so much powder had been deposited in the barrels, then mounted Target and rode east.

_____

Back at the Mitchells, Jessie was sitting in the bathtub with her bar of lilac soap in her hand. She was smiling and not washing as she thought about Earl and wanted him to come back as soon as possible. Her parents had been pleasantly surprised by her return, and she told them both about what had happened and how her discovery of Elmer's presence had rattled her. Both were aware of Elmer's violent tendencies, but only her mother knew about what had transpired in their bedroom.

After her father had gone out to the fields, Jessie told her mother about Earl's promise to return and begin courting her. She confided to her mother that he had explained how he had been waiting for the right woman and had told her that she was 'the one'. Her mother was as happy for her daughter as imaginable. After what she had endured at the hands of that monster to have someone as kind and thoughtful as Earl for her husband would balance the scales.

_____

Earl continued to press the chase. After another five miles of traveling due east, the five had turned northeast, heading toward Boston, which made sense to Earl. Outlaws didn't steal money to set aside for rainy day. They wanted to have a good time and that's what made tracking them easier. They would only move quickly when they thought there was pursuit. Once they thought they had eluded any posse, they would look for a place to spend their money. For this group, it would be Boston.

Now that he didn't have Jessie with him, he could make more use of the local law if he needed it.

He stopped once more about ten miles short of Boston. It was getting late and he'd rather arrive in the daytime, so he found a decent campsite, unsaddled Target and brushed him down. After a cold dinner, he began dry practice with his weapons. Now that he knew he could hit his targets with both guns, he just needed to work on smoothing his draw. He worked for two hours, just dry firing, until he was satisfied with his performance and turned in for the night.

As he lay in his bedroll, he decided not to waste any more time thinking about the probable confrontation and let his mind roam into the much more peaceful and enjoyable thoughts of Jessie.

Since he first saw the adult Jessie in those bib overalls, he suspected that she might be the one, and it didn't take long for that idea to grow as he listened to her and even when she threatened to follow him. It was only then that he began to understand that maybe she hadn't tried to join him to try and catch Claude at all, but simply wanted to be with him. What made him sure was that her essential personality was still the same as it had been when he'd gone to war. She was still Jessie.

Now, for the first time in his lawman career, United States Deputy Marshal Earl Crawford wanted to come back from a mission unscathed for more than just the more obvious reasons of not wanting to absorb any more lead. He wanted to return to Jessie.

He let the images of Jessie take control of his mind as he drifted into a peaceful sleep with very pleasant dreams.

―――――

He left the campsite next morning at daybreak, knowing it would put him in Boston just as their normal workday would be starting. He had skipped another cold breakfast, preferring to eat at a local café in town.

It was probably around seven o'clock or so when he entered the town. It was bigger than White Oak, and probably had a sheriff and two or three deputies, but he'd wait to see if he needed them. First, he went to fill his stomach.

He did just that, ordering six eggs and ham, biscuits and coffee and making short work of every bit of it after the waitress set it on his table with a big smile.

He was still drinking some coffee as sat back contentedly looking through the window at the street as it filled with early-morning traffic. He just studied the town and wondered if his targets were still here but doubted it. They would have arrived here three days ago. As a rule, men like that would stay a day to enjoy themselves, get totally whiskey-fried and whore-burned that they'd get up late the next day and move on. It was just what they did, and it was time for him to do what he did.

Earl paid for his breakfast and walked out into the street. He never mentioned to Jessie that he rarely bothered to submit an expense voucher. He hated the paperwork and besides, he would have spent the money on the same things if he was back in Fort Worth.

He walked across the street to the sheriff's office, smiling as he wondered why cafés and sheriff's offices were always located so near to each other.

He entered the office and found a pleasant young deputy behind the desk, showed him his badge and said, "I'm United States Deputy Marshal Earl Crawford. Is the sheriff in?"

"Yes, sir," he replied, then said, "Follow me," stood and led him down a long hallway past the jail cells to a large office and knocked on the door jamb of the open door.

"Sheriff Smith, this is United States Deputy Marshal Earl Crawford. He needs to speak to you."

Earl was impressed with the deference shown by the deputy, so after the deputy waved him inside, he entered and saw an older man about fifty with a shock of white hair and large droopy mustache.

"Come on in, Marshal," he said as he waved him in.

Earl entered as the sheriff stood and offered his hand, saying, "Joe Smith."

Earl shook his hand and offered and equally short introduction, replying, "Earl Crawford."

"So, what is a United States Deputy Marshal doing in Boston?"

"I'm hunting a gang of five bank robbers that held up the White Oak bank four days ago and tracked them here. They should've come through three days ago. More than likely, they stayed here and passed on after having a night enjoying themselves."

"I remember that crowd. One of my deputies pointed them out to me as potential trouble. I looked 'em over, too. I didn't have any descriptions to work with, or we would have picked them up.

I might be wrong, but I think only four of them left two days ago. I think one might have gotten attached to a whore over in the Palladium. It's a fancy name for an ordinary bar and whore house."

"You have a whore house in a nice town like this?" Earl asked with a grin.

"They keep it quiet and the ladies' guild doesn't complain about it, so we let it go."

"Wise decision. Do you think he might be there?"

"Either there or in the hotel. Did you want some help?"

"No. Can you give me description of the one that stayed?"

"Another deputy watched them leave and said the guy with the white streak in his hair wasn't with them. At the time, he wasn't sure if he had departed earlier or stayed. Now, we think he stayed, but I'm not positive."

"Which way were they headed?"

"They were going south, toward Lindan."

"I'll go do some looking around, Joe. I appreciate the help. You guys run a tight ship. Say, one of your deputies wouldn't want the sheriff's job over in Hopewell, would he?"

"Why? Did someone kill the old one?"

"Nope. I'm going to remove both the sheriff and deputy for incompetence when I finish finding this crowd."

"They were that bad, huh?"

"Worse. There was a double homicide in their jurisdiction, and they didn't even investigate or mount a posse to go after the prime suspect."

"You're kidding me. You shoulda hung the bastard on the spot. I'll ask around. What happened with the murderer?"

"He's with the gang that knocked off that bank. He's my brother and murdered his wife and six-year old son."

His reply stunned the sheriff, as Earl knew it would.

"I hope you get him."

"I will. Count on it."

He shook hands with the sheriff and left the office, then once outside, quickly mounted Target and thought he'd check the hotel first. He rode halfway down the long main street and pulled up to the hotel, stepped down and looped Target's reins over the hitch rail.

When he entered, he noticed the nicely appointed lobby and a pretty young lady behind the desk. She was already beaming at him when he walked to the counter.

He showed his badge and said, "Good morning, miss. I'm United States Deputy Marshal Earl Crawford, and I'm trailing some men. Do you have male guest who's about five feet and eight inches tall, black hair with a full beard and a white streak above his right ear?"

"No, sir. We haven't had any guests check in that looked like that."

"Now I'm going to ask a delicate question. I hate to ask it of such a pretty girl as yourself, but I need to know before I head over that way. Does the Palladium rent rooms to guests as well?"

She blushed and Earl didn't know if was because he called her pretty or because of the question itself.

"Yes, sir. They do. They are the only competition for customers of the hotel."

"Thank you. That means that more than likely, he's over there. I think I'll go and arrest the gentleman, although to be honest, he's far from being one."

He smiled at her and tipped his hat, which had the expected but unintended effect, generating a sparkle in her eyes as he left.

Earl sighed as he stepped across the lobby, wishing it wasn't like this.

He didn't bother mounting Target but loosened his right-hand Colt's hammer loop, walked across the street and stepped onto the boardwalk. It was too early to visit a bar, but he wasn't going there to drink.

He entered the open doors to the Palladium, which surprised him because it wasn't even nine o'clock. He couldn't understand why until he went through the doors and found clients at tables eating breakfast.

"Of course," he thought, "if they had rooms, then their customers would need to eat, and they may as well make a little extra money on a captive audience."

Earl scanned the room, not seeing Elmer but wasn't surprised as he walked to the bar.

The barkeeper also must have served as the maître de as he asked, "Would you care for some breakfast, sir?"

"No, thanks. I'm looking for somebody. You wouldn't happen to know my friend Elmer, would you? He was supposed to be coming to Boston with some other pals, but I can't find him at the hotel."

"What does Elmer look like?"

"Shorter than me, black hair, beard, has this weird white streak over his ear. Some of the fellas tried to call him 'Whitey' because of it, but he wasn't too keen on the name. He can have a temper, so we all dropped the idea."

"Yeah, he's here. I'll send him a message. He's in back with a lady."

Earl got a pained look on his face, and said, "I hope not, friend. He's right nasty with women. He killed this one whore down in Athens. He likes it rough, so we try to keep him away from the ladies."

"Damn!"

"What room is he in? Maybe I can talk him out of there before he hurts the woman."

"Go ahead. He's in room six upstairs at the end of the hallway. I knew he had been a bit rough with Sally, but I didn't know it got that bad."

"I'll take care of it."

Earl quickly climbed the stairs, then walked quietly down the hallway to room six and could hear giggling from room four as he passed by. There was no giggling from room six, but there were other, more violent sounds. Knowing that Elmer didn't know him from Adam, he rapped on the door.

He said loudly, "Sally? You're needed up front right away."

He heard a muffled, "No! You're staying here," followed by a loud, "Go away! We're busy!"

Earl pulled his Colt and reached with his left hand, turned the doorknob and yanked the door open. When he looked inside, he saw Elmer with a heavy rope around Sally's neck and his pants were around his knees. He saw her googly eyes and tongue out and realized that he was choking her to death.

Earl didn't bother saying anything as he took one long stride, then swung the Colt and crashed it down on Elmer's head, collapsing him on top of Sally.

Earl grabbed the unconscious man by his shirt collar and yanked him unceremoniously to the floor then quickly loosened the rope around Sally's neck. He could see that her lips were already blue, despite the heavy lipstick.

She coughed as Earl took the rope off her neck and he could see the burns. He sat down on the bed and sat her up to let her breathe. Sally was young for a prostitute, no more than Jessie's age, he guessed. She wasn't overly pretty, and her makeup was in bad shape, which made her look almost comical if it wasn't for her bruises.

She began to come around, and her eyes finally focused when she saw Earl's face not six inches from hers.

"Who are you?" she asked in a scratchy voice.

"United States Deputy Marshal Earl Crawford, ma'am. Elmer here almost killed you with that rope. He's not conscious right now."

"Why didn't you kill him? That bastard wouldn't take no for an answer and kept getting worse. This time, I thought he was going to kill me."

"It was a close thing, Sally. I'm going to take him to the sheriff's office now. Did you want to take a kick or two while I'm not looking?"

"Only two?" she asked.

Earl smiled and picked up the rope for evidence, then he put his Colt back in his holster and walked to the other side of the room slowly adding his hammer loop as he listened for Sally to administer her revenge. He had to wait a minute before she was able to get enough strength to get out of the bed, but once on her feet, she used them viciously.

After the third hard kick, he turned and said, "Okay. Sally, I think it's time I moved him. I'll notify the sheriff. I don't know if they'll press charges because of your occupation and the fact that you're still alive, but I'll tell him what happened and that will be his decision."

"You mean he could get off with no punishment at all?"

"No, I didn't say that. He's wanted for bank robbery in White Oak, too. I'll have the sheriff hold him in his cell until I come back through after taking care of his pals or the sheriff from White Oak comes and picks him up."

"Okay," she said, then administered one last hard kick to his chin.

No man's vengeance, thought Earl, could match that of a woman wronged, even a whore.

Earl grabbed the comatose Elmer, flipped him on his back and pulled his drawers back up. Then he easily picked him up and threw him over his shoulder before he walked into the hallway, closed the door behind him, then headed for the stairs.

The bartender saw him coming and as Earl reached the barroom floor, asked, "Was he passed out?"

"Nope. I had to pistol whip him or you'd have had to replace Sally. He had almost choked her to death with this," he said as he held up the rope.

"She's a good girl. Too bad she couldn't get payback."

"She did. I let her have a few good kicks before I picked him up. This bastard deserved it."

"Thank you for that. Where are you taking him?"

"To the sheriff's office. He's also wanted for bank robbery in White Oak."

"Who are you, anyway?"

"I'm United States Deputy Marshal Earl Crawford. This is one of the five men I'll be bringing to justice."

"Thank you, marshal. Stop by some time and I'll buy you a drink."

"I'll be moving on shortly, but thanks for the offer."

Earl stepped across the barroom floor and exited the Palladium. He kept on the boardwalk capturing the stares of dozens of onlookers as he walked to the sheriff's office.

Once there, he opened the door, swung it wide, and stepped inside with the load.

The deputy stared at him as he said, "Good morning again, Deputy. Got a cell where I can leave this piece of trash?"

"Yes, sir. Come with me."

The deputy led him down the hallway to a very tidy cell area. There were six cells, and none were occupied. The deputy opened the door and Earl dumped Elmer on the cot. He was still out.

"You might want to have your doc check up on him," said Earl.

"I think so. What happened?"

"Let's go talk to the sheriff, so I only have to explain this once."

The sheriff was standing right behind them and said, "Okay. I'm ready to hear this one."

Earl straightened, then said, "I checked with the hotel, but he wasn't there, so I went to the Palladium. I asked the barkeep if he had someone matching his description staying there. He said he did, and I told him that he was rough on whores, so he told me where he was. I went up there, knocked on the door and told the girl, her name was Sally, by the way, that she was needed out front. But Elmer here told me to go away that he wasn't finished. I opened the door and he had this rope wrapped around her neck while he was humping her. She was almost dead. Her lips were already blue.

"Elmer looked up as the door opened and I coldcocked him with my Colt. I took the rope from Sally's neck and she finally came around and was none too pleased with Elmer. So, while I was on the other side of the room and putting my Colt away and hooking my hammer loop in place, she kicked him. Now, you know how long it can take to get that pistol placed just right and that hammer loop on snugly, so the by the time I could get back to stop her, Sally had let him have three more hard kicks. I suppose I'll have to apologize to Elmer for letting that happen."

The sheriff was holding back a laugh as he said, "No, I don't think that will be necessary. We'll have the doc look at him sooner or later. I don't know if I can get the prosecutor to file on this one, though."

"I know. That's what I told her, but I'll notify the sheriff at White Oak that the first of the bank robbers is in your jail and he can send someone over to pick him up."

"Thanks. We'll hold him for them. How did you know he was rough on whores?"

"He used to live in my hometown down in Hopewell. Rumors like that float around."

"True. You off to get the other four now?"

"Yup. Right after I send the telegram. Oh, and Joe?"

"Yeah?"

"You can take your time with the doc. A little pain might do him some good."

"I intended to."

Earl shook his hand and that of his deputy, then left the office and stepped up on Target, heading for the Western Union office.

He stepped inside and wrote:

US MARSHAL GRANT FORT WORTH TEXAS

CAUGHT AND ARRESTED ELMER JACKSON
CHARGED WITH BANK ROBBERY
CAUGHT STRANGLING PROSTITUTE
HAD TO USE FORCE TO SUBDUE
WILL PROCEED AFTER REMAINING FOUR
TWO DAYS BEHIND NOW
PROCEEDING TO LINDAN

US DEPUTY MARSHAL CRAWFORD BOSTON TEXAS

He wrote out a second message:

SHERIFF WHITE OAK TEXAS

ARRESTED ELMER JACKSON IN BOSTON
HELD AWAITING TRANSFER TO YOUR JURISDICTION
ONE OF THE FIVE WHO ROBBED THE BANK

US DEPUTY MARSHAL EARL CRAWFORD BOSTON TEXAS

He handed the sheets to the operator, then said, "I'll need the one to Fort Worth also sent to the following address in a separate message and handed him a third sheet.

It simply read: Jessie Mitchell Farm Hopewell Texas.

"That'll cost you double, you know. If I just add the address to the top, it'll only add a nickel."

"I know. One is business and the other is personal."

"Oh. That makes sense, then. That'll be a dollar and ten cents."

Earl paid the money and received his change. He didn't wait to hear the message being sent because he needed to move, but first, he needed to add to his supplies. He stopped by the dry goods store and added four more cans of beans and some more coffee, knowing he'd be mighty tired of beans by the end of this trip.

Five minutes later, he mounted Target and headed south toward Lindan.

———

Two hours later, there was a knock at the Mitchell farm. Ada Mitchell went to the door and found a messenger there holding a telegram, found a nickel in her dress pocket and handed it to him, then took the message into the main room and looked at the name on the outside of the folded sheet.

"Jessie. You have a telegram."

Jessie was out in the kitchen rolling biscuits when she heard her mother. *A telegram?* She had never received a telegram before. She hoped it wasn't bad news as she stepped quickly into the main room, wiping her flour-covered hands on her apron.

Her mother handed her the telegram and stood by anxiously as her daughter unfolded it and read it, then saw Jessie's face broaden into a wide smile.

"It's from Earl," she said as she handed the message to her mother.

Ada read it and said, "I wonder how much force he had to use to subdue Elmer."

"I have a feeling it was a bit more than he needed to use."

"Jessie, Elmer tried to kill a prostitute by strangling her," her mother said.

Jessie's hand went involuntarily to her neck as she said, "I know."

"Do you think Earl knows?"

"I told him that he had wanted to do bad things to me in the bedroom, but I wasn't specific because it was too difficult to even say what I did tell him."

"Well, I'm sure he knows what he did now."

"I think so."

"He's a good man, Jessie. I'm sure he wanted to kill Elmer for what he did. Many men would have, and he had the authority to do it, especially if he found Elmer trying to kill the woman. It shows just how good he is when he refrained from exacting the punishment he wanted to inflict."

"I know, Mama. He's all I've ever wanted in life."

She hugged her mother and felt safe, except that Earl was still out there.

CHAPTER 6

Earl was still out there, and he was closing in on his prey. He had departed Boston immediately after getting his food and made good time. He ate his lunch, a strip of jerky and some water from his canteen, on Target's back as he pressed southward. He finally had to make camp fifteen miles outside of Lindan.

He tied Target to a tall bush near what barely passed for a pond, unsaddled his gelding and brushed him down, apologizing for the rough treatment he had undergone in the past few days. He then sat on a rock and thought about what he would do the following day.

He was at a disadvantage because he didn't know what kind of horses were being ridden by the gang. None of the witnesses had paid that much attention in White Oak. The best he had were a 'brown with some white patches' and a 'maybe black or gray with a star'. It was odd because most Texans paid more attention to the rider's horse than the man on its back. He had picked up their trail, though. One of the horses had an odd crescent shape in on the right side of its rear right shoe, probably from a missed hammer blow by an apprentice farrier when he was learning to shoe the horse. It was hard to estimate how far behind he was, though, but it should be a day and a half or so.

He feasted on cold beans and jerky before practicing with the two guns for an hour but didn't waste any ammunition. He was getting pretty smooth using both weapons at the same time, and it helped that his hands were large which made pulling the hammer back with his thumb easier.

145

———

The next morning, he was up early and made the two-hour ride into Lindan, which was about the same size as White Oak. He entered the town by midmorning and debated about going to the sheriff's office or just looking around before deciding to scan the town and see if he noticed a four-horse grouping with two horses that matched the vague descriptions he had been given.

He didn't find anything of interest, so he walked Target to the livery, stepped down and looped the reins over a hitching post, then walked into the livery where he found the liveryman scooping hay into the stalls.

"Morning," Earl said, making a rapid appraisal of the man, wondering if he would answer questions better to a stranger or a lawman.

"Howdy, what can I do for you?"

"I'm United States Deputy Marshal Earl Crawford, operating out of Fort Worth. I've been trailing some outlaws who robbed a bank in White Oak. There were four of them and should have arrived a couple of days ago."

"I seen 'em. Not friendly lookin', either. Got here two days ago and asked me to check their horses and change any shoes that needed replacin'."

"One of their horses had an odd crescent shape in his right rear shoe."

"Yup. It was a missed hammer mark. The shoe itself was okay, so I left it on. Had to shoe two of the others, though."

"Can you tell me what the horses looked like?"

"You bet. The oldest, the one with the hammer mark, was a mare, brown with a black mane. She had two white marks on her left rump, but that was all. Another was this dark gray gelding. Had a white stocking on his left front and a star on his forehead. The prettiest of the four was this young gelding roan. He was a chestnut with a nice white pattern on both sides. The last was a run-of-the-mill brown mare with no distinguishing marks at all."

"That helps a lot. Did they stick around or head out?"

"They lit out of here yesterday, heading toward Jefferson. They even balked at paying for getting the shoes changed. One of them, looks a little like you to tell the truth, threatened to go to the sheriff. I told him to go ahead and he backed off."

"Yeah, sounds like him. He always was a cheap bastard."

"You know him?"

"Only too well. He's my older brother. Aside from being involved in the bank robbery, he murdered his wife and six-year-old son. He's the one I aim to see hang."

"I can understand why you'd want that. Anything else you need, Marshal?"

"No, thanks for the information. I'm going to be heading out right away because I need to close that gap some more."

Earl shook his hand and remounted Target. Now he could identify the horses which was a real advantage. That, and they still didn't know he was on their trail.

He kept Target on a nice trotting pace for four more hours before he broke for lunch, not so much for himself, but for his friend. He might need him for serious work later. He unsaddled him and let him graze and drink his fill from a nearby creek. While he was eating, Earl ate four more strips of beef jerky and water, filling his two canteens before he left thirty minutes later.

The next town on the stop was Jefferson, and he thought he might find them there. They hadn't stopped in Lindan for very long, and that surprised him. Jefferson was smaller and not likely to have the same variety of pleasures offered in the bigger towns. But it did have a reputation as being a hard town, so that's why he bet they'd stay there. He expected to reach the town in two hours.

Almost exactly two hours after leaving his camp, Target carried him into Jefferson in the middle of the afternoon. In a town this size, there was no reason to check with the sheriff or city marshal, or whatever they called him because, at best, he would be inexperienced. At worst, he'd be no better than the men he was chasing. Technically, sheriffs were supposed to be for counties and local lawmen were supposed to be city marshals, but a lot of towns still preferred their lawman to be called sheriffs for some reason.

If this one was in his office, he probably wouldn't be much help. He trotted down the street looking at horses. For such a small town, he noticed that it had an out-of-proportion number of saloons. He counted four, and none looked very stylish. Then, standing outside one of the saloons, he noticed two of the four horses he sought, at least he was pretty sure it was two of them. There was the gray gelding with the white stocking and star beside a nondescript brown horse. He was unsure of the other two horses' whereabouts, which meant he had to decide. *Did he try to take down these two, or did he wait until they were together?* He chose to act.

He walked Target to the neighboring saloon's hitch rail, dismounted and tied him off. He loosened his right Colt's hammer loop and walked down what passed for a boardwalk but was really just two connected front porches.

He entered the saloon, let his eyes adjust to the lower light, then walked inside through the squeaking batwing doors. He purposely hadn't shaved since leaving Jessie to develop a harder look.

He walked up to the bar, ordered a beer and when it arrived, he tossed a nickel on the bar, took his beer to the corner table, then sat down and nonchalantly scanned the room. The only one who might recognize him would be Claude, but Claude wasn't there. He soon spotted Weasel Holland sitting in the opposite corner playing cards. He had never seen him before, but for once, the wanted poster was very accurate. He couldn't find either Atherton or Overton, but one of them might have his back to him at the card table, so he drank his beer and waited.

Halfway through his beer, he saw the hidden card player's face as he turned to order another drink. It was Atherton, so he unhooked the loop on his second Colt for insurance and slowly removed the badge from his shirt and pinned it to his vest, then scanned the room one more time for other possible threats. There were only eight other patrons in the bar room and three were so far gone in their liquor, they probably didn't know their own names. The bartender might pose a threat, especially if he had a scattergun under the bar, which they almost all did. Three of the remaining five looked affable enough. That left one of the other two card players and one gent sitting at a table in the other corner on the door side.

The possible threats identified, it was time for him to move.

Earl quickly stood, drew both pistols, then rapidly stepped across the room, glancing once at the stranger in the corner, then cocked both Colts and said loudly, "Holland and Atherton, I'm United States Deputy Marshal Earl Crawford, and I'm arresting you both for bank robbery. Stand slowly and drop your weapons. I have you covered."

Earl took a half second to glance at the barkeep who was staying motionless understanding that it was a dangerous situation and he wasn't about to challenge a United States Deputy Marshal with two cocked Colts in his hands.

Holland and Atherton were momentarily stunned by Earl's warning as they had been so sure that no one had trailed them.

Atherton must have been the smarter of the two as he put his right hand into the air and slowly stood as he began undoing his gunbelt with his left hand, but Weasel Holland tried to play it cagey. He lifted his left hand and started to stand. He had been facing Earl, so when he had looked up, he could see the two Colts aimed in his direction, then glanced left and right quickly to see if he had any support but didn't see anyone.

Earl saw Weasel's eye movement and growled, "Don't even think about it, Weasel. These Colts are both cocked and ready to let loose hell in your direction. You'd better think again. A couple of years in the slammer is a lot better than forever in damnation."

Atherton's gun belt hit the floor with a loud thunk before Earl said, "Step back slowly, Atherton. You're making a smart move. Nobody was hurt in that holdup. You'll be out before you know it."

Atherton backed away. He didn't want to die yet. Not for this.

Weasel thought he had a plan when he suddenly yelled, "Shoot him, barkeep!", then went for his revolver.

Earl didn't even glance at the bartender. He knew he would have spotted any sudden motion in his peripheral vision, but as he watched Holland's pistol clear leather, he pulled both triggers. The double firing of the large pistols echoed in the room as Weasel Holland was slammed back into the wall behind him. Atherton then watched his partner slowly slide to the floor, his eyes wide and unseeing.

Earl had cocked both hammers quickly for any possible threats and scanned the room. The bartender appeared almost disconnected from the whole scene and the other relatively sober customers were non-players as well.

"Atherton, come over here and I want you on your knees facing away from me with your arms behind your back."

Atherton complied willingly, having witnessed the damage that two Colts could inflict at close range.

After he had knelt on the floor, Earl lowered both hammers and replaced his Colts. He pulled Atherton's Colt New Army from his holster and put it in his waistband, then removed a pair of handcuffs from his pocket and locked them around Atherton's wrists.

He pulled Atherton to his feet and turned to the bartender.

"Bartender, which direction to the sheriff's office?"

"It's south, three doors down and across the street. I'm sure he'll be here soon, anyway."

"Sorry about the mess. Write up the damages and I'll give you a chit, so you can get reimbursed."

"I'd appreciate that."

Earl turned Atherton toward the door when a young man, maybe twenty, if that, came racing through the door with his gun drawn. Earl saw the badge on his chest and thought he must be a new deputy.

"What's going on here?" he shouted, pointing his pistol at Earl, despite the badge on his chest.

"Put that damned gun down, Deputy. I'm United States Deputy Marshal Earl Crawford. I have a warrant for the arrest of this man and the dead one in the corner over there."

The kid stood there and continued to aim his pistol in Earl's direction as he said, "I ain't no deputy, I'm the sheriff in this town. And how do I know you are who you say you are?"

Earl sighed. A baby sheriff. Great.

"Can't you see the badge on my chest? If you get close, you'll see that it reads United States Deputy Marshal in capital letters, too. Now, if you want to keep your job as sheriff, you'll let me get this man into your jail and arrange to get the other one picked up by the undertaker. Tell him not to go through his pockets. That's evidence."

Finally, it dawned on the baby-faced sheriff that he was dealing with a United States Deputy Marshal and not some imposter. He lowered his pistol and put it in his holster.

"Sorry, Marshal, I had to make sure you weren't going to shoot me."

"Let's go to your jail. I need to talk to Mister Atherton here."

"Okay."

He turned and led the way out of the saloon.

There were a few rubbernecks watching the two lawmen, well, one lawman and one wannabe lawman, escort the prisoner across the street and down to the sheriff's office. They went inside. It was a cheap building as befit the town. The cell looked adequate though, so Earl put Atherton inside after removing the cuffs.

The sheriff went to notify the undertaker of a business opportunity, so Earl pulled a chair to the outside of the cell and sat down.

"So, Joe, tell me what happened. You don't seem quite as stupid as some of those other guys."

Joe looked like a kid caught with his hand in the cookie jar as he stared back at Earl and replied, "We were just gonna knock off the bank and head out of Texas and have a good time. But Charlie wanted to get some more money, so he wanted to go south to Marshall. He kept complaining about how little we got at White Oak. Weasel and I didn't want any part of that operation, so we cut loose. So, how come a United States Deputy Marshal is following us for such a small job?"

"Don't you know? Claude Crawford killed his wife and six-year-old boy just a couple of days before the holdup. He's the one I'm after. The rest of you guys are just dressing."

"That low-life bastard! I knew there was something wrong with him. I hope you hang him by his privates!"

"Trust me, I'd like nothing better. So, they're planning on another bank job in Marshall?"

"Not a bank job. There's a rancher outside of Marshall, who runs a spread called the Circle K. He's supposed to have a lot of cash in his house."

Earl had a sinking feeling. They were going to hit a residence which was much more likely to result in innocent deaths than a simple bank heist. He had to get on the road to Marshall soon.

"Where is the Circle K?"

"Charlie said it was north of the town. They had a big sign right on the road."

"Thanks. Which horse was yours, Joe?"

"The gray gelding. He's a real good horse, Marshal."

"Well, I aim to borrow him for a spell. When you get out of the pen, come and see me outside of Hopewell. Just ask for the Crawford ranch. I'll have your horse waiting for you in good shape. It's a lot better than having this burg take him. One more thing, Joe. You're a young man, and you don't seem like you've committed to this life. Now, if you can promise me that you'll go straight, I'll tell them to go easy on you. I hate to see someone get roped into a miserable life.

"That's what it is, you know. I've arrested or killed dozens of outlaws, and not one had more than thirty dollars on him. They were lonely, dirty and just plain unhappy men. Now you strike me a young man who wants a better life than that. You probably want a real girlfriend that can be proud of you as a man. No woman is proud of her man being an outlaw, so you think about it."

"Thanks, Marshal, I will. And you're right about not wanting to go this way. It just seemed easy at the time. As far as the horse, that's right kind of you. Did I hear you say Crawford ranch? Like Claude Crawford?"

"Yeah. He's my brother," he replied before he slid the chair back and stood.

He walked outside and stepped quickly toward the saloon already hearing the clock his head ticking down the time to get to the ranch. He found Joe's gray and unhitched him. There was a Winchester in the scabbard, then just before he led him away, he he grabbed Weasel's saddlebags from the dead man's horse and threw them over the gelding's saddlebags.

He led the horse down next to Target and ran a trail line from Target to the gelding, then he turned to go back into the saloon.

The undertaker was getting ready to move Weasel when Earl arrived and said, "Hang on for a second."

The undertaker paused and Earl said, "Go ahead and go through his pockets."

The undertaker pulled a total of $87.55 from his pockets, putting a lie to his intentional fib he'd told Joe Atherton about what he found in outlaws' pockets.

"Give it to me."

The undertaker sadly complied and handed over the cash.

Earl accepted the money, then looked at the man behind the bar and asked, "Barkeep, what were the damages?"

"Twenty dollars should cover it."

Earl knew that there wasn't that much in the way of actual damages. A good cleaning should clear up the blood but handed him a double eagle anyway.

"How much to put him in the ground?" he asked the man in the dark suit.

"I can provide a nice burial for twenty dollars."

"Here's ten dollars. That's all he's worth. The rest will go back to the citizens of White Oak."

He pocketed the rest and went back outside, looked for telegraph wires and found them leading to a small building at the end of the road standing by itself. He smiled as he remembered Jessie telling him to look for the wires.

The youthful sheriff interrupted his reverie by walking up behind him and asking, "What am I supposed to do with the prisoner, marshal?"

"Just hold him until someone from White Oak comes to get him. It should be in the next couple of days. They have to pick up another one in Boston. Have him empty his pockets and any money he has belongs to the bank at White Oak. Give it to the deputy who picks him up and get a receipt, so they don't blame you for keeping it."

"Okay."

"Joe told me to take his horse. I need to get down to Marshall quickly. That brown one over there is Weasel's. Dispose of it and the rig as you see fit. You might want to keep his gun rig yourself, too. His is a lot better than yours."

"Thanks. I never thought of that."

"I need to send a few telegrams and then I'm going to ride hard for Marshall."

He shook the kid's hand, then turned to the horses. He might make a good lawman if he lives long enough.

He led the horses down the street to the telegraph office, stepped inside, and began to write:

US MARSHAL GRANT FORT WORTH TEXAS

**FOUND HOLLAND AND ATHERTON IN JEFFERSON
ATHERTON SURRENDERED IN JAIL WAITING PICKUP
HOLLAND DEAD IN SHOOTOUT
CLAUDE AND OVERTON HEADING TO MARSHALL
PLAN TO ROB HOUSE AT CIRCLE K
WILL TELEGRAPH SHERIFF THERE
PROCEEDING TO MARSHALL WITH ALL SPEED**

US DEPUTY MARSHAL CRAWFORD JEFFERSON TEXAS

He then wrote out a second message:

SHERIFF WHITE OAK TEXAS

**ARRESTED ATHERTON IN JEFFERSON
IN JAIL AWAITING TRANSFER TO YOUR JURISDICTION
ONE OF THE FIVE WHO ROBBED THE BANK
ATHERTON COOPERATED DESERVES CONSIDERATION
WILL ASSIST IN YOUR PROSECUTION
ONE ROBBER KILLED IN SHOOTOUT**

US DEPUTY MARSHAL CRAWFORD JEFFERSON TEXAS

Then he wrote out a third:

SHERIFF MARSHAL TEXAS

**TWO CRIMINALS HEADED TO ROB HOUSE AT CIRCLE K
DANGEROUS MEN AND WELL-ARMED
HEADING YOUR WAY WITH ALL SPEED**

US DEPUTY MARSHAL CRAWFORD JEFFERSON TEXAS

He handed the three messages to the telegrapher, and said, "I need the last one sent out as fast as you can get it there and marked for urgent delivery. I'll need the first one sent out to this location separately. I know it costs more, but it's personal."

He handed the operator a short note that read:

Jessie Mitchell Farm Hopewell Texas.

"Very well, sir. That will be $1.25."

Earl handed him the money and said as he left, "That one to Marshall could save some lives if it gets there soon enough."

"Understood, sir. I'll send it first and they'll have it in minutes."

"Thank you."

He stepped outside, mounted Target and set off south at a fast trot. It was another long ride to Marshall, and he wouldn't take a break except to water the horses. Atherton's gelding would let him move faster, and he needed every minute.

———

Outside of Marshall, Claude and Charlie sat on their horses in a large copse of cottonwoods overlooking a large ranch house.

"You sure there's a lot of cash in there?" Claude asked.

"I used to work at this place. I know it like the back of my hand. The old man didn't trust banks 'cause he lost a lot of his money when the first bank in town went belly up. I'll bet he's got five thousand dollars in there."

"You know where he keeps it?"

"Not exactly, but we grab his wife or his daughter and point a gun at their heads, he'll tell us. He really cares about 'em."

"Won't one of the hands come over?"

"Nah. The bunkhouse is a good quarter mile away. This is perfect, Claude. We get the money and then hightail it to Mexico."

"Won't they be able to identify us?"

"Not if they're dead."

Claude grinned and replied, "That's a good idea."

"We'll wait for the sun to go down. And then we hit 'em fast."

———

As Earl fast trotted the horses south, another messenger arrived at the Mitchell farm and received another nickel, this time from Jessie. She anxiously opened the telegram as her parents walked up behind her and asked what Earl had written. After she finished reading, she handed them the message.

"He's gotten three of the five now," said Tom. "But he has to get to Marshall fast if he wants to stop those last two."

"He was in a shootout with two of them, Papa. Do you think he was shot?"

"No, Jessie, he would have said so in the telegram. This is just a copy of the one he sent to his boss. He's sending a copy to you to keep you informed of where he is and what he's doing. It looks like he's quite fond of you, Jessie."

"He told me he wants to court me when he returns, Papa."

"Well, that's wonderful news, Jessie. And when did he tell you this?"

"Before he left."

"And why am I just finding out about it now?"

"I didn't want you to think anything happened out there on the trail."

"I would never have thought that might have happened for a moment. I know you both and you are very moral young people."

Then Jessie almost blurted out, "I wish that it had," but she bit her tongue.

CHAPTER 7

Earl was still moving fast. He had watered the horses an hour ago and was on Joe's horse now. It had a bouncy gait, so it was a jarring ride, and he wished he was back on Target, but he needed the speed and Target needed the break. He was still eight miles out of the town when the sun grew lower in the sky and was nearing sunset, leaving him with maybe another hour of sunlight. He hoped that the Circle K was at least two miles north of Marshal and that the where waiting for darkness before they mounted their attack.

———

Charlie and Claude were getting anxious. They had been sitting next to the horses for a few hours now in a small clump of trees just a couple of hundred yards from house end of the long access road. Charlie had gone through dozens of cigarettes and was running low on tobacco and was irritated that Claude didn't smoke.

"How much longer do you reckon, Charlie?" Claude asked.

"About an hour or so. The sun will be down in thirty minutes and then it won't be dark enough for another thirty minutes after that. I don't want to give anyone a chance of seeing us moving in. They always ate a late dinner, so we'll catch them eatin'."

Claude grinned as he not only thought of the money, but the power he would feel when he saw the look of terror in the women's faces, followed by the shock on those same faces when he and Charlie pulled their triggers.

He replied with just a simple, "Okay."

_____

Earl saw the sign over the ranch's long access road just as the sun was giving away to the night, and hoped he was on time. As he pulled onto the ranch's access road, he dismounted and changed back to Target. He needed to be sure of the horse's behavior under fire. He then started Target forward at a walk, not wanting to run into those two accidentally. The access road was a one of the longest he'd ever seen. It must be an enormous spread. But he hadn't seen any commotion, which meant that they hadn't made their move yet or maybe decided to go somewhere else. A ranch this large would have a bunkhouse full of cowhands, and he wondered why they even thought of robbing the place. A bank would be easier than taking on a dozen armed ranch hands.

_____

Charlie thought it was dark enough, and said, "Let's go, Claude."

Claude replied, "Let's get rich!", before boarding his horse as Charlie stepped into his saddle.

Two minutes later, they tied off their horses in front of the house, checked for any nearby ranch hands, then Charlie slowly climbed the porch steps, opened the front door and walked inside as Claude followed. Both had their pistols drawn.

_____

As he walked Target down the access road, Earl could see smoke from what was probably the cookstove in the kitchen, but he couldn't make out the house yet. As the access road made a final, gradual turn toward the house, the roof of the huge house came into view.

He stopped, dismounted, then led the gray gelding to a nearby tree and tied him to a low branch so he could crop grass. He quickly trotted back and hopped into his saddle and soon resumed the slow walk toward the ranch house, wondering if they might have changed their minds about trying to rob the ranch. If some ranch hands had seen them coming, they probably would have just ridden on.

As more of the house came into view, there was enough light for him to see two horses sitting out front, recognized them both, and knew that they had to be inside the house. He kicked Target into a fast trot and unhooked his hammer loops but slowed when he was closer to minimize the sounds of his arrival.

———

Inside the house, Claude and Charlie were moving quickly on their tiptoes, looking for victims.

The King family was sitting down to dinner and heard their muffled footsteps, and Brandon King looked questioningly at his wife Abigail. She raised her eyebrows as if to say, "I don't know."

Mister King started to rise from the table as the two invaders entered the room with their guns drawn.

"Don't anybody move!" snarled Charlie.

"Charlie Overton! *What the hell do you think you're doing?*" exclaimed Brandon.

"What does it look like I'm doing, you overblown moron? Me and my partner are gonna take every dime you've got in this place, or your dear wife and cute little daughter are going to die. It's your choice. Get us the money or we'll begin shootin', startin' with your wife."

Brandon knew Charlie. He had fired him two years ago for being the kind of man he saw before him. He also knew that money or no money, they were all going to die, and he needed to stall for time.

"You're not killing anyone tonight, Charlie. I'll get you the money."

"Well, that's the first smart thing you've said so far. Stand up and come over here."

———

On the porch, Earl had listened to the opening tirade as he stood beside the door. He pulled his right-hand Colt, cocked the hammer, then slipped through the front door that they had conveniently left wide open. He stepped into the front parlor and could hear them still threatening in a back room; probably the dining room as it was supper time. He looked around for the best position to stand, knowing that they'd be exiting that room soon. It sounded like there were three possible innocents in the room from what Overton had just said: the ranch owner, his wife and his daughter. If the two bad men both came out it wouldn't be too bad, but it was more likely that one would stay with the hostages, and he'd have to gamble. He had heard that Charlie knew the ranch owner, so he'd probably stay with him to get the money. That meant Claude would stay with the women, and Claude was unpredictable. He just didn't know where the ranch owner would lead Charlie. He knew the kitchen was always in the back of houses, so unless there was another office somewhere else in the house, he guessed that they'd soon be entering the front parlor because the office door was open nearby.

He had barely had time to draw his conclusion when it was confirmed with the sound of approaching bootsteps and he realized that they were headed his way. He quickly pressed himself against the wall on the left side of the hallway and waited for Charlie and his captive to enter the front room.

It was ten seconds later that he saw Brandon King come through the doorway with the muzzle of a pistol at his head. Earl noticed that the hammer wasn't even cocked, but his was and he had it aimed at head level. He'd have to take the shot and then rush Claude. It was the only option he had.

He kept his pistol aimed at the oncoming Charlie Overton as the ranch owner passed with his eyes focused in front of him. After just one more step, Charlie's head came into view and Earl fired. Then all hell broke loose even as Charlie's body crumpled to the floor.

The two women screamed, thinking Charlie had shot Brandon. Brandon was shocked as he heard the explosion behind him and realized that he was still alive. He turned and saw another stranger in his house, heading down the hallway toward his wife and daughter with a loaded pistol. He looked around for a weapon, not realizing that he was their rescuer, then picked up Charlie's pistol, and cocked the hammer.

Earl walked quickly down the hallway not paying any attention to the man behind him. *Why should he?* He'd just saved the man's life.

In the dining room, Claude was in a state of panic. *What happened? Why did Charlie shoot the rancher before he got the money?*

He turned and began to walk to the door as Earl almost reached it. Both had their pistols drawn, but unlike his deceased partner, Claude had his hammer cocked.

The women saw a new man wearing a badge suddenly appear at the door just as Claude aimed his gun and he was the first one to fire. Earl felt the bullet hit the top of his right shoulder halfway to the neck, then dropped his Colt and luckily, it didn't go off. The wound was only a deep crease. He reached for his left-hand Colt before Claude could cock his hammer again and was ready to pull his trigger when another shot rang out from his left and Earl fell to the floor, his finger yanking his trigger as he fell, the .44 drilling through the dining room wall as blood began running from his head.

Claude ran out the door and saw Brandon King standing at the end of the hallway with a smoking gun, then quickly changed direction and ran out the kitchen door as King started chasing him.

Claude hit the ground and ran for his life around the house and reached his horse, leapt into the saddle, then set his horse to a gallop and disappeared down the access road into the night. He had seen that face looking at him and instantly recognized Earl even after all these years and felt a measure of satisfaction knowing that he had killed his brother. He hadn't been able to beat him for a long time before he ran off to war, and that one bullet had made up for it.

Claude may have been pleased with killing Earl, but he knew he was in deep trouble now. He had ridden out of the ranch without much thought about where he would go after he made his initial escape, so when he arrived at the road, he stopped briefly. He was going to go to Marshall when he heard the rumble of made by a number of horses coming from the south and somehow knew it had to be a posse. Someone had tipped off the law, so now he was hunted. He turned north and rode away as quietly and quickly as possible, grateful for the darkness.

———

In the house, Brandon King stopped at the kitchen door and closed it. He had to stay and protect his family and make sure that his wife and daughter were safe, so he turned and began walking quickly to the hallway.

Meanwhile, his wife and daughter had huddled over the wounded lawman, and when Brandon exited the kitchen and saw them trying to help him, he was stunned.

He shouted, "*What's the matter with you women?* That man is a murderer! That's why I shot him!"

"You shot a United States Deputy Marshal, Brandon!" his wife shouted back.

"*What?*" he asked in shocked disbelief as his stomach twisted.

His wife returned to look at the wounded man and said, "He was trying to save us. He shot the man that was behind you and then came in to stop the other one. The other one shot him in the shoulder and the marshal was just about to shoot him when you shot him in the head."

"Oh, my God! What have I done? Is he dead?"

"No. He's bleeding badly, though and needs a doctor. Can you ride into town and get him quickly? Annie and I will do what we can to stop the bleeding. Go!"

Brandon didn't waste any time, realizing there was at least one horse outside the front door, so he ran out front and started to mount the horse when he heard, "Stop right there! Get your hands in the air! This is Sheriff Hopkins."

Brandon yelled back, "Bill? This is Brandon King. Come in quickly. We need to get the doctor here as fast as we can."

Sheriff Hopkins turned to his best deputy and said, "Go get Doc Faircloth and make it quick. Go!"

The deputy ran to his horse and hopped into the saddle, then wheeled his horse around and spurred him down the access road.

Brandon King dismounted and said, "I screwed up, Bill. The marshal had stopped Charlie Overton from killing me and my family and then he was shot by the last man but as the marshal was getting ready to shoot him, I shot the marshal thinking he was one of them."

"Things happen like that when the shooting breaks out, Mister King. Let's go in and see the damage."

They walked into the house and the sheriff saw where Earl had blown Charlie Overton's head apart. It was a mess, but it just needed a cleanup. He turned to another of his deputies and said, "Put a cloth under what's left of his head and drag that bastard out of the house. Hold off putting him on a horse until we figure out whose horse is whose."

"Yes, sir."

They then walked into the kitchen where the women had slid Earl because of the added light and the water pump. There was also a large supply of towels nearby. They had already soaked a towel in water and wrapped it tightly around his head. Brandon King's shot had tapped the very crown of his head but hadn't penetrated the skull. Earl had been right about the shoulder wound. It had creased along the top of his shoulder and neither was a life-threatening wound.

The sheriff looked down, saw the badge and said, "I think I know who he is. He sent me this," then handed the telegram to Brandon.

"When did you get this?" he asked as he read it.

"It was delivered less than an hour ago, which frosts me a lot. The deputy marshal had them mark it urgent and the messenger delivered it two hours after it was sent. We could have stopped them if the damned telegrapher had gotten off his ass."

"But he did stop them, Bill. He rode over thirty miles in less than three hours and got here and killed one and would have stopped the other if I hadn't shot him. I feel like a heel."

"No use feeling bad, Mister King. Things happen."

Earl heard voices, so he wasn't dead after all. *How had Claude gotten a second shot off?* He knew that he had him because his second Colt was armed and ready to go, it would have killed him but somehow Claude had gotten off his second shot first. His shoulder hurt, and he had a headache but none of that mattered now. He had to find Claude. His eyes popped open and he saw a very pretty face smiling at him like it always happened in the dime novels.

"He's awake, Mama!" cried Annie.

"Got to get Claude," croaked Earl.

"You're not going anywhere for a while, Marshal," said Brandon.

Earl struggled to sit up, but someone was holding him down.

"I'm all right," claimed Earl in a more normal voice.

"You've been shot twice, Deputy," said the sheriff. "We got your telegram late, so we didn't get here on time, but we'll hunt down that last one for you. Don't worry. We'll find him."

"He's my brother. He killed his wife and little boy ten days ago."

Everyone, including the hardened sheriff were dumbstruck by his comment.

Earl then said, "I need to notify my parents in Hopewell that he's loose. He may head there for safety."

"I'll get a telegram sent as soon as we get back. We've got a doctor coming. He should be here shortly."

"He's got to fix me up so I can travel. Can you notify my boss in Fort Worth?"

"Sure thing. You did a hell of job here, Deputy Crawford."

"That's a bunch of horse manure. I get shot by my brother twice and he gets away. I screwed this one big time. I'll probably get fired for it, too. It's just as well. I'm getting tired of getting shot."

As he was talking the women had cut away his shirt to staunch the bleeding from his shoulder. His head wound had already congealed, and the bleeding had slowed to almost nothing.

Earl then passed out again from the blood loss.

Meanwhile some quick-thinking deputy had figured out that Earl's horse was Target by measuring the length of the stirrups. No one noticed the gray gelding tied up in the trees who was spending his leisure time mowing the grass.

———

At the Crawford ranch, Jessie was in the front room talking to Earl's mother while Ray sat on the other side of the room reading. Since she had returned from her shortened ride with Earl, Jessie had been a regular visitor and had brought both telegrams to Lydia, so she could be informed of Earl's progress in finding Claude.

There was a knock at the door. It was a bit late for visitors, so Jessie said, "I'll get it."

She had her derringer in her pocket and her hand on the little gun as she opened the door and was surprised to see the same messenger she had seen twice before standing at the door.

"Evening, ma'am. I have a telegram for the Crawfords."

"Thank you," said Jessie as she tipped him a dime and accepted the message.

She walked in and handed the telegram to Lydia.

Lydia opened it and began reading. Suddenly her hand went to her mouth and she said quietly, "Oh, my God!" as the telegram slipped from her hand. Ray's head snapped up to look at his wife.

Jessie picked up the message and read:

CRAWFORDS CRAWFORD RANCH HOPEWELL TEXAS
US MARSHAL DAN GRANT FORT WORTH TEXAS

EARL CRAWFORD SHOT TWICE
SHOULD RECOVER
STOPPED ROBBERY AND MURDER AT CIRCLE K
SHOT BY CLAUDE CRAWFORD WHO ESCAPED
POSSE SEARCHING
WILL ADVISE

SHERIFF BILL HOPKINS MARSHALL TEXAS

Jessie's eyes filled with tears, then walked over, handed the message to Ray, then slowly stepped over to Lydia and both women embraced, sharing a mutual concern for Earl's welfare.

———

Earl finally awakened a second time an hour later, noticing that he had been moved to a cot and his shoulder and head had been bandaged. He had no shirt and could hear the doctor outside talking to someone explaining what he had done to repair Earl's wounds. The head wound only needed four stitches as the bullet had ricocheted just off the crown of his head leaving more of a puncture wound than a streak. He had put some salve on it and bandaged it. The bandage would need to be changed daily. The shoulder had required twenty stitches to close. It would be stiff for a while but should heal nicely. The sutures would have to be removed in ten days.

Someone thanked the doctor and Earl heard him leave the house. He tried to sit up, finding it difficult at first, but after a while he managed to get upright. He was dizzy, but not as bad as he thought he'd be. His shoulder was tight and pulsed with pain, but again, not as badly as he expected. He was glad to see he was still wearing his pants and boots as he sat and waited until the dizziness stopped. He began moving his head back and forth to test just how much he could get move before the dizziness became too big of a problem. When he tried too quickly, the dizziness returned in earnest, and he had to wait again. After two more minutes, he braced his left hand on the side of the cot and stood and thought it wasn't that bad. He was tired of getting shot, and he'd been hit twice this time. That made nine bullet wounds, and being a target is a bad way to make a living, unless you were a horse and that was your name.

He carefully stepped out of the room and tried to orient himself as he balanced himself by keeping a hand on a wall. He was on the ground floor and must be in a sitting room, although he had no idea where the they had gotten the cot. He walked out into the hallway and began to grow more confident, so he pulled his hand from the wall and walked down the hallway.

He patted his hip and found only his britches. *Where were his guns?* He remembered having them in the kitchen and wandered that way, finding the room empty, so he began to look for his guns. They were nowhere to be seen, but he did find his hat, and noticed the two holes. He carefully put it on his head and continued his search. After a few minutes, he figured he wouldn't find them and if they weren't there, so be it. Then he remembered he was set up for traveling fast and had left his Smith & Wesson with Jessie. Then he winced as he recognized the error that he had made in having the sheriff send that telegram. He probably told them he had been shot. If his parents told Jessie, she'd be worried to death, as would his mother. He should have told the sheriff to just tell them that Claude may be heading their way, but it was too late now. He had to find his Colts and his badge. He needed his badge.

He found his vest near his hat. It had a rip along the top more than a hole but wasn't as bloody as he expected and still had the badge on the front. He slid the vest on and walked out of the kitchen hunting for his weapons. He needed to go and stop Claude.

He stepped out into the hall and was met by Abigail King coming the other way.

"Excuse me, ma'am, but do you know where my guns are? I've got to get going."

"Marshal, you've been shot twice less than two hours ago. You need to rest."

"I beg to differ, ma'am, but I've got to go. I need to stop my brother."

"The sheriff has his men combing the area for him. They'll catch him and you need to rest. And, by the way, when was the last time you ate?"

"I'm not sure, to tell the truth, but I feel fine now. I appreciate all you've done for me. Tell the doc to submit his bill to the United States Marshal's office in Fort Worth," he said, then added, "Heck, never mind. I'll pay it myself."

Earl reached in his pocket and pulled out some bills. He handed them to Mrs. King, saying, "That should cover it, ma'am. Now if you could give me my weapons, I'll be out of your hair."

"You are going nowhere, Mister Crawford! You will stay here until I say you leave! Do you understand?"

"Normally, ma'am, I'm very subservient to the gentle sex, but this is more important. It's my job. If you won't return my weapons, then I'll just do what I can."

Earl walked past the protesting woman and left the house, then saw Target still hitched to the rail. He quickly crossed the wide porch, walked down the four steps, untied him and climbed into the saddle. As he turned and headed down the access road, he could hear a female voice threatening to come and drag him back into the house. She reminded him of his mother.

He got almost to the end of the road and found the gray gelding where he had left it, then turned Target into the trees, untied the horse and attached the rope to his saddle. He guessed that it must be about ten at night as he led the gelding out of the ranch and turned south toward Marshall.

He was almost to the town that was close to becoming a real city an hour before midnight and realized how odd he must look, so he pulled off the road onto the grass and searched his saddlebags for his spare shirt. He found it, and after removing his vest, gently pulled the shirt over his already stiffening right shoulder, but it was still somewhat useful. He put his vest back on and then moved his badge back onto the shirt. He went back to his saddlebags and looked for something else he could use. He had no pistols and no knife. He still had his Winchester and four boxes of cartridges, but he really wanted those Colts.

He also realized that the lady had been right. He was ravenously hungry, but he'd see what he could do about it later. Then he remembered the two sets of saddlebags on the gray gelding, so he went over to the horse and pulled Weasel's saddlebags off. He put them on the ground and opened the first one. The moon was up and casting a good amount of light, although it was far from a full moon.

He found the usual contents, a shirt, some socks and a pouch with the makings for a percussion revolver. Then he opened the second and almost didn't see anything in the low light and was about to give up on it as well when he found another pouch on the bottom. He looked inside, hoping it might be a pistol, but it was stuffed with cash. He wasn't sure, but it looked like the money from the White Oak holdup. *Why did Weasel have the money?* He knew he'd never get the answer to that, so he took the pouch and put it in his saddlebag.

Then he inspected the two saddlebags on the gelding and to his disappointment, found nothing of use. There was a Henry in the scabbard, so it wasn't a total loss.

He mounted Target, regained the road and began walking him to Marshall.

————

Fifteen miles so to the north, Claude was having a worse time of it than his younger brother, despite his lack of gunshot wounds. He hadn't eaten since breakfast and had no food in his saddlebags. He didn't want to return to Jefferson, and he had almost given up on his next move when he arrived at the Big Cypress River, the same river which ran about six miles east of the Crawford ranch. His mood improved immensely when he realized its significance. He'd follow the river cross country and be at the family ranch by noon. His father would cover for him and tell any lawmen that he wasn't there. He could go to his old house and eat and relax until he could safely leave. He probably could even get his old man to cough up some cash to help him on his way. He smiled as he directed his horse down into the brush alongside the river.

———

Earl entered Marshall just around midnight. He had no idea where he would go and then he thought he may as well press on through and take the road leading back to Hopewell. It was another long ride, about thirty miles, but he had the time. He had little else, but he had the time.

He exited Marshal a few minutes later and headed north. He and the two horses just moving along, and Earl wasn't too sure at what speed. He began to doze and realized that he wasn't going to last much longer in the saddle, so he pulled the two horses off the road and led them to a large grassy area. There was no water nearby, but he had two, no, three canteens.

He took off his hat and filled it with one of the canteens and offered it to Target. He had to hold his fingers over the bullet holes to keep the water from draining out too fast. Target drank most of the water, so he refilled it for the gray gelding. He took a drink out of the third canteen, and despite its metallic taste, he was so thirsty he almost drained it.

He sighed and remembered that he had three cans of beans, but without a knife or a can opener, they were just dead weight. He did manage to find two sticks of jerky which made him laugh. He had more than five hundred dollars on him, between his money and the bank's, but it didn't matter. The nearest town, Gilmer was ten miles away, so at least he'd be able to get some breakfast there.

With no other real options, he took out his bedroll, removed his boots and slid inside. He was asleep in less than a minute.

———

It seemed like just a few seconds later when he was awakened by a harsh voice shouting, "You'd better come out of that bedroll empty handed, mister, or you're a dead man!"

Earl popped open his right eye and saw a deputy sheriff leveling a Winchester at him.

"Good morning, Deputy. Glad to see you're on the job. Did you guys catch my brother last night? Mrs. King said you were all out searching for him."

"Don't give me no sass, mister. Just slide out of that bedroll."

Earl sighed and did as he asked, despite the pain from his shoulder and his noggin.

When he was all the way out, he asked, "Could I at least shake my boots to get out any nasties that might have crawled in there?"

"Go ahead but do it real slow."

Earl shook each boot and then slid them on, before asking, "Now, Deputy, I'm going to very slowly pull back my vest, okay?"

The deputy noticed that he was unarmed but suspected he might have a shoulder holster, so he cocked the Winchester.

"Go ahead, but I'll blow a hole in you if I see something that shoots in there."

"The Kings kept my Colts, but I sure could use a pistol."

He slowly raised his vest, revealing the badge pinned to his shirt.

"I'm United States Deputy Marshal Earl Crawford. I was shot twice last night, and I don't really want to go for a third so soon. So, could you please lower the Winchester?"

"Oh, sorry, Marshal. We're still hunting Claude and I wasn't sure."

"You're okay, Deputy. I don't blame you a bit. You had to be careful with him. He killed his wife and son and tried to kill me. He's not a good man."

"Doesn't sound like it. How come you're out here if you were shot twice last night?"

"For the same reason you are. I've got to find my brother. I need to stop him. Right now, I'm awfully hungry and I need to get riding, so I can get some breakfast at Gilmer. I really need to get going. Tell the sheriff and the Kings that I'm sorry that I left so abruptly. I have a job to do."

"I'll let him know what happened. Do you need anything?"

"I need everything. Oh, and, Deputy? Before I go, I need to give you something that I found last night."

He walked to his saddlebag and pulled out Weasel's pouch.

"I found this in one of the bank robber's saddlebags. He was the one I killed in Jefferson yesterday afternoon. It's the money from the holdup and it looks like all of it, too. I have no idea why he had it all, but if you could, give it to your boss and have him wire White Oak that the bank's money has been recovered."

"I'll do that. Don't you want a receipt?"

"No, I'll trust you. I don't have the time to do otherwise."

Earl shook the deputy's hand, wincing as his shoulder protested, then turned and mounted Target. He was set to hit the road when he heard the hooves of a fast trotting horse, then he and the deputy both looked quickly to the source, expecting to see Claude coming at him with a Winchester pointed their way. He started to reach for his rifle, when he saw that it was obviously not Claude. It was the daughter of the rancher. She saw him and waved.

"Now what is this all about?" he asked himself.

The deputy watched in awe as this pretty young lady with long blonde hair came smiling up to Earl and handed him his gun rig. It was so heavy, her arm drooped.

"Thank you, ma'am," Earl said, as he accepted his missing weapons from her, "I'll probably be needing these shortly."

"My mother told me that I'd never find you, but I remember you said you were from Hopewell, so I thought you might be headed this way. She said if I found you to tell you that you were an ill-mannered young man and that if you ever came back this way, she'd give you a harsh word or two, but I think she was just saying that. She was really worried about you. So was I. My father said he really owes you a lot for what you did and said he felt really bad for shooting you."

"He shot me? It wasn't Claude?"

"No, sir. Your brother shot you first and then when you were getting ready to shoot him, my father shot you. He thought you were part of the gang and had a falling out."

"Well, that explains that. I was confused and thought I had my brother dead to rights and then I blacked out."

"He said to tell you he was sorry."

"Tell him it was only a mistake and not to worry. Thanks a lot for bringing my guns."

"My mother also sent this, but I helped."

She handed him a paper bag and said, "We made some bacon and egg sandwiches. She said you hadn't eaten in a while and needed the food."

"Tell your mother I sincerely apologize for being rude. It's not my normal nature. It's just that I need to do this job. I need to stop him before he hurts someone else. But thank you both for the food. It will save me time."

"The sheriff said you were the bravest man he'd ever seen. We think so, too."

"I'm really just doing my job, miss. But I really need to get back. I think I know where my brother's going."

"One more thing, please, Marshal?"

"Anything. What can I do for you?"

"Let me give you a kiss."

"If you insist," Earl replied with a smile.

She leaned across and instead of the peck on the cheek he was expecting, she kissed him on the lips as if they'd been courting for a while and were close to walking down the aisle.

She leaned back smiling broadly and said, "I wanted to do that while we were helping you, so now I feel better."

"Well, I'm glad I could help. Could you escort the deputy back to his office? I think he's lost."

She glanced over at the stupefied deputy and laughed before replying, "I will."

Earl held his smile as he waved and turned toward Gilmer and the ranch. He belted his Colts on as he rode which was a bit awkward with only one fully functional arm, then pulled each one and checked the loads. He still had two empty shells in his right-hand pistol, so he replaced those with two from his belt. He didn't want to waste time digging around in his saddlebags.

Having the Colts back in place made him feel less naked as he set the horses to a fast walk. Then he remembered the sandwiches and when he opened the bag, the aroma of the bacon was heavenly. As he reached in for a sandwich, he pulled out a piece of paper.

He opened it and read:

Deputy Marshal Crawford,

The King family will be forever in your debt. Your actions last night were nothing less than heroic. If I hadn't overreacted, you would have been able to shoot the other man.

I've sent a telegram to Marshal Grant. If you ever need anything, don't hesitate to ask.

Brandon King

Earl smiled. At least he had done some good on this trip. He took one of the three sandwiches and took a huge bite and rolled his eyes upward. The taste was a bit of heaven itself.

———

Claude woke up to a much less desirable situation. He had been bitten by mosquitoes for most of the ride and when he had finally stopped, he had to avoid being bitten by a water moccasin. He hated snakes, despite the kinship. He finally had found a reasonably safe place to bed down.

Now, after he had awakened, he found himself hungry and itching all over. At least he knew that no one would be following him, and no one knew where he was headed. He believed that he was home free.

———

In White Oak, Elmer Jackson couldn't believe his luck. No one could recall seeing him at the holdup and Joe Atherton hadn't been returned yet, so he was grinning as they removed the handcuffs and the sheriff told him to get out of town and not come back. They even had to give him his horse and gun back. His head still hurt from where he had been cold-cocked, and he really wanted to ride back to Boston and give that whore a good licking but figured nothing good would come of it. Maybe he'd just head back to Hopewell and see if he could fit back in. The only crime he was accused of had melted away. He was still grinning as he mounted his horse and headed out of town.

CHAPTER 8

Earl stopped in Gilmer just to water the horses and refill his canteens. There was another twenty miles before he reached the ranch and needed to get there to warn his parents, convinced that Claude was heading that way. He hoped that his murdering brother didn't get there first but hadn't expecting him to ride cross-country in a reasonably direct route. There was also the chance that the posse had tracked him down, but his gut feeling was that they hadn't found him, especially after the deputy had misidentified him as his brother.

He remounted on the gray gelding and left the town at a medium trot.

––––––

Claude was only ten miles from the ranch, but he had rougher going and his horse was tuckered out. He didn't care about the horse and could always get another animal at the ranch, so he pressed on.

––––––

Earl decided to pick up the pace even more as his level of anxiety kept rising but didn't know why, maybe it was his own worries playing against him. Regardless of the reason, he had the gray gelding moving at a fast trot. Claude may not have known that Earl was on his way after the shootout. Earl was dead as far as he knew, but Earl was positive that Claude was somehow going to try get to the ranch. It wasn't even a guess anymore. He just knew, and he had to get there first.

———

At the ranch, Jessie had already arrived to talk to her new best friend, Lydia Crawford. They hadn't heard a word from Marshall, so they both stayed in the main room talking, expecting a messenger to arrive at any minute. Every once and a while, one or the other would walk out to the porch and scan the road for the messenger. Jessie went more often, because she was really scanning for Earl.

———

Claude finally saw the ranch buildings in the distance. He was hungry and felt miserable, but he had made it and was immensely relieved. He knew that he was home free as he exited the open country and crossed over the road to the back of the ranch. He would approach from the west where no one could see him in case the law was already there. He unhooked his hammer loop and smiled.

———

Earl was two miles south of the ranch, had eaten the second sandwich earlier and was now just finishing the last one before he washed it down with fresh water from his canteen. He hoped he would make it in time as he envisioned Claude riding onto the ranch with his pistol drawn.

———

Claude walked his horse up to the west side of the house and dismounted. He didn't care about the horse, so he just stepped away from the exhausted animal. The horse needed water badly, so he slowly walked to the trough.

Claude stepped onto the porch and crossed to the open screen door. Everyone inside was talking and didn't hear his footsteps as he pulled his Colt out of his holster, then opened the door as three faces turned to him expectantly, hoping to see Earl.

"Well, well. What do we have here?" asked a smiling Claude as he took one step into the room and stopped.

After the shock of seeing Claude subsided, his mother growled, "You get out of this house, Claude! You are no longer a member of this family. You are a monster!"

Claude laughed. Papa would put her in her place, so he turned to face his father.

"Papa, do you hear what she said? She can't do that. You're the head of the family and only you can do that, but I know that you won't. I can stay, can't I, Papa?" he asked in his most pleading voice.

Claude was stunned when his father said firmly, "No, Claude, you can't stay here. You make me ashamed to have given you my name. You aren't my son. You must leave; and leave now. Your brother is hunting you and will find you."

Claude laughed louder, before he said, "Earl? That wimp? I killed him last night. Shot him right in the chest and watched him go to the floor and stay there. He's dead, Papa."

Jessie would have none of it and snapped, "You're a liar as well as a wife and son killer!"

Claude turned to her and said, "So, Jessie, what's the matter? Don't like the idea of your hero being dead? It's too bad, isn't it? Well, folks, whether you like it or not, I'm staying. Papa, I don't know what's gotten into you. You always knew how people lied about me. I had to kill Earl first, Papa. He had his gun out and was going to shoot me."

His father glared at him and replied sharply, "Claude, Earl is a good man, and a better man than you could ever hope to be. If he had his gun on you, he would have warned you to drop your weapon. I'll bet that you had your gun on him before he even saw you."

Claude was getting angry and it was bordering on an insane rage. His father, who had protected him all those years was turning against him. He didn't deserve this kind of treatment. *Who the hell did his father think he was? He's defending Earl, for God's sake!*

Claude's eyes scrunched into slits as he snarled, "Papa, you take that back right now. You always told me that I was your favorite son. You knew that I was going to be great someday. Well, that day is now. I have power over all of you. I can kill all of you if I want, and then I can stay here as long as I want because it will be my ranch."

He laughed at the thought. *It would be his ranch, and those two old people were in the way.*

Claude had drifted into the depths of insanity, and those watching him could see him sink into the abyss as his eyes returned to that wild look that Jessie had seen as he rode away from the murders.

———

Earl arrived at the ranch and turned on the access road then quickly slowed down when he saw the horse at the trough still wearing its saddle. Claude had somehow beaten him to the ranch, and he had a serious problem now as he angled left toward the barn. When he was close, he stepped down and let the horses go to the trough themselves. He'd tend to them later because he needed to tend to Claude now.

————

Inside, Claude was doing everything but frothing at the mouth. He was looking wildly from victim to possible victim as he tried to choose the order of their deaths. *Who should he shoot first? The girl? No, she wasn't even in the family. She goes last. His mother? No, she was always against him. It would cause her more pain if she saw her husband die in front of her. It had to be the old man. That would begin to set everything right.*

He pointed his muzzle at his father and almost shouted, "I'm going to kill you all for not believing me. You're all wondering who will be the first to die, don't you? Well, I've made my decision!"

Then he laughed and as he shifted his sights to his father, he announced in his crazed voice, "And the first one to die is…."

He paused for effect and didn't hear the door open behind him before he heard the voice from the beyond the grave.

"Claude Crawford, you are under arrest for the murder of Eva and David Crawford. Drop your weapon and put your hands behind your back."

Claude didn't hear Earl's voice. It was Death calling to him.

But that was all wrong! The answer should have been 'Ray Crawford'. Why had the voice of Death said 'Claude Crawford'?

He turned to correct the voice and saw the handsome face of his dead brother. *How perfect! He could kill him again!* He lifted his pistol to return him to his grave where he belonged.

Earl didn't hesitate and fired both Colts at point blank range. He had made sure that no one was behind him as he pulled the triggers.

Claude looked at him with crazed eyes and a smile on his lips as he dropped to his knees, then fell face first onto the floor.

Earl quickly returned his pistols to their holsters and stepped into the room where everyone was still in a state of shock. They all knew they would die at the hands of the madman in just moments, and then incredibly, he was lying dead on the floor. And yet, there was Earl, whom he claimed to be dead, standing there with his head wrapped in a bandage. Then he spoke, breaking them out of their trance.

"Mama? Papa? Jessie? Are you all okay?" he asked.

Jessie recovered first as she quickly popped to her feet, flew across the room and threw her arms around his chest.

"Earl, you're okay!"

"Mostly," he replied as he grunted.

"Oh, I'm sorry," she said as she released him, "You were shot twice yesterday, weren't you?."

"That's all right, Jessie. It was worth it," he replied as he smiled at her.

His parents approached him slowly, neither looking down at Claude's body. His mother wrapped her arms around him much more gently with her eyes full of tears. Not for the son that was lying on the floor dead, but for the one that had returned to them.

His father reached him and said softly, "Thank you, Son. He was about to kill us all."

"He was going mad, Papa. I could see it when I confronted him at the ranch. His eyes were demonic when he shot me. That's why it was so important that I get here. I knew this was the only place he thought he could be safe. They wanted to keep me at the ranch house for a couple of days, but I knew I had to get here. I'm glad I made it in time. Papa. Why don't you take Mama and Jessie into the kitchen? I'll take care of moving Claude. It's my job."

"Alright, son," he said as he smiled at Earl and patted his good shoulder.

"Ladies, would you accompany me to the kitchen at the request of the marshal?"

Lydia nodded and stepped toward her husband as Jessie looked at Earl and worried about his recent wounds. She could see that one was on his head somewhere, and saw the ripped vest and some blood, but didn't know how serious they were.

"Go ahead, Jessie. I'll be all right. Please?" Earl asked.

She smiled at him and said, "Alright, Earl. I'll be here when you return."

"I'll be looking forward to it, Jessie," he said as he smiled back at her.

After they were gone. Earl looked down at Claude's body. This was going to be difficult. He didn't want to pop any stitches and start bleeding again.

He blew out his breath and reached down with his left hand, lifted Claude and flipped him over so he didn't streak as much blood across the floor. He then grabbed the front of his shirt and began sliding him across the floor, then reached the doorway and slid him out onto the porch and released his grip.

He looked at the three horses outside. Claude's horse was in bad shape, so he left the porch, then went to the gray gelding and led him to the left side of the porch and tied him to a porch support post. Then he slid Claude's body across the porch and when it was near the edge, he summoned every bit of his strength and lifted Claude's body with his one good arm, flipped him across the saddle and then had to rolled him over onto his stomach, so it could hang over the saddle. He exhaled sharply and quickly inspected his right shoulder for any seeping blood. Not seeing any, he stepped off the porch, went around to the gelding and tied the body down.

Earl led the gelding over to where Target still stood watching them, tied a lead line to Target, mounted and then set off for Hopewell. As he came to the Mitchell farm, he decided he'd better go and pay a visit to let them know that their daughter's murderer had paid the ultimate price, so he turned Target down their short access road and stopped in front of the house.

He stepped down, flipped Target's reins around the hitching rail and walked up the steps. After knocking on the door, Ada Mitchell opened it and saw Earl smiling at her.

"May I come in, Mrs. Mitchell?" he asked, as she noticed the bandage on his head.

"Of course, you can, Earl? How are you doing? Jessie said you were shot just last night."

Earl followed her inside while Tom was in the kitchen working on the pump.

"Yes, ma'am, but I'm fine. Can you have Tom come in, please?"

"I'll do that and we'll be back in just a moment."

She was getting nervous. She knew Jessie was over at the Mitchells and hadn't ridden in with Earl.

Fifteen seconds later both Mitchells were sitting in front of Earl.

"First, I need to tell you both that Jessie is fine and still with my parents."

They both let out the breaths that they had been holding.

Earl then went on to tell them of the events of the past day, ending with Claude's death.

"That's the whole story. I just wanted to let you know that Jessie is safe, and that Eva and little David can rest in peace now that their killer had been brought to justice."

The Mitchells had listened to the tale with a combination of awe and horror. Claude had almost killed their second daughter, but Earl had stopped him.

"Earl, I don't know what to say after that," said Tom, "It's almost too much to absorb in one sitting."

"Just accept the end results knowing that Jessie is safe. I need to get Claude's body to the undertaker and send a telegram to my boss. If you'd like, you can go to my parents' place and talk to them and Jessie. I'm sure Jessie would be happy to see you."

"We'll do that, Earl, and thank you so very much," Ada said as she rose, crossed the few feet to Earl and gave him a gentle hug.

Tom shook his hand, and both followed him out the door. They looked at Claude's body draped over the gelding, but neither said a word.

"I'll go get the buggy ready, Ada," Tom said as he walked toward the barn.

Earl mounted Target and turned his gelding and the grizzly cargo toward the access road and then north to Hopewell.

He arrived ten minutes later and walked the horses to the mortuary. He stopped out front, hitched Target and went inside. After talking to the undertaker, he brought the gray gelding around the side and the undertaker and his assistant removed the body. Earl paid the fee for his burial and was asked what he wanted on the marker. He had them put his name and the dates of his birth and death but nothing more. The undertaker, having heard all the stories about Claude and Earl's mission to bring him to justice understood completely.

He then walked to the Western Union office, and even though he knew where it was, he looked up at the wire and smiled.

He went inside and wrote:

US MARSHAL GRANT FORT WORTH TEXAS

CAUGHT CLAUDE AND OVERTON AT CIRCLE K
HOSTAGE AND ROBBERY ONGOING ON ARRIVAL
KILLED OVERTON
CLAUDE ESCAPED
RETURNED TO HOPEWELL WITH HASTE
FOUND HIM ABOUT TO EXECUTE PARENTS
AND JESSIE MITCHELL
HAD GONE TOTALLY INSANE
SHOT AND KILLED CLAUDE
WILL MAKE FULL REPORT
LEAVING TOMORROW FOR FORT WORTH

US DEPUTY MARSHAL CRAWFORD HOPWELL TEXAS

He handed it to the operator who read the message and looked at him.

"That'll be fifty cents, Marshal. And I have one that came in for you about twenty minutes ago."

Earl handed him a half dollar and received the telegram.

US DEPUTY MARSHALCRAWFORD HOPWELL TEXAS

SHERIFF WIRED ABOUT CLAUDE AND OVERTON
RETURN WHEN YOU CAN TRAVEL

US MARSHAL GRANT FORT WORTH TEXAS

Earl sighed. It sounded like Dan wasn't pleased with what had happened. He had let one get away and then violated the doctor's orders, which was breaking an important rule. Well, he wasn't surprised. This mission had started out strange and had gotten worse as it went along.

He went back outside and picked up the gray gelding and walked out to Target, then mounted and was getting ready to leave Hopewell when he swore that he saw Elmer Jackson walking into the saloon. He walked the horses to the hitching post and stepped down, walked into the saloon and released his left-hand Colt's hammer loop. He looked around the bar and damned if his eyes hadn't told him the truth when he spotted Elmer Jackson sitting at a table drinking a beer.

Elmer looked up and saw Earl looking at him and immediately recalled the face from the whore house in Boston. *He was the bastard who had pistol-whipped him!*

Earl walked over to the table, but Elmer hadn't done anything yet, so Earl left the Colt in its holster.

"Elmer, what are you doing out of jail?" he asked.

"And who are you to be askin'?"

"I'm the United States Deputy Marshal that gave you that crack on your skull to keep you from strangling that whore to death in Boston," he answered loudly enough for the few patrons to hear.

"We was just havin' fun, and you stepped in and tried to be the big man."

"If you were just having fun, then why did Sally kick you four times when you were down? She'll have rope burns around her neck for the rest of her life, you low-life bastard."

"Well, Mister Marshal, there's nothing you can do about that or the bank robbery, either. Nobody in White Oak could identify me, so I'm free of the law, and I can stay here as long as I like."

Earl was surprised that Joe Atherton hadn't fingered him for the bank job and wondered if he'd changed his mind. He'd have to find out later.

He stared at Elmer and growled, "You'd better keep your nose clean, Elmer. I'll be on you like buzzards on a dead carcass. I've killed your pals Weasel and Charlie, and I just dropped Claude off at the undertaker. You're next if you so much as sneeze wrong."

Earl then turned and left the bar seething, knowing that there was nothing more he could do, especially not with that worthless sheriff still in charge.

Earl wondered what was wrong with the law that scum like Elmer are free to walk the streets and innocents like Eva and David are six feet under the ground.

He mounted and left the town heading south. He knew he'd have to tell Jessie, and both sets of parents that he'd seen Elmer. They'd have to protect her while he was in Fort Worth, but he had to go. It was the final step in this mission and at the very least, he'd have to write his lengthy report, which might be the last one he ever wrote.

Thirty minutes later, he turned onto his parents' access road, and could see the Mitchell's buggy. He was exhausted, but at least he understood why. He walked both horses into the barn, removed their gear and brushed them down, having to work around his shoulder wound. He put them in stalls and made sure they had plenty of oats and hay, then he went outside and had to hunt down Claude's mistreated horse. He wasn't a poor horse, but just needed some food and care. Earl led him into the barn as well and removed his saddle and blanket and saw several large saddle sores. He had some salve in the corner for those and spread it liberally across the sores on the animal's back, then he brushed him down, staying away from the sores. He gave him oats and hay and left him in the stall to rest. He deserved better treatment than this.

When he was satisfied that he was done, he felt his head and thought about removing the bandage around his skull. Then he realized, almost in shock, that it had only been sixteen hours since he'd been shot. No wonder he was so tired. Somehow that night seemed days away rather than just hours. He put his Stetson back on, its holes obvious, and started back for the house.

He stepped up onto the porch and walked into the main room where he was met with five sets of wondering eyes.

"Is Claude taken care of, Son?" asked his father.

"Yes, Papa. He's at the mortuary."

"Good."

"As long as I have you all here, I have some disturbing news. When I was dropping Claude's body, I saw Elmer Jackson walking into the saloon. I had a talk with him, and it seems that he wasn't charged for almost killing the prostitute in Boston, but that's not surprising. Most prosecutors won't touch a case involving violence against a prostitute short of murder, and sometimes not even then. But the kicker was that none of the witnesses in White Oak identified him as being with the gang and obviously Joe Atherton hadn't fingered him when they picked him up, so they set him free. There's nothing I can do about it except what I did. I warned him that I'd be watching him like a hawk and would shoot him if he strayed. He probably knows what I can and can't do, but hopefully, the threat that I'm watching him will help."

Jessie's eyes widened at the news. She thought she had been freed from that fear. Now she couldn't go into town with the almost terrifying prospect of seeing him again.

"Earl, am I in danger?" she asked quietly.

"Not immediately, but over time, I'm not betting against it. Always keep that derringer close. Mister and Mrs. Mitchell, you both need to keep an eye out as well. Mister Mitchell, do you have any other weapons besides that squirrel gun that Jessie had?"

"I have a shotgun that I use for keeping varmints away."

"That's helpful, but not if you only have bird shot. You'll need to pick up some better shells for protection later, maybe some double aught shot. There are also several guns in my packs that I left with Jessie. Feel free to use whatever you need. I'll be heading back to Fort Worth in the morning. My boss seems to be mad with me for screwing up a few things and I need to write my report. I'll be gone five days or so."

"Earl, how could he be mad at you? You saved at least six lives on your trip and caught every member of that gang," Jessie asked angrily.

"I let Claude escape and disobeyed a doctor's orders. The second one is a real no-no. It shouldn't be too bad, but I'm kind

198

of tired right now. If it's okay, I'll wander over to the other house and take a nap. I'll answer any questions you might have in a couple of hours. Okay?"

Before anyone could reply, he waved, then turned and headed out the door. He needed to clean his guns, too, so he went into the barn and found his saddlebags, removed his gun cleaning kit and headed for the house.

He opened the door and found all the smells of death gone. He walked into the kitchen, sat at the table and removed his Colts one at a time, shucking empty and full shells into his hand and then laying them on the table. When both guns were empty, he began to clean the weapons. As he was cleaning, he heard small footsteps in the main room and knew it was Jessie.

"Earl?" she called.

"In here, Jessie."

She stepped into the kitchen, saw him cleaning his guns and said, "I thought you were going to take a nap."

"I am, but I needed to take care of these right away. If I didn't, they'd start to corrode from the powder residue. Have a seat."

Jessie sat down and looked at his drawn, but still handsome face.

"Earl, what are you going to do next?"

"Just like I said I was going to do, Jessie. I'll get back to Fort Worth and take my medicine, write my report, and then take the two weeks leave we get whenever we're shot. I'll come back here and start courting you, Miss Mitchell. You did give me permission, if I recall," he said as he smiled at her.

"You meant what you said?"

He stopped cleaning and put the rag down.

"Jessie, did I or did I not tell you that you were the one that I had been searching for over most of my life?"

"Yes," she whispered.

"And, Miss Mitchell, did I not kiss you?"

"Yes," she whispered again.

"And finally, Miss Jessie Mitchell, did I not tell you I'd come courting when I returned?"

"Yes, but when you told me, I was still upset and wasn't sure you meant it."

"Well, Jessie, I most certainly did mean it. If I get my way, I'll court you for as long as you think is proper and then I'll marry you. I don't want to spend the rest of my days without you, Jessie."

"Earl, I want nothing in this world more than to be your wife, but there's something you need to know before you even start calling on me."

Jessie sighed, and her eyes began to well with tears and Earl had no idea what could be worse than what she'd already told him.

"Go ahead, Jessie. I want you to understand one thing before you start. I love you, Jessie Mitchell. Nothing you can say will ever change that. Do you understand?"

"Yes," she squeaked.

Then she continued in a subdued voice, her eyes lowered, "When I was married to Elmer, he hurt me, Earl. I know you found out about how he used the rope. That terrified me more than you can imagine. But he did other things to me. He hurt me in other places."

She paused, her tears falling to the table. Earl wanted to hold her, but knew she needed to release the demons that were inside her.

"Earl, he hurt me where a woman is a woman. I had to see a doctor and that's when my father drove him away. The doctor said it should heal, but he wasn't sure. It took months before I even had my monthlies again. I feel normal now, but I don't know if I'd be able to be a wife like a husband needs a wife to be. Earl, I love you so much. I've loved you since I was ten, and now, I have that chance to be your wife. Before I met Elmer and he did those horrible things to me, knowing I was going to be your wife would have made me happier than you could ever imagine. But now, I'm so afraid of not being able to make you the wife you deserve that I feel miserable. I'm sorry, Earl."

Earl stood and walked over to Jessie whose head was still down. He lifted her chin and gave her a gentle kiss.

Then he took her hand and said, "Come with me, Jessie."

He led her into the main room and sat her down on the couch, then sat next to her and put his good left arm around her shoulders. She naturally leaned her head against his chest.

"Jessie Mitchell, before I tell you anything else, you must understand that I never lie. I always will tell you the truth. Always. Now, about your problem. First, you should never apologize about anything to do with your marriage. It was Elmer's fault, not yours, and I'll find some way of making him pay for what he did to you. Trust me. People like him always think they'll get away with something. I'll dig around in his past and when I return, I'll have something that will get him hanged. So, forget about Elmer for a while. Let me talk about my favorite, subject…us."

Earl took a breath and continued.

"When I was away fighting in the war. Even before I received my mother's letter telling me that Eva had married Claude, I found myself thinking of your eyes and the wonderful times I spent with you as we just talked. At the time, I wondered why I spent more time thinking about you than the girl I had been visiting. After all, you were just a young girl without all those mesmerizing bumps and curves that attract a man's eyes. After I did receive that letter, I began to realize just how much I enjoyed your company. You were important to me, Jessie, even then. It was you who carried me through the rest of that war.

"If I had been halfway smart, I would have returned to Hopewell and waited for you to reach marrying age. But I was a coward, Jessie. I couldn't let Claude have his satisfaction, so I stayed away. Remember I told you I was always looking for the one woman I knew I could spend my life with? Well, there was my problem, but I was too ignorant to realize it. I had already met her, but she was a girl and not a woman. In my mind, you were still a girl and I couldn't connect you to the wonderful young woman I have beside me now.

"So, Miss Mitchell, I am going to tell you honestly and without a doubt that I want to marry you. I love you so completely, Jessie, that I'd rather spend the rest of my life with you even if it means having to just hold you close and nothing more. I'd much rather have you that way than being intimate with any other woman. I love you, Miss Mitchell, not the package that you live in. Do you fully understand that?"

Jessie found it difficult to believe that any man, especially one as masculine as Earl, would even think of giving up that critical part of love for a lifetime together as she looked into his eyes.

She finally asked softly, "You really mean that, don't you, Earl? You'd be willing to give that up and still marry me?"

"Yes, my love, I most assuredly do mean that."

She began to cry again and wrapped her arms around him. He held her tightly, vowing to punish Elmer Jackson for doing what he did to Jessie.

Finally, she looked at him and said quietly, "Earl, did you want to try it now to see if we can be man and wife?"

"No, sweetheart, and for one very good reason. I'm not going to give you any excuse for getting out of marrying me. If we tried now and it hurt you badly, then you'd want to call off our marriage. Now, I know that it will probably be fine, but I'm not going to take the chance of losing you, Jessie. We'll wait until our wedding night for that reason alone. I love you too much to risk it. I want you to just prepare for our wedding when you think the timing is right. If you want to wait a few months, I may not like it, but I'll wait as long as you want me to. But I'm not giving you up because you are the one, Jessie."

Jessie was both relieved and amazed at his answer, so she asked, "So, you'll marry me when you get back from Fort Worth?"

"If you'll give me a few days to get these stitches removed. It's only been a day since the doc put them in. I need another nine days or so."

"I'm sorry, Earl. I had forgotten about your being shot. Does it hurt?"

"Not as badly as it should. The doc says I need to change my head bandages daily but didn't say for how long. I think two days is good. The sutures can come out in nine more days. I'll see Doc Simpson when I get back to Fort Worth."

"Earl, how many sutures did you need?"

"I think he said twenty in the shoulder and four in my noggin. It's not bad, though."

"Earl, I'm being selfish. I was worried about me and I should have been worried about you."

"Jessie, you were worried about me earlier. Some women would marry the man first and tell them later. You are not selfish at all. You're the same selfless, considerate and warm soul that I love."

"I love you, Earl," she said as she sighed.

He leaned over and gave her a long and deep kiss as she responded and held him.

"Well, Miss Mitchell, now that we have the marriage question out of the way, do you know what you can do for me?"

"Anything."

"You can move you cute behind back to the house and let me get some sleep. I'll be back over in time for dinner. Okay?"

"You like my behind?" she asked with a slight giggle.

"I like your behind and your front and everything in between, above and below. So just move all those cute parts back to the house and I'll finish my cleaning and get to my nap."

She smiled at him, gave him another kiss and left the small house not even feeling her feet touch the earth as she returned to the ranch house.

Earl was still smiling when he finished cleaning his Colts. He loaded them each with five rounds, put them back in their holsters and took them with him to one of the two bedrooms. He took off his holey hat, carefully laid down on the bed and was asleep in less than a minute.

Jessie had practically floated back to the house. She had been so afraid of telling Earl about her injuries that she dreaded it more than when Claude had entered the room. But he not only told her that it didn't matter, he had told her that he loved her and even showed how much he did by refusing her offer to let him take her to bed. She didn't think she could love him more than she had earlier that day but found that she did, and she was going to be his wife.

Her mother noticed the change when she entered the room, and for a brief moment, she thought that they had been intimate in the short time she was gone, but then realized that her hair wasn't mussed, and her clothes were exactly as they had been when she left. She wanted a few minutes alone with her daughter to find out why she was so exquisitely happy.

Jessie told them that Earl had been cleaning his guns when she had arrived and was going to nap after she left. Then she told them that he had asked her to marry him when he returned to Hopewell. They all were very happy for them both and gave her hugs of congratulation before Lydia announced that she was going to prepare lunch.

Jessie passed a look to her mother that suggested she had more news for her, and Ada announced that she and Jessie were going for a short walk and would be back shortly.

Ada hooked her arm through her daughter's, and they left the house. Once they reached the ground and began walking toward the pastures to the west, Ada turned to Jessie and asked, "So, what's the rest of the story?"

"Mama, I can't believe he loves me as much as he does. It has me flummoxed a bit, really. I told him of my concerns with the damage Elmer had caused, and he told me that it didn't matter. He said he loved me for what's inside and that he'd live with whatever we discovered after we married. Mama, I even offered to go to bed with him right now to see if it would be okay. I know it makes me sound like a cheap harlot, but I had to know."

"But I can tell that you didn't, Jessie. Why did he refuse?"

"For the most extraordinary of all possible reasons, Mama. He told me that he wasn't going to let me use that as an excuse not to marry him. Can you believe that?"

Her mother's eyebrows peaked as she replied, "I have to admit, I do find that hard to believe, knowing men's fondness for romps in the bedroom. Are you sure he likes women at all? I mean all these years with women practically throwing themselves at his feet causes one to wonder."

"Trust me, Mama. I know he likes women. I could tell. When he kissed me when we were in the house, both sitting on the couch close together, it was quite obvious that he was excited to be so close to me. It was going to be painful for him after I left, I'm afraid. I asked him when we were on the trail why he never married after I had seen a telegram that he had received from the marshal in Fort Worth. The message said that Teresa O'Toole had been chasing after him after he had saved her from being kidnapped."

Her mother interrupted, asking, "And you think that's a problem?"

Jessie shook her head and replied, "No, it was what started our conversation. Anyway, I asked him about all these beautiful women that chased after him and why he had never married. He told me that he knew that all of them saw him as a handsome face and nice body and not past that. He said it's like men do when they see a good-looking woman, and he didn't like that, either. He said he wanted to find the one woman that saw him as he was inside not just on the outside.

"Then he said that he always enjoyed talking to me when he was courting Eva. He said he'd rather spend the time with me, but I was just a girl. During the war, he said he always remembered those times just talking with me, and when he came back from the war, but didn't return home, he told me that he was always searching for the one woman he knew he could be with.

"When we returned after that one night we spent talking, he was getting ready to leave and his last words to me were 'you're the one'. That's when I knew, Mama. I knew he wanted to marry me, but I had that one giant worry; my terrible secret that I thought would ruin my chances to be the wife he needs. It weighed on me, Mama. I was frightened to tell him, but I knew I had to. And when I did a few minutes ago, Earl made me the happiest woman in the world."

Ada processed all the information. She had never heard of a man so much in love as to forego having marital relations if it meant hurting his wife. Earl was truly an amazing man; one she could have easily fallen in love with if she were twenty-five years younger.

"I'm very happy for you, Jessie, and I'm very proud of our future son-in-law. I've never met his like before and will unlikely meet one in the future."

"Mama, I only pray that I can make him completely happy as his wife."

"I think you already have, dear."

Mother and her very contented, happy daughter then returned to the house.

They had lunch and spent time talking about recent events, including the reappearance of Elmer Jackson. They all knew they were waiting for Earl to awaken from his nap, so they could ask questions about the missing holes in his excessively concise story.

Three hours later, Earl's eyes snapped open, and had no idea where he was for a moment. It took him a full minute to remember where he was and why he was there. His shoulder was throbbing from lifting Claude onto the horse and ignoring it for the past twenty hours. He swung his feet onto the floor and discovered that his boots were still on his feet, so he wandered into the kitchen. He took off his shirt gingerly and looked at the bandage over his shoulder. There were a few bloodspots, but not many. He felt his head, then removed the bandage. There wasn't any fresh blood, so he left it off.

He began pumping water until he had a good flow and plunged his head under the cold water, then took a towel and gingerly patted the top of his head. He looked at the towel and found no new blood and was satisfied that he could go without the bandage. He ran his fingers through his hair and searched the house and found Claude's razor in the same bedroom he was using. He really would prefer his own, but it was out in the barn, so he took some soap and built up a good lather and scraped the stubble from his face, causing only two nicks, so he was happy. He ran more water and rinsed off his face and cleaned the rest of his chest with soap and clear water.

Now that he was reasonably clean, he felt human again, and a hungry human at that, but had no idea what time it was. His internal clock had been reset, so he looked out the window at the shadows and guessed it was close to five o'clock. He put his shirt back on and then his hat. He was going to take his Colts, decided against it, then remembered Elmer, and put them on.

Refreshed, he walked out of the small house toward the main house. Jessie was standing behind the screen door and as soon as she saw him step out of the small house turned and said, "Earl's awake and heading back. It looks like he took his head bandage off, too."

She scurried back to the room and sat down, not wanting to appear too anxious.

"Afternoon, everyone!" Earl said as he entered.

He received a chorus of various welcomes, but he only looked for Jessie who was beaming at him and smiled back at her.

"When's dinner, Mama?" he asked.

"In about an hour and a half. I have a roast in the oven with some potatoes."

"That sounds good. So, I guess I need to fill in some blanks about what happened since I left."

Jessie's father asked, "The biggest question we all have, Earl, is how did you do it? In less than twenty-four hours, you left Jefferson, rode down to Marshall, stopped two men from murdering a family, killed one, took two bullets, left after two hours, then rode sixty miles, and got here in time to save your parents and Jessie. That's almost impossible for a man in good condition to do. How did you do it?"

Earl simply answered, "It's my job, Mister Mitchell."

"It has to be more than that!"

"No, it's not. I've been a Deputy U.S. Marshal for seven years now. I've learned how far I can push myself. I have to do that all the time. This case was even more important because it involved family. I know that I pushed the limits, but I had no choice. I knew the posse down in Marshal, no matter how competent they were, wouldn't find Claude. I knew where he was probably headed, so I needed to get out of the house and on the road. They thought that keeping my Colts hidden would keep me from leaving, but I had to go. Having them returned to me was a godsend, but I would have used the Winchester if I had to. I had no choice. I was not going to fail in this."

"You can make it sound like it was routine all you want, Earl, but no one here will buy it. So, what are you going to do now?"

"I'll spend the night here and then in the morning, I'll head back to Fort Worth to make my report. I'll take a day there doing all the administrative necessities and then come back to marry Jessie. What happens after that will depend on what my boss will say. I may not be a deputy marshal much longer. No one should have more than nine bullet holes in his carcass anyway, so I probably won't miss it much."

"When are you and Jessie are getting married?" asked his father.

"We just agreed to the formalities before I had my nap. I had told her I was intending to court her when I returned, but we both thought that whole process was a waste of time. Isn't that right, my betrothed?" he asked as he smiled at Jessie.

"You're correct as usual, my future husband," she replied as she grinned back.

There was more discussion about the events of the return ride from Marshall. Jessie was particularly interested in Annie King's appearance and subsequent kiss and wondered if that would continue after they were married. She realized she was probably doomed to it for the rest of her life, but it was a small price to pay.

After a dinner that finally satisfied Earl's hunger, he said, "Folks, I know it's early. But I need to pack what I need for my trip to Fort Worth. I'm going to try to make this trip out and back in five days. It may take me longer, but I'll try. Target has given me eighty miles in a day before, but never back-to-back. I'll take the gray gelding along and switch off. I'll take a bag of oats, so I can give them both something better to eat. If anyone wants to ask anything else, I'll be out in the barn getting my saddlebags ready. I'm planning on leaving very early, Mama, so don't bother getting up early to make me breakfast. I'll be fine."

Earl didn't wait for a response before he waved and headed out to the barn and make his choices about what he'd be taking. He'd be traveling fast and light, but was going to be a hard two days, especially on the horses. If he left around five o'clock, he'd see how far he could go.

He emptied his saddlebags and began tossing things he'd be taking onto the worktable. One bar of soap, his razor, two cans of beans, the bag of jerky, a box of ammunition, his bedroll and slicker. He stepped back, ran the numbers in his head and added another can of beans, then loaded them into his saddlebags and set them aside. He filled four canteens and put them alongside the saddlebags. Finally, he took his other set of saddlebags and filled them with oats to supplement the grass the horses would eat when they finally bedded down for the night. If he left tomorrow, which was a Tuesday, he should be able to make Fort Worth Thursday morning, get his work done and start back Friday morning. He would probably have to take a slower pace on the way back or the horses might break down. A lot depended on what would happen in Fort Worth.

He was satisfied with his choices and then examined both horses. They had already made that long ride the night before but showed little evidence of being overworked. Their joints felt good and there was no swelling anywhere. He'd have to watch them closely on the trip, though. What really drove him crazy was the absence of railroads. For almost forty years now, there had been plans to build railroads throughout Texas. First there were all the bad financing schemes, then the war came followed by Reconstruction. If the Yankees had stayed out of it, there might be more railroads in the state, but now it looked like they'd start building them. It just didn't help him now.

He heard noise out front and saw the Mitchells boarding their buggy to return home and noticed that Jessie wasn't with them. With Elmer around, it made sense to leave her here where she couldn't be found. He waved to them as they turned the buggy around. They both returned his wave before the buggy rolled down the access road.

He ambled over to the small house. He needed to sleep, but it would be hard to find after the long nap. He entered, closed the door, and when he turned, he saw a smiling face on the couch and smiled back at Jessie.

"And what, Miss Mitchell, are you doing here?"

"I just wanted to spend a couple of hours with my fiancé before he left on another crazy journey."

"Well, in that case, you're welcome to my temporary residence."

"Are you ready to go, then?"

"Yes, ma'am. I'll just need to saddle the horses in the morning, and I'll be off."

"I wish I could come with you."

"So, do I, but it's going to be a hard ride, and I'm not too sure of what will happen when we get to Fort Worth."

Jessie stood and walked close to Earl.

"Earl, I can't tell you how happy you've made me today. I was so worried over these past few days since you left. Between my personal problems and worrying about you getting shot and being in danger all the time, the relief from all of those concerns is so uplifting."

She stepped closer until she was pressed against him. He pulled her closer still and kissed her deeply. He could feel her against him as her full breasts pushing into his chest and her hips slid across his. She could feel the impact she was having on him as she had planned as it was the reason that she had been waiting for him in the small house.

He suspected her purpose, which wasn't difficult, but even after turning down her last offer, he was finding it difficult to restrain himself now. She was just so perfect.

"Please," she whispered.

Earl was beyond being able to resist Jessie and as he kissed her again, he caressed her breast with his left hand, causing her to gasp.

Jessie was far from virginal but having Earl touch her as she felt his passionate kiss made her knees weaken and she wanted this probably as much as she knew he did, and not just to see if she could be the wife he needed and deserved.

Earl then took her hand and led her slowly to the bedroom as their eyes stayed locked together.

Once in the room, Earl continued to kiss her then as he began kissing her neck, let his hands wander over her soft curves as she felt his hard muscle.

For a man who had never been with a woman before, Jessie was enthralled with how much Earl was doing to make her unexpected lust simmer to a boil inside her.

As he began removing her clothes, he would kiss her wherever a new part of her was exposed, giving her goosebumps and driving her to a heightened sense of desire.

She was undressing Earl just as quickly as she could and soon, they were both naked and engaging in frenzied caresses and kissing on the bed, but even after she asked him to take her, he kept driving her passion to heights she thought was impossible.

Earl, despite his own extraordinary need for Jessie, had tried to be as gentle as he could. Any moment, he was expecting her to cry out in pain as he touched her with more pressure than he had intended. But she only responded with more sounds of intense pleasure and begged him to do more. He was beyond rapturous himself. Making love to the one woman he needed was even beyond what he had anticipated after all those years of waiting.

After what seemed like hours of constantly heightening levels of pleasure and desire that had her begging for Earl to take her and having totally forgotten any concerns about her possible injuries in the throes of passion, Earl finally could delay no further. When he at last succumbed to their mutual demand for fulfillment, there was no pain for her, just unrivaled pleasure. She was in a world of ecstasy for so many reasons: the physical pleasure, the relief at knowing she could be a wife in every way possible, and most importantly, the overwhelming sense of love that they shared.

When they had passed the ultimate in ecstasy, they collapsed onto the bed, and as she lay naked and sweating, wrapped in his arms, she whispered to him, "I never knew it could be like that, Earl. I was lost in a place I could never have imagined and want to visit there as often as I can, but only you can ever bring me there. The best part is knowing that I can be your wife in every way possible now."

Earl kissed her softly and said, "I never thought you wouldn't, Jessie. As a complete novice at this, I wasn't sure if I could make you feel the physical needs that I know women have, but society condemns. It's such a stupid thing. Why shouldn't I make you enjoy what we do?"

"Well, husband, I definitely enjoyed it. So much, in fact, I wouldn't mind making absolutely sure that everything is working right."

"Jessie, I'd do anything that you ask. If I can put your mind at rest, then I'd be only too happy to help."

She giggled as Earl pulled her close and began kissing her again.

By the time evening had fallen, Earl looked down at a sleeping, naked Jessie and smiled. What a wonderful woman he was going to marry, and in fact, already had in his mind. He traced his finger along her side and down her thigh and could see signs of scarring on her side and back. He wanted to crush Elmer Jackson for that. She had remarked on his scars when she examined his naked body and he had to explain each gunshot wound and the one knife cut. Now, there were no secrets at all between them.

He reached down, slid a blanket over them and watched a slight smile play across her lips. She was satisfied that theirs would be a perfectly wonderful marriage, and he had never even paid a bit of mind to the pain in his shoulder. He'd found the ideal pain-killer.

CHAPTER 9

Earl awaked while it was still dark with Jessie was still snuggled against his left side, but he knew he had to leave. He needed to complete his mission, so he tried to slip out without waking her, but found it impossible.

He tried to lift himself over her but his shoulder was reminding him that it wasn't a good idea, when her eyes opened, and she asked sleepily, "Do you have to go?"

"Jessie, I'd much rather stay in bed with you than anything else, but yes, I need to be going. It'll be a long ride and I want to get back to you as soon as possible."

Jessie slid out of bed to let him reach the floor without her acting as an obstacle, then stretched while Earl marveled at the perfection of her naked body, scars and all. She turned and smiled at him, noticing once more the reaction she had on him.

He stood and as he pulled her toward him, he said, "I suppose I could delay my departure another half hour, my love."

———

Forty-five minutes later, Earl, washed and dressed, then walked into the kitchen. Jessie was wearing her shirt, but nothing else as she cooked him breakfast. He smiled at her and ran his hand across her naked smoothness.

"I thought you were leaving, Mister Crawford," she said as she smiled.

"I am, I just thought one more caress to keep my mind occupied on the trip would be nice. Besides, that is one enticing behind you have there, Miss Mitchell."

"It's yours now, so you'd better like it. I made some bacon sandwiches for you to take with you. It'll be better than jerky."

"I thank you, my wife."

She turned and kissed him before she said, "I'll go and finish dressing. You go ahead and eat."

"Yes, ma'am," he said but watched that pretty behind walk away and seriously wished he didn't have to leave.

He cursed himself for missing so many years with Jessie for so many reasons.

He finished his breakfast quickly, then stood and snatched the paper bag with the sandwiches from the table. He was ready to go but needed to say good-bye to Jessie, so he waited.

She appeared two minutes later fully clothed. To the average person, there would be no noticeable difference, but to Earl he could see how her face radiated her happiness after the last possible obstacle to a happy marriage was gone.

He hugged and kissed her one more time before saying, "That was one hell of a sendoff, Mrs. Crawford."

"It was I the least I could do for my wonderful husband. Come back to me soon, Earl."

"You know I will, sweetheart."

He turned and left the house before he couldn't leave at all. The sky was growing lighter as he rode Target and led the gray gelding out the access road and turned left toward Hopewell. Jessie watched his shrinking form until it was gone from sight, then walked into the house to fix breakfast for his parents.

Lydia was first up and walked into the kitchen where she found her future daughter-in-law.

"How are you doing, Jessie?" she asked.

Jessie turned to her future mother-in-law and beamed a smile as she answered, "Just wonderful, Mrs. Crawford."

"Jessie, I think you should start calling me mama or Lydia, whichever you prefer."

"I'd enjoy calling you mama, if that's alright."

"Perfect. So, how did it go?"

Jessie was caught off-guard and asked, "How did what go?"

"I talked to your mother last night. She told me all the awful things that Elmer had done to you, and also told me of your concerns and of Earl's promise to you. When you left the house last night, I knew what you had to do. The question I have is to make sure that everything is still all right between you and Earl. I know how much you two love each other, but I do understand your concerns."

Jessie relaxed and said softly, "Mama, it was wonderful. Earl was so kind and gentle. For a man who had never been with a woman before, he knew everything he needed to do to make me feel like a loved woman. I never imagined it could be like this. All the love between us made it so perfect. I can't begin to tell you how happy I am."

"I can see it in your face, Jessie. I'm very happy for you both. I know Earl would write to me often about never being able to find the right woman. He had looked for years and almost given up, Jessie. But he almost always added that he wondered why more women couldn't be like Jessie."

"He told me last night that the biggest problem he had while he was away was that he could never picture me as a woman. He had only seen me as a young girl. When he brought me home after the short trail ride, as he was leaving, he told me 'you're the one'. Then he rode off."

"You are definitely the one, Jessie. He told me that before he left, too. He said, 'take care of Jessie, Mama, because she's the one'."

"Now we'll see what happens in Fort Worth and when he comes back. I hope he's wrong about being disciplined for making mistakes. How could they do that after all he did? I'd imagine that no other U.S. Deputy Marshal, or any other lawman, for that matter, did more in such a short time," Jessie said.

"I agree with you, dear. Now let's make breakfast for us and my husband. By the way, it may come as no surprise that he knows none of this."

"I'm sure my father doesn't either."

They laughed and began cooking.

———

By the time Jessie and Lydia finished cooking breakfast, Earl was twelve miles west of Hopewell and had Target at a fast trot. He estimated they were moving at ten to twelve miles an hour. He would stop for a rest in another hour or so and let them drink and munch on some grass. He'd hold off eating one of Jessie's sandwiches until it was later in the day when he was hungrier.

An hour later, he pulled off near a pond, dismounted and led them both to the water. He let them quench their thirst but pulled them back to keep them from drinking too much. He let them eat some grass and walked them to keep them from stiffening. He let them have more water and then mounted the gray gelding, then set off at the same pace. He knew it wasn't a demanding pace, but it ate up the miles.

By early afternoon, he estimated he had gone almost fifty miles. Again, he found water and grass and repeated his care of the animals. Twenty minutes later, he was atop Target and they were trotting again. Despite his worries, both horses seemed to be enjoying the test.

He finally stopped for the day just twenty miles outside of Dallas. Despite his worries, they had trotted closer to ninety miles that day and he was proud of both horses.

He walked them to a pleasant campsite beside a clear brook, took off their saddles and rubbed them both down after letting them drink and crop some grass. When they appeared satisfied, he took the saddlebag with oats in it and walked to Target and let him eat from one of the pouches until it was half empty. Then he opened the other side and let the gray gelding do the same.

He hobbled both horses and laid out his bedroll. Then he reached into the saddlebag and pulled out the bag of Jessie's sandwiches. He hadn't had one yet because he was too concerned about the horses when he had stopped. He pulled out the first one and wasn't surprised to find a note.

He read:

My beloved Husband,

As I made these sandwiches, I hope I didn't forget to add the bacon because my mind was filled with thoughts of you. You have made me the happiest of women, and I know that it will be that way for the rest of my life.

With all my love,

Jessie

Earl felt so warm inside he felt like he was developing a fever. He folded the note and put it into his pocket to read again later.

———

He slept well and awakened before the sky turned pink. It was the gray predawn, and soon began packing for the last ride. He saved the last two sandwiches for the road and saddled both horses. It was the gray's turn to go first. He checked over their joints and legs before starting out and they were on the road before sunrise. After ten minutes of walking to get their muscles ready, he picked it up to yesterday's pace.

They entered Dallas around breakfast time, and passed through, having to slow just a bit going through town. He changed over to Target as they left Dallas and headed toward Fort Worth. They were setting an amazing pace. After they left Dallas, Earl ate another of Jessie's sandwiches and reread her note. Thirty minutes later, he had stopped for a break and let the horses drink, then let them chew on some grass and gave them the last of their oats. They had surely earned them.

It was around noon when the first buildings of Fort Worth appeared on the horizon. They had traveled more than a hundred and fifty miles in thirty hours. Less than an hour later, he rode to the office's livery stable and dismounted. He walked the two horses into the barn, unsaddled them and removed the rest of their tack. He brushed them both down and thanked them both as he loaded their stalls with hay and oats, then filled their trough with water, took his saddlebag and left the livery, heading toward the office of the United States Marshal.

He walked in the door and saw Ed off to the corner. He was just about to call out to him when Ed turned and face broke open into a giant grin.

"Earl! How the hell did you get back here so soon? Didn't you get shot a couple of nights ago?"

"No, I think it was three nights ago. How are you, Ed?"

"Well, I'm fine but you're in a heap of trouble."

"I kinda figured that. Dan's telegram hinted that I was facing consequences from my screw-ups."

"If you wanna call it that."

Just then, Dan Grant came walking out of his office. He had heard Ed's greeting but thought he'd give his deputies a chance to at least pass a few words.

"Earl, can you come back to my office for a minute?"

"Sure, Dan."

Here it comes. thought Earl as he followed his boss.

He entered the office, and the marshal said, "Close the door and have a seat, Earl."

The double-whammy, Earl noted, as he closed the door and sat down in the hot seat.

Dan leaned back in his chair and said, "Earl, when you left, I thought you'd be gone a month at least. Now, you're back in eleven days. You were shot twice three nights ago and were told by the attending doctor to stay put. Not only did you leave two hours later without your weapons, you then returned here two days after that. Can you explain that?"

Earl smiled and replied, "Just anxious to see your smiling face, I guess."

"Do I look like I'm smiling, Earl?"

"No, sir. Dan, you need to understand. I was lying in that bed outside of Marshal and I knew what Claude was going to do. There was no one else who could stop him. I didn't feel that bad. I still had my Winchester when I left. I had to ride hard, and even then, only made it with seconds to spare. If I had waited even another five minutes, I'd have lost my parents and my future wife."

"Now that's a new twist. Your fiancée was with your parents?"

"Yes, sir. She was there waiting for my return. She didn't know that Claude was on his way."

"Well, all that aside, Deputy Crawford, I want to show you something," he said as he reached into his desk and pulled out a stack of papers over an inch thick.

"This is all the grief you've caused me and the United States Marshal's Service. Do you know how much work this has caused me and how much it has cost the service in telegraph fees when we had to reply?"

"I apologize, Dan. You know, I was thinking of leaving anyway. I've been shot nine times already, and I'm not eager for a tenth. So, if it's all right with you, I'll just write my resignation after my final report."

Earl started to stand, and Dan stopped him when he growled, "Sit your ass back down. I didn't say you could leave!"

"Dan, you don't have any authority over a civilian. I'll write my report and be out of your hair in another hour or so. It's a long report."

Then Dan's tone changed dramatically as he said quietly, "Earl, please sit down. I've taken this too far. I just wanted to pull your leg a bit. I didn't mean to get you that angry."

Earl saw his contrite face, relaxed and said, "It's okay. It's been a long two weeks. I really screwed up at the King's ranch, Dan. I know that, but you can't imagine how it felt to be riding to try to stop your own brother from killing your parents and then just getting there to watch him holding his gun at them and telling them he was deciding who was going to die first. He was totally insane, and I almost missed it."

"No, Earl. You didn't screw up at all. Mister King admitted you would have shot Claude if he hadn't shot you. You did everything right."

Dan showed him the pile of papers and said, "Earl, these are telegrams from everyone that you've encountered over the past two weeks, and from some folks you didn't, including the governor and the head of the service. As your telegrams began coming in and they were expanded by others from sheriffs and the Kings, and even other citizens, it was easy to see that what you were doing was beyond extraordinary. Around the service, it's already being simply called *The Mission.* I know you were worried about breaking protocol about disobeying a doctor's orders, but we all have to one degree or another, but to leave on a sixty-mile ride just two hours after being shot twice was incomprehensible. How are you doing, by the way?"

"The head is fine, but the right shoulder is stiff. I should go and have it looked at after I finish my report."

"Good idea. But what this all boils down to, Earl, is that there is an opening for a U.S. Marshal in Kansas City and the chief wants you to take it."

"I appreciate the offer, Dan, but I need to run that past Jessie, my fiancée."

"I understand, Earl. You'll have a couple of weeks to decide. You're on sick time as of now."

"Thanks. Anything else before I go and fill out my report?"

"No. By the way, when did you leave home?"

"Yesterday morning."

"You rode over hundred and fifty miles in less than thirty hours?"

"I had good horses. I'll probably use the same two on the way back tomorrow morning."

"Don't you want to hang around a day or two?"

226

"No. I have my Jessie to think about."

"As many women that have thrown their caps your way, I imagine she's one hell of a woman."

"She's the one, Dan."

"Speaking of women, what do you want me to tell Teresa O'Toole? She's been even stopping by looking for you."

"Tell her I've gone back home to get married," then stood, smiled at his boss, opened the door and walked off to do his report.

Earl entered a small office and began writing. He left out all the personal things, but the report still took him two hours to write and filled eight pages.

When he was done, he took his report to his boss.

As he was handing it to the marshal, he asked, "Dan, do we have any applicants for positions that didn't get accepted for some reason or another?"

"I have two in town right now. Why?"

"I'm going to head back and relieve that sheriff in Hopewell and want to put someone competent in his place.'

"Of the two, I'd recommend Pete Procter. He only missed out because he had an issue firing the rifle. No matter how much they worked with him, he never reached the minimum."

"Can I talk to him after I get back from the doctor's?"

"Sure. I'll send someone over. And, Earl?"

"Yes, sir?"

"Get something to eat. You look terrible. At least for you."

"I'll tell you what, Dan, you go and find Pete and I'll take him to lunch when I get back."

"Speaking of lunch, I don't suppose you want to submit an expense report for this trip, do you?"

"Nah. It wasn't bad."

The marshal grinned and shook his head before saying, "Go and see the doctor."

Earl left his office feeling much better than when he entered. He wondered how Jessie would feel about moving to Kansas City. He'd find out soon enough, but any thoughts of a leisurely return trip were long gone.

———

After the doctor examined Earl's most recent wounds, he said the healing was faster than it should have been considering the abuse he had put himself through. The stitches all held, and his head wound had scabbed over nicely. He told him to get the stitches out in a week and then he'd clear him for duty in two weeks.

Earl sauntered back to the office as his rumbling stomach complained mightily of neglect.

He walked in finding several of his fellow deputy marshals in the office. He was greeted like a celebrity, with handshakes and backslaps, until he winced when someone hit his stitches, then he made his way back to Dan's office after the extended congratulations, which included those normally given to a bachelor friend about to end that status.

When Earl entered his office, he found Dan talking to a tall young man, about twenty-five or so. He had an open, good face with a shock of dark brown hair and blue eyes. Earl liked him on sight.

"Earl, this is Pete Procter," Dan said.

Pete turned, stood and shook Earl's hand.

"I've briefed him on the sheriff's job and he's very interested."

"Great. Pete, can you be ready to ride tomorrow morning?"

"Sure, but I don't have a horse."

"Dan, do we have any recent acquisitions in the corral?"

"Four. Three of them look pretty good. Pete can take his pick."

"They all have tack when they were acquired?"

"Yep. In the barn."

"We'll go check them out after lunch. I know what his first job will be, too."

"What's that?"

"Help me find something to hang on Elmer Jackson. He got off on the robbery charge because no one would identify him. He also got off on almost killing a prostitute because they didn't want to prosecute."

The marshal said, "Elmer Jackson? I just got a warrant on him. Seems that Joe Atherton, the only other survivor of the robbery is singing like a bird to the prosecutor. Someone had dropped the ball and thought he was dead. He named Elmer as the other member of the gang."

"Well, my day is made, then. Can you give me a warrant to take with us?"

"It'll be my pleasure."

"Just to let you know, Dan, because I need to be up front here. He used to be married to my fiancée and beat her badly. She still has scars from where he hit her, and they've been apart for over a year and a half. I'd rather beat him to a pulp, so he can feel the pain, but I'll be satisfied with sending him to prison for five years."

"I trust you to do what's right. I'll get you the warrant while you're out to lunch with Pete. By the way, we both read your report. It was even better than a dime novel, and it's making its way around the office now."

"Thanks, Dan. One more thing before I go, so I can explain it to Jessie. What does a marshal make, anyway?"

"A hundred and fifty dollars a month, plus room and board. If you're married, they kick in an extra fifty to save them some money."

"You ought to get married yourself, Dan," Earl smiled.

"Never met the one, Earl. You're a lucky man."

"I know it. We're off to lunch."

Earl and Pete walked across to the diner. When they walked in, several patrons stared at Earl and he wondered how they even knew who he was.

They sat down, and a buxom waitress bounced up to the table and literally batted her eyelashes at Earl.

"What can I get for you, Deputy Crawford?"

"Well, why don't you take Pete's order first. I'll think about it."

"I'm not sure yet," he said, and Earl guessed his cash supply was low.

Earl said, "Tell you what, get us a couple of steaks, some potatoes and biscuits and lots of coffee."

"Of course, I'll be right back with your orders."

Pete looked at Earl, and asked, "Does that happen often?"

"Way too often, to be honest. It may sound strange, but it gets annoying after a while."

"I thought she was going to knock me over with those things."

Earl laughed and said, "You have a point there. Of course, she had two."

Pete joined him in light laughter before saying, "So, tell me about Hopewell."

"It's a nice town. Quiet, usually. Now that my brother and his gang are almost gone, it should be a lot quieter. The current sheriff and his deputy are pathetic. They ignored a double homicide in their jurisdiction and didn't even mount a posse to chase after him. They're like that about most things. When I told him that I was going to remove him from his office while he was stuffing his face at the café, you should have seen the smiles across that room. You do a good job and you'll be respected, and you'll have your pick of the ladies in town. All except mine, of course. I'll help you get settled in while I'm on sick time.

"The two horses you'll be using tomorrow will be yours permanently. They're what we refer to as acquisitions. When we pinch bad guys, or have to kill them, the rule is that any unaccounted money that they have on them, up to say fifty dollars we get to keep along with any weapons they have. The horses and larger sums of cash we turn over to the office. The horses are eventually sold, and the money returned to the service, but we usually keep them in the corral for a month or so in case any of us lose our animals.

"Now the two I rode in on are different. Target was always mine. The gray gelding belongs to Joe Atherton, the one I arrested in Jefferson. Joe didn't seem like a bad sort, and I needed a second horse to make it down to Marshall quickly, so I told him I'd keep him at my parents' ranch until he got out. He's a great horse except for a bit of a jarring ride, and I'm sure Joe will be happy to get him back."

"How long do you think it'll take to get down there?"

"I'll take it slow this time. I took thirty hours to get here, so I think two and a half days getting back should be right. When we get there, you can stay at the ranch. There's a spare house that my parents built for my brother when he got married."

"Is that the house where…"

"Yes. But it's all cleaned up now. I slept there last night."

Earl didn't add, '*sort of*' to the statement.

"Alright. How much does it pay?"

"Good question. I'll talk to the council. Now they paid that fat-ass sheriff fifty dollars a month and his useless deputy another forty a month. Now you won't need a deputy, so, I think sixty dollars a month plus room and board sounds pretty good."

"I'll say. That sounds better than I expected."

"Good."

The waitress brought their food and almost shoved her expansive bosom into Earl's face when she put the steak in front of him. She had undone her top button, so Earl was rewarded with a few inches of cleavage as sort of a pre-luncheon entertainment package.

After she left, Pete looked at Earl and they both snickered.

They finished their steaks and Earl left two dollars on the table, which was an enormous tip. He looked at Pete and said, "Enormous deserves enormous," and they left the diner laughing.

They swung by the office, where Earl picked up the warrant for Elmer, then they walked over to the corral and studied the four horses.

"What do you think, Earl?" asked Pete.

"I like the strawberry roan and the tan gelding. They both have long legs and look young enough to give you years of service."

"Okay. How do we do this?"

"We leave them there, and in the morning, we saddle them up and take them. They already have the USMS brand on them, so if anyone questions you, and they won't, tell them that Marshal Dan Grant provided them for you."

"What's next?"

"Do you have a bedroll, slicker and other things you need for the trip?"

"No."

"How about a gun rig?"

"No."

"Okay. Let's head over to the dry goods store and pick up some things."

They walked to the store and Earl began loading up supplies as he and Pete brought beans, bacon, a new cooking grill, frypan and coffeepot, two tin plates and forks and spoons, and two cans of peaches, just because Earl felt like having some. He also bought Pete a bedroll and a slicker.

Then, just before he finished loading items onto the counter, Earl looked down and noticed Pete's boots.

"Pete, are those the only boots you have?"

Pete looked sheepishly as he answered, "Yeah. I've been meaning to get another pair."

"Well, go get a pair as long as we're here and get a few pairs of socks, too. You can use those boots as your traveling boots."

Earl followed him back and said, "You also need a couple of vests. A black one and a gray one will be good. A sheriff should always wear a vest. I do, too. It's good to put your badge on the vest or hide it behind the vest, depending on circumstances. How many shirts and pants to you have?"

"Two shirts and another pair of pants."

"Get two more shirts and two more pairs of britches. I think that should do it."

Pete picked out the items that Earl told him to get.

When they loaded it all onto the counter, the storekeeper said, "$52.45."

Earl wrote out a bank draft and handed it to the man. "Can you pack the clothes into a bag, so we can carry them on a horse?"

"Sure thing."

When they left, Pete asked, "Earl, you just spent a lot of money. Are you rich or something?"

"No, not at all. You'll find out that if you don't spend it, it'll just accumulate on its own. Now, the service pays me sixty a month and room and board. If they're paying for food and my bed, what do I need to spend the money on? I don't smoke or drink or whore, so I don't spend that much. I don't wind up spending a third of my pay each month. It may not sound like much, but I've been doing this for seven years, plus a couple of years as a deputy sheriff, so run the numbers yourself."

Pete's eyes bulged as he said, "You have over three thousand dollars?"

"Yup. You can do the same, Pete. Just be careful what you do with your money."

"I will. I never thought about it that way."

"Not too many of us do. Speaking of spending money, I need to go and drop more cash at the jewelers. I need some wedding rings."

They unloaded the packages at the livery barn, and Pete followed Earl to the jewelry shop. Once inside, Earl found what he was looking for easily. He asked the clerk about sizing for his bride's finger and the clerk assured him that most women's fingers fit the size he was buying. As he was looking at the rings, he noticed a nice necklace with a silver chain and a nice-sized amethyst. The purple color reminded him of the streaks in Jessie's eyes, so he had to buy it, of course. He also decided to finally buy a nice pocket watch for himself. He paid for his purchases with another bank draft. He was done for the day, but happy he had stopped by.

That left only one more thing to do, so they headed to the Western Union office.

Earl wrote out his message and handed it to the telegrapher.

JESSIE MITCHELL FARM HOPEWELL TEXAS

LEAVING FORT WORTH TOMORROW
EVERYTHING GOOD
YOU ARE THE ONE

EARL CRAWFORD FORT WORTH TEXAS

236

He paid the forty cents and they left the office.

"Can you read Morse code, Pete?"

"No, why?"

"Just curious, really. It's a good skill to have. Some operators either make mistakes or drop something out that they don't think is necessary, even though you paid for it. They don't think anyone will notice, but if you can read Morse, then you can point out his error. They don't like it, either. It shouldn't matter much as a local sheriff, but it sure helps as a U.S. Deputy Marshal. So, Pete, where are you staying?"

"I'm at the hotel."

"Good, I'll go get my stuff and get a room. That way we can find each other in the morning."

Earl got his room and found he and Pete were just two doors apart. After he had put his things away, Earl pulled out his new watch and said, "Well, Pete, it's 5:17, what say we go and have some dinner?"

They decided to use the hotel restaurant rather than risk another display at the café. The waitress at the restaurant was older and just smiled a lot at Earl. They had more steaks and potatoes and Earl told Pete that the ride starting tomorrow would be hard, but not too bad. Earl told him that he'd tap on his door at six o'clock.

They turned in and Earl started the habit of winding his watch every night and used the alarm feature on the watch to ensure that he was out of bed early.

_____

At exactly, 6:02, Earl rapped on Pete's door, and was pleased that he only had to wait a minute for him to appear. They had a fast breakfast at the hotel restaurant, then crossed the street and walked to the livery. Earl retrieved the strawberry roan and the tan gelding, then led the two horses into the barn.

They saddled all four horses and packed their supplies, including Pete's new clothes and hit the road at 6:47 by Earl's new watch.

_____

Early the next morning, as Earl and Pete departed Fort Worth and were well on the road, Elmer Jackson was still sleeping. No one had offered him a job, not that he really wanted one. He was really scouting out loose items that might be lying around for lifting when the opportunity presented itself.

_____

Just south of Hopewell, a messenger arrived at the Mitchell farm and delivered a telegram. Jessie was at her family home, knowing that Earl was still in Fort Worth and hoped that his boss wasn't really mad at him.

When she received and read his telegram, she felt as giddy as she used to be when she was a girl and Earl walked into the house. Earl was coming home and would be there in three days. He even added the last line that warmed her heart.

_____

Earl and Pete were moving faster than Earl had anticipated. Target and the gray gelding seemed used to the speed they had taken on the way in, and Pete's mounts wanted to keep up. They stopped once before Dallas and again for a quick lunch fifteen miles southeast of the city. They rested the horses, let them graze and drink and were on the road again twenty minutes later. By the time they were ready to stop for the night, they had put almost eighty miles behind them.

As they were setting up their camp, Pete asked, "Do you always travel this fast? My butt feels like lead."

Earl laughed and answered, "Not usually. The horses must feel comfortable at this pace. I had only planned on fifty miles the first day."

"Even that is a long day."

"It is. I guess they're as anxious to get home as I am."

"You're getting married?"

"Yup. I never thought I would after a while because I never met the right woman until I met Jessie. The odd thing is that I met her years ago when she was only twelve and I was visiting her older sister. I went off to war and her sister married someone else. I just couldn't picture Jessie as an adult. I enjoyed being around her a lot when she was a kid, and until I met her again a few weeks ago, I didn't realize how much I loved her even then."

"Wow! That's something. So, did the sister marry someone you know?"

"You might say that. He was my older brother. The one I had to kill three days ago."

"*The guy who killed his wife and boy?*" Pete asked with a shocked face.

"The same one. He was always a bully, and finally he just snapped."

"Are you going to take the Kansas City job?"

"I don't know. It depends on what Jessie wants to do."

"How far will we be going tomorrow?"

"However far the horses want to go."

"What will we do when we arrive?"

"The first thing we'll do is head to my parents' place to get you settled in the house. Jessie will probably be there because I wired her that I would be coming home. Then, the next day, we are going to replace the sheriff and his deputy, and I'll serve that warrant on Elmer Jackson and put him in your lockup. We'll notify the sheriff at White Oak that he is available for transport and wait for them to send someone down to pick him up. Oh, before I forget, I'm going to swear you in as a temporary U.S. Deputy Marshal, so you'll have authority when we need to arrest anyone."

The idea really appealed to Pete, even though it was just temporary, so when Earl swore him in and gave him the badge, he was all smiles as he pinned it on under his new vest.

After the short ceremony, they enjoyed a hot supper that Pete prepared, which impressed Earl. They spent another hour discussing what Pete might expect and Earl expanded what Pete had read in his report on his mission before they turned in, knowing that they had another long ride in store tomorrow.

———

The day's long ride began just hours later, when Earl and Pete were up at the first signs of daylight. Earl handed Pete a can of peaches and he had the other, making for a fast, but unusual breakfast. They were packed and on the road by 6:11, according to Earl's new timepiece and he wondered why he hadn't bought one years ago.

By nine o'clock, they had passed the century mile mark and were taking a break where they switched horses and were back on the road thirty minutes later.

Earl's original intention of taking more time on the return trip had fallen by the wayside long ago in his anxiety to see Jessie again. He couldn't wait to tell her the news of the Kansas City job, and his only concern was that it would take her away from her family for the first time in her life.

He wished that she wouldn't be upset to leave Hopewell after all those years. He knew that she hadn't ever even been to a real city before, and it could be intimidating. He might have to sell the idea based on the number of stores and shops nearby that would be available for her to use some of his increased pay.

———

In Hopewell, Elmer was grumpy and frustrated. He didn't seem to know anyone that liked him and wondered what had happened to Claude. How he didn't know was strange in itself as everyone else in town seemed to know. It had even made the front page in the local paper. Part of the problem may have been Elmer's difficulty in reading and the other was his inability to get along with folks. He only associated with other thugs, and their number had been significantly reduced while those that remained treated him like poison. The rumor that Elmer was under Earl's magnifying glass was as bad as if he'd been identified as a snitch.

His frustration and isolation pushed Elmer to hunt down the one man that he could trust, so he decided that maybe he'd go and pay Claude a visit that afternoon. Maybe Claude even had the bank money with him, and if he did, then that would set him up for a while as his share should be over a hundred bucks. He only had $5.43 left on him, so it seemed like the thing to do.

———

Jessie had already said goodbye to her parents and mounted Butter for the short ride to the Crawfords, beginning to feel as if she had two sets of parents now. It was close to the truth because in a few days, they would be her parents-in-law.

As she had been walking out the door, she had stopped and returned to her room to retrieve the derringer, not wanting Earl to think she wasn't protected. Besides, he had given it to her and that made it special. She had a feeling that he might make it faster than he said he would and smiled at the thought that Earl was coming home. She slid the small pistol into her riding skirt's pocket and walked out to saddle Butter.

———

By noon, Earl and Pete were only ten miles out of Hopewell. The horses were still trotting well without any signs of stress. Taking care of them on their breaks had helped immensely.

"So, what am I going to do for guns?" asked Pete.

"I have a nice Smith & Wesson Model 3 and a gun belt you can have. It's stored at the Mitchell farm. I used it exclusively for two years. I only got this rig on my last mission with Ed before the last one. Crazy Jack was wearing it, and I gave the rig to Ed, but he gave them back when I started on the last mission. He's still partial to his older weapons, or so he said. More than likely, he was just being his usual generous self. Now, the sheriff's office should have long guns and a shotgun. If not, I have a nice Henry you can have."

"Thanks, Earl. You've been like a big brother to me."

"Hopefully, I'll be a better big brother to you than mine was to me."

"That wouldn't take much."

"Nope."

———

Elmer finally got out of bed when his stomach began to complain of neglect and his bladder was even more demanding. He decided to head over to the café and get something to eat and then ride down to the Crawford's ranch and visit Claude.

Twenty minutes later, he left the room that he was renting and stepped out onto the street under the hot Texas sun. Before he had his first meal of the day, he crossed over to the rooming house's barn where he saddled his horse, mounted and walked the gelding to Mama Smith's Café. After stepping down, he tied up at the hitchrail and went inside to fill his stomach before he headed south to find Claude and get his share of the bank money.

———

Jessie and Lydia were talking about Earl's return and the plans for the wedding. It wasn't going to be a large ceremony, but a simple family affair that suited the couple. They had already talked to Reverend Lawless, which wasn't really a good name for a man of the cloth, and he said he would be very pleased to marry them. He had read about *The Mission* and how important Jessie was to Earl.

Lydia told Jessie that she thought the minister was hoping to gain a measure of fame for performing the ceremony and they still laughed about it. Neither realized that the good reverend really was hoping for an increase in his congregation's size with the corresponding increase in donations. The added fame would be just frosting on his clerical cake.

————

Elmer finished his breakfast/lunch and paid for his meal, not leaving a tip from his diminished funds. He mounted his horse and headed south. If he had even paid attention to the conversation from a nearby table, he would have heard Claude's name used in the past tense by one of the diners.

————

Earl and Pete had just entered Hopewell from the northwest. It was just after one o'clock, making the second ride in thirty-two hours.

When they entered the town, Pete said, "So, this is where I'll be living. It's about the same size as my hometown, and is even laid out a lot like it."

Earl replied, "We'll come back and get rid of the sheriff and deputy tomorrow, Pete. I'm a bit anxious to see Jessie and I don't want to see his face today if I can avoid it."

Pete snickered then said, "I can understand that, Earl."

———

Elmer continued trotting toward the Crawford ranch. He passed the Mitchell farm and for a passing moment thought of going in and seeing his ex-wife. He knew that she had divorced him, but to Elmer it didn't matter. He had her once and could take her anytime he wanted.

———

Jessie had begun her *'Earl's coming'* watch, stepping out on the porch every few minutes and scanning the road, even though she knew he might not make it until very late in the day or possibly not until the next morning.

Lydia watched her and smiled, happy that Jessie and Earl had finally found each other. All the time that Earl was away, she had watched Jessie blossom into an attractive young woman with a deep and warm personality. In her letters, she had tried to convince him to come home without describing Jessie physically because she thought that he might think she was matchmaking, which is what she was doing anyway.

Suddenly, Jessie saw a rider approaching from the north. *Earl was home already!* She started to wave and then realized that there was only one horse, not two. and it wasn't black like Target. *Who was riding to the ranch?*

She turned to Lydia and said, "Mama, someone is coming and it's not Earl."

"Who is it?"

"I'm not sure. He's too far away."

245

―――

Elmer could see the ranch and a female figure on the porch looking at him and thought she must be Claude's mother. He wondered if he'd have a problem with her after what Claude had done before he left, but then remembered that Claude had told him that she didn't matter anyway because his father was the one who was in charge and his old man had always backed him.

In a rational world, even the thought of Claude living on the ranch after murdering his wife and son made no sense at all. But Elmer understood the lengths that Claude's father had gone to protect his son, so to Elmer, it was perfectly understandable that Claude was now enjoying life in the small house where he'd killed Eva and their kid.

―――

In the afternoon sun, Jessie had a better view than Elmer, and finally recognized the rider and quickly turned to Lydia.

"Mama, it's Elmer!"

Lydia glanced at the oncoming rider and said, "Go into the kitchen and lock the back door so he can't get in. Ray is too far away to help. Do you have your little gun?"

"Yes."

"Good. Make sure you have it handy. Did Earl tell you not to cock it until you were ready to fire?"

"Yes, Mama."

"Okay. Go back into the kitchen. I don't want him to know you're here."

"Okay."

She scampered back into the kitchen, her hand wrapped around the derringer, but hoping Lydia could simply turn him away.

Lydia remained on the porch watching Elmer approach, feeling an eerie sense of déjà vu after the recent confrontation with Claude.

Elmer turned on the access road and had momentarily seen another woman on the porch before the first one went inside and wondered who the second woman was. He had recognized the one who had stayed longer on the porch to be Claude's mother, but she had gone inside soon after he spotted her.

———

Earl and Pete were fast trotting past the Mitchell farm, and Earl pointed it out to him.

"So, that's where your bride lives. Aren't we going to stop?"

"Nope. Jessie will be waiting at my parents' ranch, just as she was when Claude arrived and tried to kill them all."

"That must have been a scary time for everyone."

"I can't imagine how it must have felt to know you were going to die and had no way to stop it. I still get a chill when I think about how close it was."

"But you did stop it and now you're marrying the girl."

Earl grinned at Pete and replied, "Wait until you meet her, Pete. When you do, you'll understand why I'm so anxious to get back to her."

Pete grinned back and could almost feel Earl's anxiety and wasn't surprised when Earl nudged Target into a faster pace.

———

Elmer stopped a hundred feet from the Crawford house and looked around to see if he could see either Claude or his horse. He didn't spot either, but he did see Butter and a smile grew on his face. His wife was here for some reason, but he still needed to find Claude. He even wondered if she was here because Claude was using her.

He dismounted, hopped up the steps to the porch and knocked on the screen door. He thought it was odd that they'd have the regular door closed on a hot day, but it didn't matter.

Lydia delayed opening the door, so after another series of louder knocks, Elmer walked to the closest window and peered inside. He saw Claude's mother standing in the room watching the door but didn't see Claude. Suddenly, whether or not Claude was there was now secondary to him. His wife was inside the house somewhere and obviously Mrs. Crawford didn't want him to see her.

He returned to the screen door, pulled it open and began pounding the inside door with his fist.

After almost another minute without a response, Elmer shouted, "I know you're in there! I saw you through the window. You'd better open this door, or I'll bust it in!"

248

Lydia smoothed her dress, then took a deep breath and stepped to the door to let him in, hoping that she could reason with him, but after that horrifying experience with Claude, she didn't believe it was possible. Elmer was just another Claude, but not as good-looking.

———

Earl and Pete turned to the access road and Earl noticed the figure at the door shouting. He also spotted Butter and his stomach flipped knowing who was at the door and why he was trying to get inside. He had to act quickly to keep Jessie safe, but he needed to get Elmer's attention first to get him away from the door. He pulled out his right-hand Colt and quickly fired a shot at the ground near of the porch steps, knowing that he had no chance of being any more accurate than that at this range.

As soon as he fired, he released the gray gelding and let Target race toward the house. He'd be there in seconds.

Pete released the roan and followed, completely baffled by what Earl was doing.

———

As soon as he heard the pistol report, Elmer whipped to his right and saw two men riding quickly toward him and knew instantly who one of them was, even if he didn't notice their badges. He turned, ran down the end of the porch and leapt off the end. His horse had wandered off, so he mounted Butter and headed south across the pastures, taking hurried looks behind him.

Earl turned to Pete and shouted, "Go to the house and make sure everyone is safe! I'll take care of Elmer!"

Pete waved and turned his horse toward the house as Earl chased after the fleeing rider.

Elmer kept nervously glancing over his shoulder as Jessie's mare thundered across the grassy field at her top speed, knowing that if he let Earl catch him, he'd be a dead man. He finally realized why Jessie was at the ranch and she must have told Earl how she had been treated while she had been married to him. He didn't doubt that Earl would make his death as painful as possible.

He was losing ground on the slower mare as the big man on the black horse was rapidly gaining on him. With his options running low, he pulled his pistol, cocked the hammer and fired, hoping that it would at least give him more room when Earl had to start zigzagging.

Earl saw him fire and had no intention of altering Target's path and didn't even wince. If he was going to take his tenth bullet, it would happen and there was nothing he could do about it by the time he saw Elmer's pistol blast smoke and sound after his bullet left the muzzle.

Elmer threw two more shots at Earl who was now less than fifty yards behind him but waited until he was even closer, and he felt that he couldn't miss before he fired twice more, but still missed anyway as Butter bounced along the uneven ground.

Earl maneuvered Target to Elmer's right and was only twenty yards away now.

Elmer took care with his final shot. He aimed carefully at the pursuing lawman, pulled the trigger and felt his Colt rock back as it fired, but even at that range, with the horse rocking beneath him, he missed again. *Damn it!*

Earl knew he was empty now and had no chance to reload that old pistol. He gave Target his head and he made up the last twenty yards in ten seconds, pulling up to Elmer's left side. Then Earl reached across the gap between the two racing animals, grabbed the back of Elmer's shirt and yanked.

Elmer flew from the saddle and bounced once on the hard Texas ground before he rolled to a stop in a large cloud of dust.

Earl brought Target to a rapid halt, then quickly onto the ground. He unbuckled his gun belt, hung it from his saddle horn, then stalked toward Elmer, who was scrambling to his feet, uninjured from his forced tumble from the horse.

Elmer had seen Earl remove his pistols, so he knew that he had a chance, and then smiled when he realized he had and advantage now when he pulled his knife, then flashed it in the afternoon sun to let Earl know he was in control.

As Earl strode toward him, Elmer grinned and said, "Looks like you're gonna get stuck, Marshal."

Earl didn't say a word but kept walking until he was within six feet of Elmer then stopped.

Elmer had hoped that he would have gotten closer, but as soon as Earl halted his approach, Elmer took one long stride forward and thrush his long blade at Earl's stomach.

Earl had been in many knife fights before and had learned from the first one that had given him one of his scars. He knew that even with that step, Elmer didn't have the reach to put his knifepoint close enough to cause any serious damage, so he acted as if there wasn't a knife just an inch from his stomach before Elmer withdrew the blade. He didn't react when Elmer stepped back after the failed stabbing, knowing that he'd soon try again and then he would give Elmer a second opportunity.

Earl took one step closer and Elmer knew he had him. He swiped with his knife in a long arc across his front, sure he'd catch his victim at some point. Earl waited until he started to move his knife hand, then leaned back and brought his left fist down hard, timing it to meet Elmer's wrist as it passed. His clenched big hand missed the wrist but slammed into Elmer's forearm, making him drop his blade as he shrieked in pain from the blow. causing him to drop his only weapon. Earl kicked the knife away and Elmer looked up at Earl's volcanic face and knew he couldn't stop him now. He threw up his fists to make a show of defense but expected that it wouldn't make any difference. He was right in his assessment of his situation.

Earl then lit into Elmer with his incredible anger and need to inflict pain on the man who had hurt Jessie. He didn't care about the badge on his chest as he wasn't a lawman, he was Jessie's man. For all the pain Elmer had caused Jessie, he would experience much, much more. He didn't care about his own injured shoulder or anything else in his state of rage.

He slammed his right fist into Elmer's stomach, then, as he knifed over in pain from the blow, Earl crashed a savage left into his ribs on Elmer's right side, then as soon as his punching bag turned to avoid another blow, he buried an even harder blow into the right side of his chest.

Even though he had expected to be pummeled, Elmer was still stunned by the fury and power in Earl's repeated shots. He was in serious pain already, so even though he was still standing, he bent over, then covered his head with his arms as if he was in the fetal position on the ground.

Earl didn't care if Elmer wasn't even pretending to fight back. He wanted the bastard to feel more pain and didn't let up as he unleashed one blow after another to Elmer's exposed torso and their protecting arms. He stayed away from any head shots so Elmer would remain standing as long as possible so he could inflict as much punishment as possible.

Earl was working up a sweat when Elmer finally sank to his knees, his arms still over his head and Earl relaxed his fingers.

Elmer was sobbing as he knelt on the ground, but was grateful that Earl had finally stopped, but he hadn't. He had one last blow to deliver.

Earl stepped directly in front of the whimpering bully, then twisted clockwise, pulled his right boot from the ground and swung it back before rocketing it forward with as much power as his considerable strength possessed and with one long arcing kick, let his boot's toe pound deep into Elmer's crotch.

Elmer's screech was almost unearthly as he ripped his hands from over his head to grab his manhood. As they reached his incredibly painful nether regions, he toppled onto his left side, but was still conscious and in deep pain.

Earl stared at him and hoped that his pain would stay with him for the rest of his life as he knew that the agony that he put Jessie through would remain with her.

After he was satisfied that he had done all he could, he walked over pulled the pistol from his holster and suddenly realized the enormous risk he'd taken when he hadn't shot Elmer and then left his guns on Target. Elmer had a Smith & Wesson Schofield and not the percussion pistol that Earl had expected. The Schofield had been designed specifically for use by mounted cavalry so they could quickly reload and fire from the back of a moving horse. Elmer could have reloaded and had six full cylinders before he'd grabbed the man's shirt collar. He wondered where he had gotten the weapon as he leaned down and grabbed Elmer's knife, but relieved that Elmer hadn't had the wits to reload.

Then he pulled out the warrant and said, "Elmer Jackson, I am arresting you for bank robbery and the attempted murder of a United States Deputy Marshal," then tossed the folded sheet onto the ground near Elmer as he continued to weep and shake.

He returned to Target. slipped Elmer's gun and knife into his saddlebag, then strapped his guns back on and retrieved Butter.

He heard hooves and saw Pete, Jessie and his mother riding towards him. Jessie was riding the gray gelding and his mother was on Pete's second horse.

Each of them looked at Elmer who was still lying on the ground sobbing with his tears falling to the ground, but soon returned their eyes to Earl as they dismounted.

But once on the ground, Jessie turned back toward Elmer, and thought about pulling the derringer from her pocket and putting a .41 into him, but she didn't because she knew that her fiancé would probably have to arrest her. Instead, she walked close to him and almost repeated Earl's final blow when she landed a hard kick into his stomach rather than his crotch, then after hearing him scream from the unexpected blow, she spit on him before turning to step to Earl.

Earl was surprised that she had only taken the one shot as she approached him and asked, "Did you get shot again? We heard all the gunfire."

"No, ma'am. I had no intention of getting number ten. I reckoned that he'd miss because I saw his sights bouncing as he fired."

Pete walked up to him and asked, "What happened, Earl?"

Earl kept his eyes focused on Jessie as he replied, "You saw him take off and me take after him. He fired firing a few long shots, then a couple more when I was closer and his last one when I was just a few yards away. When I knew that he had emptied his pistol, I got Target next to him and yanked him off the saddle. He took a hard fall, then I stopped and hung up my guns. As it turns out, it was a big mistake, too. He had a Schofield and not a percussion pistol, so he could have reloaded before I went to arrest him."

"Why'd you take off your guns?"

"I didn't want him to be able grab one of mine. Anyway, I approached to arrest him, and he pulled his knife, so I had to subdue him."

Pete looked at Earl and was sure that there was no way that Elmer would have been able to get one of Earl's pistol, but he was also sure that Earl fully realized that no one really believed it either.

Earl then smiled at him and said, "Say, Pete, why don't you go over and put these cuffs on him with his hands behind his back? Take his gunbelt, too. Why not put it on, it's the easiest way to carry it. Then help him onto the gray gelding because he has a real jolting stride."

As Pete nodded, Earl then tossed him a set of handcuffs, and after snatching them out of the air, simply replied, "Okay, Earl."

"I need to talk to the ladies for a few minutes."

He gestured for his mother to join him and Jessie, and when she arrived, he put his arms around them and said, "That was the official report that will go to Fort Worth. It's not far from accurate, but I'm sure that each of you and Pete know that there was a slight deviation from the truth.

"It wasn't because I was concerned about Elmer getting my pistols that I hung my gunbelt over my saddle horn. It was because I wanted to cause Elmer pain rather than just arrest him and suspected that he'd think that he had an advantage when I was disarmed. I knew he had a knife on his gunbelt, so I walked close until he pulled it and thought he could stick me with it.

"I wasn't worried because I'd faced down other knife fighters before and knew that Elmer was probably nowhere as practiced in the technique as a man who used them often. I was right about that when he came at me with the knife and on his second attempt, I slapped it away from him. Then, it was no longer a contest when I proceeded to beat him as much as I could without killing him. I finished him off with a swift kick to the groin, which is why you found him the way he was. I just wanted you both to know. I wasn't about to let him get away with just being slapped in cuffs."

Both women smiled at Earl, then Jessie said, "Thank you, Earl. I wasn't sure my little kick was going to be enough. I was wondering why he was all curled up like that and crying, too."

"He'll be in pain for a while, especially after we drag him to Hopewell sitting in a saddle."

"You did what had to be done, Earl," said his mother as she patted him on the shoulder.

"Let's head back to the house. I'm sure papa is going to wonder what happened out here, after hearing those shots."

Jessie then asked, "Who's Pete?"

"Oh. I'm sorry. I should have introduced you. He's going to be the new sheriff if I can convince the mayor to appoint him, and I think I can. He was a candidate for a deputy marshal position but had difficulty with the rifle part of the evaluation process."

Jessie nodded, then turned and walked to Pete, who was talking to Lydia after putting Elmer on the horse. Elmer was moaning even louder now that he was sitting with his privates pressing into the leather saddle.

She held out her hand and said, "Pete? I'm Jessie. I'm pleased to meet you."

Pete shook her hand, smiled and said, "So, you're the one."

Jessie smiled back as she replied, "So, he tells me."

He released her hand and said, "I'm Pete Procter, and I'm glad to finally meet you. You were all he talked about on our ride from Fort Worth."

Earl had pulled Elmer's Schofield from the saddlebag and handed it to Pete.

As he slid it into Elmer's holster he said, "Now you have a nice shooting iron. I'll give you a box of ammunition to get you started, too. I'll keep my Russian, so we'll each have a different model."

"Thanks, Earl. This is a nice weapon."

Jessie and Lydia mounted their horses, Jessie on Butter and Lydia on Pete's roan.

Lydia looked down at Earl and said, "We'll go and get some lunch ready for you and Pete."

He waved at them before they set off back to the house.

Earl mounted Target and took the gray's reins to lead the gelding back to the house with Elmer cursing at each bouncing stride while Pete rode on his left wearing a slight smile. Earl didn't know if the smile was because he had met Jessie or because of Elmer's condition.

When they arrived at the house, Earl and Pete dragged Elmer from the gelding, then put him on his own horse, listening to his cursing and moaning as they made the change. Ray stepped onto the porch, having been given the basics from the women, but he wanted the full story.

He stepped closer to Earl and asked, "What happened, Son?"

"Elmer showed up and wanted to have his way with Jessie. Pete and I rode up and saw him trying to force his way into the house, so I fired a warning shot and he took off across the south pastures on Jessie's mare. I ran him down and pulled him from the saddle and was going to arrest him, but he pulled a knife, so I had to fight him hand-to-hand. I kind of overdid it a bit and he's a hurting bastard right now."

Ray glanced at Elmer, then said, "There isn't enough hurt for his kind. This has got to stop, though. You either have to get here sooner or at least not make it so close."

"I'm trying to improve my timing, Papa, but I don't think that there will be a need for another rescue."

258

"No, I don't think so, either. Are you going to take him into town?"

"After Pete and I have some lunch, Papa," he replied, then turned to Pete and said, "This handsome young man is Pete Procter, and if I have my way, he'll be taking over as sheriff by tomorrow, if not today."

Ray shook Pete's hand and said, "Glad to meet you. I'm sure Earl has told you about our current poor excuse for a lawman."

"Yes, sir. I hope I'll do better."

"Hell, a one-eyed hound dog would do better than that lazy bastard or his useless deputy."

————

Lydia and Jessie fed Earl and Pete as everyone else had eaten before Ray had returned from the pastures. After they had finished eating, Earl told Jessie that he was going to drop off Elmer and then have a chat with the sheriff. He asked and received permission from his parents for Pete to hang his hat in the small house until he found a place in town.

Pete asked, "I thought we were going to handle the sheriff tomorrow?"

"That was before we had a prisoner to deposit in the jail. But seeing as how we have to talk to the man anyway, we may as well give him the bad news at the same time."

"I wish I could be there to see his face," Jessie said with a smile.

"Come with me, ma'am, and we'll discuss that," Earl said as he stood and held his hand out to Jessie.

Jessie took his hand, smiled back at Lydian, then she and Earl stepped down the hallway and soon left the house.

Pete looked at Ray as he said, "I wonder if we'll be leaving anytime soon."

Ray snickered as he shrugged, unsure if Elmer wouldn't spend the rest of the day in the saddle outside their door.

After leavin the house with arms linked, they stepped across the porch, the walked past Elmer without a passing glance as they headed for the small house.

Jessie looked up at him and asked, "Is it always going to be like this for us, Earl?"

"No, I think those days are long past, sweetheart. I do have a few things I need to talk to you about before we take Elmer to Hopewell, but I don't mind leaving Elmer sitting out in the hot sun for a while."

"It's not hot enough to suit me."

"It can never be hot enough, Jessie," Earl said as they reached the small house.

After Earl opened the door and Jessie entered, he closed the door behind them, then quickly snatched her from her feet, swung her around, pulled her into his arms and kissed her.

He still had her suspended in the air as he looked deep into those wonderful brown eyes and said "I love you, Jessie. You were always on my mind when I was gone which is why I had to hurry back to you."

"I'm glad you did, Earl," she said as he lowered her to her feet and she asked, "So, what did you need to talk about?"

Earl just smiled into her angelic, anxious face before saying, "First, I need to ask if you ever planned on leaving Hopewell."

"I hadn't thought about it. Why?"

"They're offering me the position of the U.S. Marshal in charge of the Kansas City office."

"*Really?* That's wonderful, Earl! Of course, I can go with you. It would be exciting. But does that mean even more dangerous assignments?"

"Not at all. In fact, it's just the opposite. The marshal assigns deputies to missions, oversees the running of the office and is responsible for the performance of the deputies assigned to his office. The marshal may go on an assignment now and then if the manpower is low, but it's much safer."

"Then it's perfect."

"I also failed to mention that the pay is more than double what I'm making now."

"Now that is good news. What were the other things?"

"I remembered to buy these," he said as he reached into his saddlebags and pulled out the small box with the two gold bands inside.

He opened the box as Jessie's brown eyes stared.

"Oh, Earl. They're beautiful!" she softly exclaimed.

"I need you to try on yours to make sure it fits. Mine is fine."

She held out her splayed fingers and with a beatific smile on her face, he slipped it onto her finger, and almost as if it had no choice, it fit perfectly.

"Does it feel nice to have that on your finger, Mrs. Crawford?" Earl asked, his smile never having left his face since closing the door.

"Yes," she replied as she gazed at her ringed finger, then, knowing it was only temporary, grudgingly removed the ring and handed it back to him.

After returning her ring to the box and sliding it back into his pocket, Earl said, "And there's one more thing, my love."

His right hand dropped into his other pocket and extracted a second, longer jewelry box, then he held it before her as he slowly opened the cover.

Her eyes grew wide as she stared at the necklace and breathlessly whispered, "Earl, it's so beautiful! I love the purple color! What is it?"

"It's an amethyst. It's not the most precious of gemstones, but once I saw it in the jewelry store, I had to buy it. It matches the purple streaks in your eyes, and unlike the wedding ring, this is something that you can wear now."

Jessie was giddy as Earl set the box on the small table next to the door and removed the necklace from the box.

She turned and lifted her sandy brown hair as he lowered the necklace past her face and gently placed it around her neck and closed the clasp.

She turned slowly and wrapped her arms around him as she whispered, "I wish you didn't have to go back into town, Earl. I have a present I'd like to give you right now."

He kissed her and said, "I wish I didn't have to leave either, Jessie, but it needs to be done. And unless I'm mistaken, your gift is one that we can share and share often. We'll be together soon, my wife."

She sighed, but smiled up at him, and after one more kiss, they left the house holding hands.

Pete was on the front porch waiting for Earl and was a bit surprised when they returned relatively quickly. He soon realized the reason for Earl's need to be alone with Jessie when he saw the amethyst sparkling around Jessie's neck.

Jessie's hand finally left Earl's before he mounted Target.

Pete stepped into his saddle and they started toward Hopewell, trailing Elmer's horse with Elmer alternating cursing and moaning, in about a two to one ratio.

They arrived in town twenty minutes later, having taken a much slower pace than when they had on the morning's ride.

They dismounted before the sheriff's office, tied their horses and stepped onto the boardwalk before the jail, leaving Elmer in the saddle. It wasn't lunch time, so the soon to be ex-sheriff should be in, and as it happened, both the sheriff and deputy were in the office, which made Earl's job easier.

Earl stepped through the open doorway first, so as the sheriff looked up at him, he sneered as he said, "So, our famous United States Deputy Marshal has returned from his trip. What do you want?"

Earl continued to walk to the desk as he said, "I have a prisoner that needs to be placed in your jail for bank robbery and attempted murder of a United States Deputy Marshal. But before I put him in one of the cells, I want your badges. I am relieving both of you from your positions for gross incompetence and malfeasance. If you do not immediately comply, I will issue arrest warrants for each of you for obstructing justice. You have five minutes to leave your badges on the desk and leave the premises. You will take nothing that is official property."

He paused before adding, "Your time is running, gentlemen."

The sheriff and deputy both shot to their feet as Sheriff Burton blustered, "You can't do this!"

"I most certainly can. I have the authority to remove any local law enforcement officer whom I believe endangers the community through either non-performance or malfeasance, and you meet both criteria. If you wish to protest my decision, you may wire your complaint to the United States Marshal in Fort Worth."

"You're damned right I'll protest! I'll go to the mayor!"

"You have about three minutes remaining before I place you both under arrest, Burton. But by all means, go to the mayor. He's next on my list of visits after placing my prisoner in a cell, and you're now closing in on just two minutes."

Burton snatched his hat and left, but deputy stayed standing for a few seconds, then trotted quickly out the office behind him.

Earl removed the key ring from the wall and handed it to Pete, saying, "Go ahead and lock up our prisoner, then we'll go see the mayor."

"Do you know him?" Pete asked as he took the keys.

"Not well, but trust me, he'll cave on this one, despite the deputy being his son."

"*He's the mayor's kid?*" Pete exclaimed.

"It won't matter a bit in the end," Earl replied as they left the jail to retrieve Elmer.

"How can you get the mayor to fire his own son?"

As they reached the horses Earl grinned and answered, "You'll see."

Earl pulled Elmer from the horse none too gently, then they duck-walked him into the jail, where Pete hurried ahead and opened a cell before Earl set him onto the cot. Earl removed his handcuffs, then left him still moaning as Pete closed and locked the door.

The two men then left the jail, and headed down the street to the hardware store, which was owned by the mayor, Gregory Henderson.

As they walked, Earl said, "If there's one lesson every lawman has to learn is how to deal with politicians. I've been at this for a long time, and it's rare when one deviates from that mindset."

Pete asked, "All of them?"

265

"Pretty much. I have met a few that really want to do a good job, but most of them are there to feel important or just gain power."

Pete felt a growing anticipation to witness how Earl would be able to convince the mayor that it was a good idea to fire his own son, and already realized that it would be an important lesson.

Earl and Pete soon entered the hardware store and headed for the counter. The mayor was already looking their way and when he recognized Earl, he broke into that beaming smile that all politicians seemed to possess.

When they reached the counter, the mayor said, "Why, welcome back, Marshal! It seems like the whole state is talking about you, and I can't tell you how proud we all are for what you did. What can I do for you today?"

Earl didn't waste time on niceties, but replied, "Mayor, I just fired both the sheriff and the deputy."

The mayor was startled by Earl's unexpected response, and quickly asked, "Why? What did they do?"

"They were removed for non-performance of their duties and malfeasance. When a double homicide occurs in your jurisdiction and you fail to even investigate the crime or pursue the murderer, that alone qualifies as grounds for termination.

"Now, I know that the deputy was your son, but I don't believe that law enforcement was a good career choice for him at all, especially with Hank Burton as a role model. I'm sure you're aware by now that many of your citizens, if not all of the law-abiding folks in the town, don't think highly of Sheriff Burton."

The mayor was still shaken but slowly replied, "Yes, I had heard some of those rumors. But what will we do without a sheriff?"

"Before I left to return to Fort Worth, I knew I would be firing Burton when I came back to Hopewell, so I requested that the Unites States Marshal in Fort Worth supply me with a list of potential candidates for the job. He said they were all well-qualified and were being considered as United States Deputy Marshals. As you know, their standards are very high, so to even be considered is an honor.

"This handsome young man beside me is Pete Procter, and he was the marshal's top recommendation for the position and has all the training to return proper law enforcement to the town of Hopewell. I'm sure that I don't have to remind you how your decision to appoint him will make you more popular among the voters. They will see you as the honest man that you are and understand that Hopewell is growing and needs professional law enforcement rather than the shoddy job Burton had been doing. Of course, I'll be more than happy to extoll your choice to the newspaper, and the best part is that after you appoint him to the job, you'll even save the town money in the process."

The mayor had already forgotten about his son and was counting votes as he asked, "I will? How can I save the town money?"

"You're paying Burton sixty per month plus room and board, and his deputy was making forty dollars per month plus room and board as well. Now, if you pay Pete eighty dollars a month plus room and board, you'll be saving the taxpayers' money and be getting top-notch law enforcement as well.

"I can't tell you how quickly it will get around in the law enforcement community when a town does that. Suddenly, that community is no longer viewed as some backwater town that hires friends and relatives to do the exacting work of enforcing the law. It is viewed as a serious town ready to take its place among the real cities in the state."

Earl could see the mayor puff up before he nodded and said, "Why, you're right, Earl. I can see it all now. You're right about Burton and my son both. To be honest, Cecil should never have been made a deputy in the first place. By golly, this is going to be wonderful for me…I mean the town. I need to swear him in, though. Do you have the badge?"

"In my pocket, Your Honor," Earl answered as he pulled Burton's badge from his pocket and handed it to the mayor.

The mayor was still grinning as he quickly administered the oath of office, hung the badge on Pete's chest, then almost violently shook his hand.

After the mayor finally released Pete's sore hand, he said, "Thank you, Earl, and don't forget to talk to the newspaper."

"I won't. They'll do you proud, Mayor."

The mayor was popping buttons as they turned and left his hardware store.

When they were on the boardwalk and walking quickly away, Pete started laughing and said, "Earl, that manure pile was so deep in there I could barely breath."

"Now you know how to handle politicians. Did you notice that slip of the tongue when he said it was going to be great for him before he corrected it? He was almost honest there for a moment. Anyway, we are going to stop by the newspaper next. I want the town to know that you're the new sheriff."

268

"You're really going to do that? I thought it was just another piece of hogwash to make him happy."

"It wasn't. I need to let the town understand why I fired them and get you out front, so you'll have the citizens' support in case the mayor gets home and his wife gives him hell for letting me fire their idiot son."

"So, you're actually playing politics yourself now."

Earl grinned at him as he replied, "You have to fight fire with fire, Pete."

As they continued to the offices of *The Hopewell Bugle,* they'd barely walked another hundred feet when they heard loud footsteps behind them, and both turned to see a red-faced ex-sheriff stomping down the boardwalk behind them.

After stopping about twenty feet away, he exclaimed, "*What are you doing wearing my badge?*"

"Ignore him, Pete," said Earl quietly.

After not hearing an answer, ex-sheriff reached for his Colt as he shouted, "Get out of here you bastards, or I'll shoot you both down!"

Earl put his hand on Pete's chest to keep him in place before he began to step slowly toward Burton, loosening his hammer loop as he drew closer but never said a word.

Hank Burton saw the menace in his eyes and recalled all too quickly that the man walking toward him had killed a half dozen men in the past two weeks and ran his tongue across his upper lip.

Earl kept walking as Pete watched anxiously, expecting the showdown to end in gunfire, but didn't doubt who would be falling to the wooden surface.

Then, just as Earl drew within eight feet, the ex-sheriff fired first, but not with his Colt, but with his personal pistol as he committed that most humbling of acts for any man in a confrontation when he peed on himself.

Earl stopped when he was three feet from the ex-sheriff, reached across, unhooked Burton's hammer loop and pulled the gun from his holster.

He stared at Burton, who was visibly shaken and growled, "Hank, you're not suited for being a lawman. You need to find another line of work."

He then turned back to Pete and tossed him the pistol. After Pete caught the Colt, he and the new sheriff continued their interrupted walk to the newspaper.

Pete glanced back at the departing ex-sheriff and asked, "How did you know he wasn't going to draw?".

"First, I knew him to be a coward. Secondly, I could see in his eyes that he wanted no part of it. He just wanted to make a show."

"Well, he did that, but probably not in the way he intended," Pete said with a grin.

Earl smiled, then replied, "I reckon not."

Two minutes later, they entered the newspaper offices and were greeted by a pretty young lady with chestnut hair and sparkling hazel eyes. She wasn't a receptionist or secretary but was sitting at one of the two working desks.

Earl didn't recognize her, of course, but might have known her from his previous life when she was just a young girl.

She obviously knew Earl, though, and asked, "How can I help you, Marshal? I'm Barbara Willoughby. My father owns *The Bugle*, but I do most of the writing, so can I hope that you have a story for me?"

Earl smiled back as he replied, "Yes, I do, as a matter of fact, a very good story for the citizens of Hopewell. Sheriff Burton and Deputy Henderson have both been relieved of duty by my order and the mayor has sworn in a trained and well-qualified lawman."

As she slid a pad across the desk and picked up a pencil, Earl turned and said, "Miss Willoughby, I'd like to introduce you to the new sheriff of Hopewell, Pete Procter."

As Pete stepped forward, smiling at her, Barbara looked up from the pad, saw Pete and began to say, "It's a pleasure to…," but stopped in mid-sentence.

Pete hadn't even gotten that far as he simply stared at her with blank eyes.

After fifteen seconds of silence, Earl looked at the new sheriff.

"Pete," he said, then paused and said more loudly, "Pete!"

Pete blinked, shook his head and said, "Oh, sorry, Earl. I was distracted."

"I can see that. Why don't you tell the story to Miss Willoughby and when you both are satisfied that it is accurate, you can take her to dinner at the café on me. Here's ten dollars to cover the meal. You have a prisoner to care for now, so you'll have to stay at the jail for a couple of days, but I'll stop by when I can. I'll have to wire my boss to ask where he wants to have him tried."

Earl flipped a the ten-dollar gold piece to Pete, who snatched it just before it hit him in the nose, then mumbled, "I'll take care of Elmer."

Earl was stifling a grin as he turned to Barbara and said, "Miss Willoughby, for political reasons, you'll need to include that the mayor wholly supports the move to a professional law enforcement department."

She never looked back at Earl as she replied, "Oh, of course. I'll do that."

Earl was impressed that for once, a good-looking woman wasn't looking at him and had to admit that it was a good feeling.

He knew there was no point in his staying any longer, so he turned and left the newspaper office, not expecting to see Pete until late, if at all.

Just a few minutes later, he entered the Western Union office and quickly wrote out his message and handed it to the operator, who grinned at its contents, then listened as the telegrapher tapped out the code.

US MARSHAL GRANT FORT WORTH TEXAS

**ARRESTED ELMER JACKSON AFTER ATTEMPTED FLIGHT
SUSPECT FIRED SIX SHOTS NONE RETURNED
SUBDUED SUBJECT LEFT AT HOPEWELL JAIL
WAITING INSTRUCTIONS FOR DISPOSITION
SHERIFF PROCTER SWORN IN BY GRATEFUL MAYOR**

DEPUTY US MARSHAL CRAWFORD HOPEWELL TEXAS

Once that was done, he returned to the jail, untied Elmer's horse, now minus its groaning cargo, then hooked a trail rope to Target, mounted and headed south out of Hopewell.

He turned off the main road into the Mitchell farm ten minutes later because he needed to talk to the Mitchells and pick up the packs that he'd left in their barn in what seemed like months ago.

After tying off Target, he stepped up onto the porch and knocked at the front door, which was opened less than a minute later by Jessie's mother.

She smiled as she said, "You're back sooner than we expected, Earl. Jessie is down at your parents' place."

"I know. I've already been there, and I stopped to pick up those packs I left a couple of weeks ago, but I need to talk to you and Mister Mitchell before I go."

Ada Mitchell sighed and thought, "Not again."

"He's inside. Come in, Earl."

Earl stepped into the Mitchell home and saw Ray exiting the hallway with a cup of coffee in his hand.

"Welcome back, Earl. You must have burned up that road getting here."

"As a matter of fact, we did."

"We?" he asked.

"I brought your new sheriff and just left him in Hopewell. The mayor has already sworn him in."

"Lord, you operate fast. What can we do for you?"

"Why don't you and Mrs. Mitchell have a seat and I'll fill you in?"

They sat nervously anticipating what Earl was going to tell them as it seemed that every visit he'd had at the house since his return had been momentous. This one would turn out to be no different.

"First, I want you both to know that Jessie's fine. When I left the ranch, she and my mother were cleaning up after lunch."

He could hear a released breath from her parents as Earl began telling them of the latest confrontation on the Crawford ranch.

When he mentioned his final blow that he delivered to Elmer, Tom Mitchell winced and pressed his knees together, then said, "I wouldn't wish that fate on any man, except for Elmer. And, speaking for my wife, I'm grateful that you did rough him up."

"It was the least I could do for Jessie. Unfortunately, his pain will only last a few hours, but he'll have another thirty years in the penitentiary to think about it."

"Why would he get so much time for that bank job?" asked Ada.

"He wouldn't. But when I was chasing him, he took six shots at me in front of four witnesses. That qualifies for attempted murder of a United States Deputy Marshal and that is worth at least twenty-five years these days."

Earl paused, then said, "I need to be getting back, so I'll load up the packs that I stored in your barn and heading back home. I'm sure Jessie would like to see you both and we still need to schedule the wedding. Oh, and one more thing; I was offered the position of United States Marshal for the Kansas City office and Jessie was excited because it'll keep me in the office more."

"That's wonderful news, Earl," said Ada.

Ray said, "Let's go out to the barn, Earl. We'll load up the packs and hitch up the buggy. Then we'll ride over to your place together."

Earl smiled and said, "That sounds good."

Earl and Ray then left the house, went out to the barn, and while Ray was harnessing the buggy, Earl led Target and Elmer's horse inside and began loading the heavy packs that included his spare firearms and ammunition. When he had it all reasonably secure on the riding saddle for the short trip, he led the horses back outside behind the buggy.

Ada Mitchell had exited the house and was boarding the buggy as Earl mounted Target then slid his gelding behind the rolling buggy down the short access road. They maintained a slow pace and arrived at the ranch ten minutes later.

When they reached the ranch, as the Mitchells exited the buggy, Earl stepped down and led the two horses into the barn, removed the packs, then unsaddled and began brushing down both animals.

He strode to the ranch house with a light step anticipating seeing Jessie again, sure that she'd been telling her parents all of the wonderful news.

Just before he entered the house, he stopped when he heard talking and laughter bubbling from the main room, then smiled and felt a wave of peace roll over him. This is the way it is supposed to be when he returned to the house and not hiding from threats or having to wash blood off the floor. Families should be happy together. Even as he stood on the porch, he wondered if he was doing the right thing taking by Jessie away from her family now that there was peace and quiet again. After the short delay, he opened the door and walked inside.

Everyone was sitting in the main room and turned their eyes toward Earl as he entered and noticed that the only empty spot in the large room was conveniently next to Jessie on the couch. She smiled at him, patted the empty cushioned space beside her, and with a big smile, he walked to the couch and happily took his designated seat.

"So, what were you all laughing about while I was out?" Earl asked.

Jessie answered, "I know it sounds terrible, but we were all laughing about Elmer having to ride that horse all the way to Hopewell with his hands behind his back with his damaged privates."

Earl grinned and said, "I made sure that the horse bounced as much as possible, too."

Then after a short pause, he said, "Now that you're all here, I'll give you updates on what happened in town. We took the groaning Elmer to the jail but left him out front while I fired both the sheriff and the deputy. After Pete and I locked Elmer in his cell, we saw the mayor, whose son I had just fired. I laid it on really thick about how I knew how honest he was and how much the voters would appreciate having real law enforcement in the town, and he was only too happy to swear Pete in as the new sheriff."

"That's great!" said his father, "A real sheriff. What's this town coming to?"

Earl smiled then continued, saying, "After that, we left to go to the newspaper to have them write a story about the change, when Mister Hank Burton took offense when he saw Pete wearing his badge. He was full of bluster and challenged me to a gunfight."

Everyone was paying rapt attention as Earl continued in his deep, resonant tone.

"I faced him as he stood twenty feet away and slowly began walking toward him with my eyes focused on his as I released my hammer loop and his right hand dropped to his Colt's grip. Each step increasing the intensity and with each step, the stress grew. Step by step, the tension was building, and I knew one of us had to make the first move."

Earl paused as he looked at their wide eyes and then continued the mesmerizing brief narration of the showdown, saying, "Then, when I was just six feet away, I stopped and knew I had waited too long to draw my pistol when Hank Burton suddenly fired!"

Everyone rocked back slightly with bulging eyes before his father asked in disbelief, "He shot at you?"

Earl nodded before he answered, "He fired, and he didn't miss either. I simply stood in disbelief when I saw the liquid flooding his britches."

Jessie then exclaimed, *"He shot himself?"*

Earl finally grinned as he replied, "You're darn tootin', ma'am, only he didn't use his Colt. He had used the hidden weapon he had in his britches when he fired his pee gun all over himself."

The room exploded in laughter at the unexpected and incredibly funny image of the ex-sheriff's embarrassment. When they had calmed down enough so he could be heard, Earl continued.

"I just walked up to him and ignoring the smell, pulled his gun from his holster and told him to get a new line of work. I tossed the gun to the new sheriff and we went to the newspaper."

He paused in anticipation of his change to another topic before saying, "And that visit was another interesting story."

"Don't tell me you have more?" asked his mother.

He nodded, then replied, "Yes, ma'am. When we got into the office, I began explaining the story to a young lady named Barbara Willoughby."

"I know her," said Jessie, "I went to school with Barbara. She's very pretty and good at writing, too."

He smiled at Jessie then said, "She said she wrote the stories for the paper, so I began telling her about running a story about the new sheriff before I introduced her to Pete. That was the last word that either of them heard as they both seemed to be, as Pete said, 'distracted'. I gave Pete ten dollars, so he could take her to dinner. I wouldn't be surprised if he's still there staring at her, but he does have a prisoner to watch, so he'll be spending the night at the jail."

"That's amazing," commented Jessie, "a lot of boys chased after her, but she wouldn't have anything to do with any of them, yet just like that, she and Pete are an item? We'll have to see how far that goes, won't we, husband-to-be?"

"I don't think we have to worry about them too much. I do want to ask everyone something while we're all together. I know that you're aware that I've been offered the Kansas City United States Marshal's job. The only reason I might be hesitant to take it is that I don't want to take Jessie away from her family now that everything is back to normal. I want to know how everyone feels about it, especially you, Jessie."

"Earl," said his mother, "it's always been the way of children to grow up and lead their own lives and go their own way. It's not like you'll be moving onto the other side of the country. It's about five hundred miles to Kansas City. Right now, we'd have to take a stage to the nearest railroad station in Clarksville, but in a couple of years, we'll be able to board a train right here, so we can come and visit whenever we want to see our grandchildren."

Earl nodded, then looked at Ada Mitchell, who said, "Lydia expressed it perfectly. You two need to make this decision about what's right for your future. Besides, the timing will be perfect. By the time we get a railroad in here, we should be able to visit our grandchildren."

Finally, Earl turned to Jessie. Even though she had already told him that she was excited about the prospect, he wanted to know if she had considered the separation from her family.

Jessie's big brown eyes smiled at him as she said softly, "Earl, I've already told you that I'll go wherever you go. I'll miss my parents, but I'll have you. They'll be visiting just as your parents will, so take the job. Now we still need to set a date for the wedding."

"Jessie, I think a week would be about right, don't you? Say a week from tomorrow? It'll give me five more days of injury time afterward to spend with you. I'll send a telegram to Dan and let him know of our decision and tell him of the wedding. Okay?"

"A week sounds perfect, Earl. I know that we wanted a small wedding, but how small do you think it should be?"

"I'm not sure. What do you think?"

"I'd like a nice quiet wedding with both of our parents there. Reverend Lawless is already excited about performing the ceremony, so why don't we both go in tomorrow, you can send your telegram and then we'll go and chat with the minister."

"That sounds fine, Jessie."

She leaned across the couch, gave him a kiss and smiled at him, before saying, "I suppose we need to get dinner going now."

The two mothers stood, and Ada said, "Jessie, why don't you and Earl go out for a walk. It's turning into a beautiful evening and we'll take care of dinner."

Then she winked at her daughter before the two mothers left the main room and walked down the hallway to the kitchen.

Earl and Jessie were only too happy to oblige, so no sooner had their mothers left the room, the couple stood, then left the house with arms linked as they walked onto the porch. The sun was beginning to set, creating a perfect backdrop, as they stepped down and began to stroll toward the small house.

"Earl, isn't this the way it's supposed to be?" Jessie asked quietly.

"Always, sweetheart."

"Do you think Pete will be back to use the small house tonight?"

"Maybe, or maybe not. He has a prisoner to watch, but if he does show up, it won't be for a couple of hours at least."

She smiled up at him and said, "Then we have plenty of time to be alone, husband."

"More than enough, wife."

After reaching the small house, they entered the door and even as Earl quickly locked it behind them, Jessie let him know that she wasn't about to waste any time.

———

An hour later, Earl unlocked the door and they left the house with looks of complete contentment on their faces.

"It'll be different in a week, won't it, Earl?" asked Jessie as they slowly stepped toward the main house.

"I think so. We'll have a lot more time to spend getting to know each other even better."

Jessie laughed and said, "I think I know quite a lot about you already."

"But not as much as you're going to know."

They reached the main house, crossed the porch, and Earl held the door as Jessie went inside.

"So, did you both walk to Hopewell or what?" asked Tom.

"No, we just enjoyed the beautiful evening," answered Jessie.

"That was a long walk, Son," added Ray.

"We needed the exercise," replied Earl as he heard a chorus of giggling from the kitchen.

Ray and Tom looked at each other not knowing what had set off their wives' merriment.

"I'll go and see if dinner is ready," said Jessie, which she followed with a quick kiss.

"Don't you ever sleep, Earl?" asked Tom, "In the last week, you've ridden over three hundred miles."

"I'm sure it'll all catch up to me sooner or later, but I have enough to keep me going for a while."

———

After dinner, Earl and Jessie sat on the porch, just enjoying the less-than-hot night air.

"Earl, what if I can't have the grandchildren that our parents want to have?" Jessie suddenly asked.

Earl was startled by her question, but quickly answered, "Sweetheart, almost every woman has that question. Some assume they'll have a whole passel of children and don't have any at all. We'll just let nature take its course. I know I will do everything in my power to help you with that endeavor."

Jessie laughed at his comment as the laughter washed away her concerns with the humor and her future husband's love.

Pete surprised them when he showed up twenty minutes later as they heard him before they saw him. When he was closer to the house, he saw Earl and Jessie and trotted his horse over to them.

"Well, Pete," said Earl, "were you able to pry yourself away from Miss Willoughby's charms long enough to remember you had a prisoner to feed?"

Pete stepped down and said, "That was a close call and it was Barbara who reminded me. We had just finished dinner and were leaving when she asked if I needed to bring some food over to Elmer. I smacked my head, then got him his food, and when he finished eating, I let him use the privy. He could still barely walk, by the way. I asked if he wanted to see a doctor and he said he'd rather see the iceman. Then I left him with a chamber pot, locked the doors and left him sleeping. Is that okay?"

"You'll need to leave early to feed him in the morning, but if you have the cell keys, you should be all right."

Earl then smiled and asked, "Is he aware that he is going to spend a long time in jail?"

"Not yet. I thought I'd let that come as a surprise."

"Good enough. What time are you going in tomorrow?"

"I'll leave here around seven o'clock."

"Jessie and I will be in town tomorrow to take care of some things, so I'll stop by and see how it's going."

"That will be great. By the way, Barbara is going to write a good story about me."

"Why am I not surprised? You go and get some sleep. Use the barn for your horse."

Pete waved and led his horse to the barn as Jessie and Earl returned to the house.

The Mitchells were preparing to leave, so Jessie said goodnight to Earl and said she'd be ready when he came by tomorrow morning.

After they were gone, Earl returned to the house and after spending another hour talking to his parents, finally entered his old bedroom to fill his need for some much-needed sleep.

CHAPTER 10

Pete had already gone to Hopewell to start his first day as sheriff by the time Earl entered the barn to start clearing out the retrieved packs before leaving to pick up Jessie. He spent an hour going through the packs, bringing all the food items to the house and smiling when he found a pack with two pairs of riding skirts, two blouses and some underwear, none of which were his size.

He unpacked his weapons and carried them to the small house, so he could sort them out with Pete. He kept two boxes of ammunition for Pete with him before he then finally saddled Target and hooked Jessie's pack over his saddlebags.

He mounted, waved to his mother and father as they stood on the porch, then left the ranch and headed for the Mitchell farm. As he turned onto their short access road, he checked his watch and was pleased to find it was 8:55; just five minutes before his promised arrival time. He rode into the yard, spotted a smiling Jessie on the porch, and watched as she popped down onto the ground.

"Good morning, soon-to-be-official-wife," he said as he pulled Target to a stop.

"Good morning to you, soon-to-be-overworked-husband," she answered.

"I could not have asked for a more joyous fate, ma'am," he said, then added, "I brought you this," as he unhooked the pack and lowered it to her.

She peeked inside and smiled as she said, "I had forgotten about these. I'll leave them on the porch until we get back. Butter is already saddled."

She turned, then quickly dropped the pack on the porch, walked to the barn, then soon emerged walking Butter out of the big doors to join him.

They exited the farm, turned north, and a few minutes later, they arrived in Hopewell where they walked the horses to the telegraph office.

Earl quickly dismounted and before Jessie could even free her right foot from her stirrup, he surprised her by reaching up and taking her by the waist to help her down.

"What was that for?" she asked as her feet touched the ground.

Earl smiled and replied, "Just so I could have an excuse to get my hands on you and not cause a scandal."

"Like we haven't been behaving scandalously for the past few days," she said with a smile.

He looked around, saw no one looking and gave her a swift tap on her behind, which caused a slight blush in Jessie's cheeks before she took his arm and they entered the Western Union office.

The operator glanced at the couple, then said, "Marshal, I have a message for you. I was going to send a messenger if you hadn't arrived by ten o'clock."

He handed Earl the short telegram and he read:

US DEPUTY MARSHAL CRAWFORD HOPEWELL TEXAS

GOOD JOB ON JACKSON
WILL PROSECUTE HERE
HOLD HIM UNTIL WE PICK UP
GLAD PETE WORKED OUT

US MARSHAL GRANT FORT WORTH TEXAS

He handed the telegram to Jessie to read while he wrote a reply, then handed the sheet to the operator.

US DAN GRANT FORT WORTH TEXAS

WILL ACCEPT KANSAS CITY JOB
GETTING MARRIED NEXT WEDNESDAY
WILL TRANSPORT PRISONER IF NECESSARY

DEPUTY US MARSHAL CRAWFORD HOPEWELL TEXAS

The operator read the short message, and said, "Congratulations, Marshal. That'll be thirty-five cents."

Earl had to smile as he said, "Thank you," then paid for the telegram, linked arms with Jessie again and left the office.

———

They next met with Reverend Lucius Lawless for half an hour and set the date and time for the following Wednesday at ten o'clock They left the church, walking with arms locked and headed to the sheriff's office.

Pete was in the office behind the front desk, chatting with Barbara Willoughby who was sitting on the desktop when Earl and Jessie entered.

Barbara turned and smiled at the couple while Pete just grinned.

She said, "So, here's the happy couple. Congratulations to you both. When are you going to get married?"

"Wednesday at ten o'clock," answered Jessie.

"I'll run an announcement in the paper tomorrow. Speaking of the paper, here's today's copy. I was just dropping it off with Pete," she said as she handed the new copy of *The Hopewell Bugle* to Earl.

Earl quickly read the article about the change of sheriffs, noticing that Barbara used a lot of typeface describing Pete's qualifications, but Earl was glad to see she had given prominent mention of the mayor's support for the change, too. He handed it to Jessie who read it quickly then praised Barbara for a well-written article.

"Marshal, could I ask you something?" Barbara asked.

"Only if you call me Earl."

"Okay, Earl. Pete was telling me more about your last mission. I only had heard parts of it before through the gossip mill and I was wondering if you would sit down with me some time, so I could document it."

"Barbara, I was just doing my job. Besides, it was all documented in my official report that's filed in Fort Worth."

"But it doesn't come close to telling the whole story. It doesn't tell the human side. It doesn't even mention Jessie, for example."

"I'll tell you what, Barbara, let's just hang on for a while. I won't make any promises, but if anyone gets the whole story, it'll be you. And it will require my bride to be there to fill in blanks and keep me from getting too racy."

Jessie laughed and said, "I'm going to stop you from getting racy? Who's going to stop me?"

Earl smiled at her as he said, "Jessie, why don't you go with Barbara back to her office. I need to talk shop with Pete for a bit. If you give us thirty minutes, we'll treat for lunch. Will that work?"

"You have a deal, Mister Crawford," answered Jessie before she gave Earl a quick kiss.

After she and Barbara left the office, Earl looked at the wall, saw two Winchesters and a shotgun and asked, "Do you have enough ammunition for the Winchesters?"

"Plenty. They fit the pistol, too."

"That's handy. Some of them shoot different cartridges. So, how are things with Barbara?"

"Really good. I can't imagine how much things have changed in a week."

"Good. Want to go and give the bad news to Elmer?"

Pete grinned as he answered, "This will be fun."

Earl and Pete walked to the cells where Elmer was sitting on his cot. He didn't look happy and Earl was going to enjoy making him even more unhappy. He had no pity whatsoever for the man.

"Good morning, Elmer. How are you doing this beautiful morning?" Earl asked cheerily.

"I feel like crap, thanks to you. I suppose you're here to take me to White Oak."

"No, Elmer, you won't be going to White Oak. You really screwed up when you went to my parents' house. If you had just stayed in whatever hole you were in, I would just have arrested you for bank robbery and you'd be out in two or three years."

"All you got is Atherton's word and I can beat that. I ain't spending no two or three years behind bars."

"No, you're not, Elmer. You'll be spending at least twenty-five years behind bars and in a Federal prison, not some swanky Texas hell hole."

A shocked Elmer exclaimed, "Twenty-five years! For what, banging on a door?"

"No, you moron, for attempted murder of a United States Deputy Marshal. I've had bullets aimed my way a few dozen times in the past seven years, and the shooters that lived to face trial before Federal Judge Harper have always received twenty-five years for the attempted murder. You fired six rounds and it was witnessed by four people, so that's bad news for you,

Elmer. They'll be sending someone to drag your ass back to Fort Worth for trial soon, so have a nice trip to Fort Worth and an even nicer one to the Federal pen. How old are you, anyway? Twenty-seven, twenty-eight? You'll be a ripe old age by the time you get out, assuming you live that long. Have a nice day, Elmer."

Earl smiled at the dumbfounded prisoner, then he and Pete turned and walked out of the jail.

Pete locked the front door before he and Earl walked down to the newspaper office to pick up the ladies for lunch.

As they strolled down the boardwalk, Pete said, "I can't believe that Jessie married that idiot."

"I asked her the same thing and even after she told me the reason, I found it hard to believe that Elmer was capable of hiding his true nature from her until after they were wed."

"I don't want to know."

"I'm never going to bring up the subject again, either. I just hope I don't have to drag Jessie or my mother to Fort Worth for the trial. They can use their sworn affidavits and that might be enough with my reputation with the judge. We'll see."

———

After finding Jessie and Barbara in the newsroom, Earl and Pete escorted them to the diner and found a nice table not seeing the ex-sheriff anywhere.

As they enjoyed the meal, Earl told Jessie about the entertaining discussion he had with Elmer and that the buffoon had no idea that shooting at a deputy marshal could carry such severe repercussions. Jessie said she had wished she could have seen it but could never be that close to him again, and even shuddered at the thought.

After lunch, Barbara and Pete returned to the sheriff's office and Earl and Jessie wandered down to the Western Union office to get their horses. Before they mounted, Earl wanted to check if he had received a reply from Dan and wasn't surprised to find one waiting.

He read:

DEPUTY US MARSHAL CRAWFORD HOPEWELL TEXAS

CONGRATULATIONS ON WEDDING
WILL NOTIFY HEAD OFFICE OF DECISION
WILL SEND SOMEONE FOR JACKSON

US MARSHAL GRANT FORT WORTH TEXAS

He handed the telegram to Jessie and said, "It's time to go home, Jessie."

She smiled, returned the telegram and took his free hand before they headed for the open doorway.

After leaving the telegraph office, they walked to their horses and when they arrived at the hitched animals, Jessie stood next to Butter, looked at Earl, then tilted her head and asked, "Well?"

Earl laughed, then stepped behind her, took her by her waist and slowly lifted her from the ground, but before he put her in the saddle, he stole a kiss on the way.

"I could get used to this," she said as she looked down at him.

Earl just smiled up at her before mounting Target. They wheeled their horses away from the office, then rode out of town heading south. Just a few minutes later, Earl dropped Jessie off at her family's farmhouse before he returned home.

———

The next day, the paper printed the announcement of their wedding, but it wasn't a short announcement on the social page. It was a front-page story. Neither Earl nor Jessie knew anything about it until Pete returned to the small house that evening and gave copies to everyone.

The only one who wasn't overly pleased was Earl. The long article made him out to be a modern Achilles, but he did appreciate Barbara's heartfelt description of Jessie and even included a mention of the amethyst necklace that Jessie had said would never leave her neck.

But he let his own embarrassment go because all that mattered in the entire story was that he and Jessie were going to be married on Wednesday.

Over the next two days, as they prepared for the wedding, Jessie and the two mothers made a new dress for the bride, while Earl had to ride to Mount Pleasant to buy a suit. As far as the couple knew, there were going to be six guests at the wedding; both sets of parents, Pete, and Barbara. Pete would be Earl's witness and Barbara would be Jessie's.

Pete had found a room Archer's Boarding House and moved out of the small house, giving Earl time to bring it up to a better condition pending the arrival of his official wife. They would stay there for three days, as Earl had received long telegrams from the boss which meant that he was going to have to return to Fort Worth to handle some paperwork and testify at Elmer's trial.

After the trial, he would be heading off to a three-week training and orientation program for new marshals. He was relieved that neither Jessie, his mother or even Pete would be needed for the trial, but their affidavits would suffice. That boon had been granted by Dan when Earl had let him know that Jessie was determined never to see her ex-husband again.

Jessie wanted to come along when he returned from Fort Worth and he left for the short course, but despite Earl's own desire to have her with him, they eventually decided that Jessie would remain in Hopewell until they moved to Kansas City. After finishing the orientation, Earl would go to Kansas City, meet his crew and try to find a house. He knew that Kansas City was a rapidly growing city with a population already past fifty thousand. Housing might be hard to find and would put a huge dent in his bank account and they may need furniture and all those other necessaries for the kitchen and bath, but he knew they'd make it work. All those years of living frugally had finally paid off.

———

The day before the wedding, it was chaotic at both families' homes, which surprised Earl because it was going to be such a small ceremony, but the mothers insisted on doing everything right. They had baked a large, two-layer cake, bought a large pork roast for dinner and all sorts of other edibles. Earl didn't know it was going to be such a production, but Jessie seemed to take it in stride.

———

Finally, the big day arrived. Earl had dressed in his suit at his parents' house and spent most of the morning pacing the main room or walking out to the small house and making sure everything was just right when he returned with his wife, as if either of them would pay the least amount of attention to their surroundings.

He had rented a buggy, and at a nine-thirty, he would drive the buggy with his parents to the church. They'd trail the gray gelding, so his father could ride back to the ranch and his mother would ride back to the ranch with the Mitchells in their buggy while Earl would return in the rented buggy with his new bride. Jessie would ride to the wedding in her parents' buggy, and they'd meet Pete and Barbara at the church. The travel logistics for such a simple wedding were beyond confusing.

Earl looked at his watch for the eighth time in the past ten minutes and couldn't understand why he was so nervous. He'd faced gunfire from four outlaws with a calmer demeanor. He knew he absolutely loved Jessie and there wasn't a doubt in his mind that she was the one. *So, why the nerves?*

Finally, at half past nine, the Crawfords boarded the buggy and started toward Hopewell. Jessie and her parents were in their buggy next to the barn, and after they watched Earl's rented buggy drive past, they waited a minute and then rolled out behind them.

Earl drove the buggy into town and soon received the shock of his life when they entered the main road. There were people everywhere lining the boardwalks, waving at him as he passed. He felt obligated to wave back despite being stunned by the unexpected reception. *What was this all about?*

Jessie was equally unsettled a minute later when her buggy turned into the town, and just as Earl had done, she waved back at the smiling faces as they approached the church.

When Earl and his parents pulled the buggy to a stop before the church, they could see that the church seemed packed and each had the same question. *What had happened?*

After they exited the buggy, it was quickly led away by a youngster who smiled at him, adding to their confusion. It was as if someone else was planning their wedding and hadn't bothered to let them know. He and his parents then slowly entered the church and Earl was surprised yet again when he was greeted by a grinning Dan Grant, who offered his arm to Earl's mother and escorted her and Earl's father down the aisle.

Pete then stepped out from the side of the church and took a very confused Earl's elbow and almost had to guide him to the front of the church, as he was lost in his befuddled state with all of the strange things that were happening. *What happened to their simple wedding?*

Jessie was no less confused as the buggy approached the church. When the buggy stooped before the steps, they stepped out of the buggy, another youngster took the horse's reins, smiled and gave her a small bow as if she was royalty. She smiled back and slowly walked up the three steps into the church with her equally disoriented mother and father and found herself in awe of the large crowd inside.

When she reached the back of the church, Barbara took her mother's arm and told Jessie and her father to wait at the back of the church until the music started.

"Music?" thought Jessie, as flummoxed as the groom was by everything that seemed so unreal.

Jessie was wearing a simple, but elegant cream silk dress, but wasn't wearing a veil. Her only jewelry was her precious amethyst necklace, even though to gemologists, it was far from that level of value.

Earl was finally coming to grips with what had happened. He concluded that it was Barbara's announcement in the paper that had created this stunning event. He was wrong but wouldn't realize it until later.

Reverend Lawless stepped out onto the altar, stood next to Earl, then smiled before he nodded to the back of the church and the organist began playing the traditional wedding march.

Jessie's father, despite having no previous instructions, understood that the music was signal to begin the ceremony, so he took his daughter's arm and escorted her slowly down the aisle. She still may have been confused, but when she saw Earl gazing at her with the love she always saw in his eyes, she disregarded everything else and just had eyes for him as he waited for her at the altar. Her angelic face then surpassed the radiance of most brides as it achieved an almost divine luminosity.

Earl watched her approach and found it hard to breath. He would have to apologize to her later as she had definitely surpassed cute. She was incredibly beautiful, but still retained that soft face that had captured his heart.

Her father brought Jessie to Earl's side, and as she placed her small hand on his, he slowly retreated to join his wife.

The ceremony itself was short and almost unheard by the couple as they continued to live in each other's eyes. After a reasonably tame soliloquy from the reverend, they exchanged vows and rings, and when Earl finally was able to kiss her as his wife, he felt such a level of happiness that he thought he'd never reach again.

Jessie was lost in her emotions as that magic moment she had dreamed about as a young girl finally arrived. A moment that she thought would be denied to her when he was visiting Eva, then when he went off to war and didn't return, and when she married that foul Elmer. But that incredible imaginary moment was here now. It was no longer a dream, it was real, and Earl was kissing her as her husband.

As they turned to leave the church, the audience broke into thunderous applause, but it didn't matter to Earl and Jessie. They were husband and wife and only had eyes for each other.

They walked down the stairs and found their buggy waiting for them. Earl thanked the boy holding the reins and held Jessie's hand as she stepped into the buggy, then walked around to the other side, stepped in and took the reins.

Jessie scooted against him and placed her hand on his thigh as he smiled at her, then snapped the reins and the buggy rolled down the street. The crowds who hadn't been inside the church waved at them as they drove down the main street and left the town.

Once clear of the noise, Earl turned to his wife and asked, "Jessie, do you have any idea what just happened?"

"Aside from becoming your wife, I have no idea what was going on."

"We'll worry about it later. Let's go home, Mrs. Crawford," he said before leaned over and kissed her.

If the newlyweds thought the day's surprises were all behind them, but they soon would discover that they were far from over.

Twenty minutes after leaving Hopewell, they turned into the ranch's access road and drove the buggy to the small house.

Earl helped Jessie out of the buggy, even though she didn't need the assistance, and quickly led her inside, then closed the door and wrapped his new wife in his arms and they enjoyed their first passionate kiss as husband and wife.

Earl then said, "I'd like nothing more than to take that beautiful dress off you and take you to our bed, but I think we have parents arriving, so we'd better behave ourselves."

"Yes, it's a shame, isn't it?"

"But I'll get that dress off you later."

"I'll hold you to that promise, husband," Jessie said as she slapped his behind.

Earl reciprocated by sliding his hand across her silk-covered and much softer bottom before they left the house and spotted the second buggy followed by Earl's father on the gelding as they arrived at the house. They waved and walked toward the main house where they met their parents before everyone went inside.

Once inside, Jessie asked, "What was all that about, Papa?"

"I have no idea. I was as surprised as anyone."

After a brief questioning among everyone in the room, it appeared that none of the family knew what had caused all the crowds or the sudden change in format. Earl still had no idea why his boss was there, but had a good guess.

He finally offered his own theory when he said, "It must have been because of that big story that Barbara wrote in the newspaper. I imagine that Dan is here to escort Elmer to Fort Worth. He could have sent Ed or someone else, but I guess he wanted to be here for the wedding."

"That's what I was thinking, at least about the wedding," Jessie said.

The mothers then went into the kitchen and forbade Jessie to set a foot into the room, so with the mothers' prohibition, Earl and Jessie took their accustomed place on the couch.

They had barely gotten comfortable when there was a knock at the door.

Earl expected that Pete and Barbara would be coming to share the food, so he just shouted, "Come on in."

Pete and Barbara entered but so did Dan Grant and then Earl grinned when he spotted Ed walk in behind his boss.

Earl stood and said, "Ed! I'm glad you could make it. I didn't even see you there."

He shook Ed's hand and then Dan's before asking, "How did you two get away?"

"We had a prisoner to transport, remember? Ed and I drove the jail wagon, so I'm sure our prisoner will have a pleasant ride back. The other reason we needed the wagon is that we needed it to transport some mail."

"Mail?" asked Earl, sinking back into confusion.

"When the word got out somehow of your pending marriage, we began getting letters and such from all over and it was quite a load, so I needed to bring it with me. To be honest, not all of it was mail. A lot was just brought to my office or to Pete's. We just consolidated it, and it's outside in the wagon. Want us to bring it in?"

"Might as well. Need some help?"

"No, we can get it."

Jessie looked at Earl with raised eyebrows as she asked, "What do you think it is?"

"Letters of congratulations, I suppose. I am the most fortunate man on the planet, you know," he replied with a smile.

Dan and Ed then returned to the room lugging a good-sized crate and set it down on the floor with a loud thump.

The marshal slid a screwdriver out of his pocket, and began to pry off the cover, as Jessie rose and stepped next to Earl to see what was inside.

After Dan pulled the top off of the wooden box, Earl and Jessie looked inside and saw piles of envelopes and boxes.

They looked at the marshal and Dan asked, "Well, Earl and Jessie, are you going to start opening these? Ed and I were a bit curious about the contents of some of them while we were on the road."

"I'll tell you what, Dan. We'll open them but only when our mothers are here. They're making a feast in the kitchen as you can tell from those delicious aromas. You will be staying, won't you?"

"We had planned on it. I could smell that food a half mile down the road."

"I'm glad that you can join us."

Dan then reached into his pocket, pulled out a thick envelope and said, "Oh, and one more thing while I remember it. Here are all the forms we need to fill out, so you'll be able to go straight to the training center. You're expected there on the sixth, so you'll have two more weeks to get there. I just need you to sign a few of these, then you won't have to even return to Fort Worth."

They walked to desk in the corner of the room, where Earl took a pen and a bottle of ink out of a drawer.

Earl signed the forms, then after he set them to dry, asked, "What about Elmer? Won't I have to be there for the trial?"

"Nope. There isn't going to be a trial. After I had a little chat with your prisoner, he agreed to a twenty-year plea bargain that I had approved by the judge before we left. We're just going to take him back with us and drop him off at the prison on the way back."

Earl was pleased with that piece of news, because he really didn't want to leave Jessie again so soon.

"Thanks, Dan. That's best for everyone."

Dan shook his hand and said, "Earl, I'm gonna miss you. You were the best man I ever had. Kansas City is going to get a great leader."

"Thanks, Dan. I had a great teacher."

———

An hour later, the food was ready, and everyone sat at a long table that had been placed outside the back of the house. It was a perfect day, and not overly hot, which was amazing for the middle of June in Texas. They ate, talked and enjoyed the company in the festive atmosphere.

When Earl and Jessie cut the cake made by their mothers, Earl held up the knife and said, "Do you think we should send some to Elmer?"

It was a measure of Jessie's healing that she said, "The cake or the knife?"

———

After everyone had finished eating and the excess food and tableware were cleared from the table, they all adjourned to the main room to watch Earl and Jessie open the mail and packages.

Most were just as Earl suspected; letter of congratulations from lawmen, people he had helped, and many he never knew. Some contained monetary gifts both small and some not so small, but there were two that even impressed Dan.

Jessie found the first when she read the name on the back, noticed the lilac scent and handed it to Earl with the comment, "I think you had better open this one."

It was from Teresa O'Toole. Inside was a five-hundred-dollar bank draft and a short note that read in flowing script:

My Dear Marshal,

I can never thank you enough for what you did that day.

Congratulations to you and your new wife. I pursued, but she won the race. She must be one hell of a woman.

Love,

Teresa O'Toole

He handed it to Jessie to read and she simply said, "She got that right. I won."

The second, unsurprisingly, was from Brandon King. Enclosed was a draft for $1043. The amount itself was stunning, but the number had Earl confused until he read the note:

Dear Earl,

Congratulations to you and Mrs. Crawford on your wedding.

My family is happy and alive thanks to you.

The $43 I added is the money you gave to my wife to pay for the doctor. The sheriff had already paid anyway. She said to tell you she really was never angry with you for leaving, she was just upset that she didn't get to kiss you as Annie did.

Thank you again,

Brandon King

The one note of congratulations that Earl appreciated the most was on a plain sheet of paper and written with a shaky hand:

Dear Marshal Crawford,

I want to thank you from the depths of my heart.

I thought I had lost my son, but after talking to you and what you did to help him, he decided to come back to me. When he was arrested, I thought I would never see him again, but you told the lawyer that he was a good boy and after he helped, they didn't charge him at all.

Now, he's home and swears he will never make that mistake again. He even has a girl to make sure he doesn't.

You gave me the greatest gift anyone could give a mother.

Thank you and congratulations to you and your bride.

God bless you both.

Claire Atherton

P.S. Joe said you could keep the horse.

Earl showed that one to Jessie. She read it and smiled at Earl, knowing that they would keep this one.

All told, the amount of cash and bank drafts totaled an astonishing three thousand two hundred and fifty dollars.

The small boxes contained mostly small, expensive and inexpensive knick-knacks. There was one flat box that had Jessie intrigued, so Earl let her open it. When she did, she found, sitting in a protective layer of excelsior, a beautiful lilac patterned plate. At first, Jessie wondered if it was meant for display, but she found a note underneath the plate that read:

Dear Marshal,

When you and your bride have your new home picked out, send the enclosed card with your address and the full dinner set will be shipped to you.

I cannot thank you enough for what you did in returning our Emma to us.

Congratulations to you and your new wife.

Sincerely,

Alan Engle

Jessie asked who he was, and Earl had to think for a few seconds before he remembered the case. The little girl had been taken hostage in a failed stage robbery. Earl had tracked the robbers to a remote cabin and had literally smoked out the three men from the cabin by blocking their stovepipe. It was four years earlier and he believed, as he always did, that he was just doing his job.

The fact that he had almost forgotten the incident was a measure of just how big an impact he had made in people's lives.

Earl asked, "So, Dan, how come all these people knew we were getting married? We didn't even set a date until last week."

"The Dallas Herald started with a story about the kidnapping attempt on Teresa O'Toole. Then they wrote about the mission itself and included a story about your pending wedding. The stories were picked up by other papers in the state. We began getting mail when you left the second time with Pete. It was showing up in such volumes that we told the post office to just hang onto them and we'd pick them up on the way out. We had planned to visit before you caught up with Elmer. By the way, can I assume that Elmer didn't have a pleasant experience during the arrest? I'd be disappointed if you tell me he didn't."

"Among other things, I can tell you he didn't want to get on a horse when we took him in. It was too bad he had his hands cuffed behind his back when we did."

"Still not enough, was it?"

"Nope."

"Well, I think we'll be getting mail for the next few weeks. I'll wait till it stops and then send it to you in Kansas City."

"That'll work. Thanks, Dan."

Earl and Jessie finally learned from Pete that the reception they got in town was almost spontaneous. The minister had arranged for the organist, but the rest of it was simply put together by a loose committee of residents of Hopewell for the man who had rid them of Sheriff Burton and had brought a great deal of pride to the town for his accomplishments.

———

The afternoon finally faded into early evening. Ada Mitchell had made a list of thank you notes they would need to write while Lydia Crawford consolidated the money and drafts and put them into one of the empty knick-knack boxes.

Dan and Ed then made their farewells before they returned to Hopewell with Pete and Barbara. They'd be leaving in the morning with Elmer in the wagon to make the long, bumpy ride t Fort Worth. The Mitchells were the last to depart, giving hugs and handshakes as appropriate to the newlyweds.

Finally, Earl and Jessie were allowed to leave the main house and go to their temporary home. Earl opened the door and scooped Jessie into his arms. His stitches had been removed the day before and his shoulder was a little stiff but had healed nicely.

He carried her into the house and closed the door with his foot. While she was trapped in his arms, he kissed her, not an unexpected nor unwelcome event. He set her down and Jessie locked the door, then she led him quickly to the bedroom to make him fulfill his promise to take her out of her silk dress.

––––––

The newlyweds lived in the small house for another ten days as they prepared for their new life in Kansas City and Earl's new job.

They would go into Hopewell occasionally, being greeted with smiles and handshakes, but they also made another trip to Mount Pleasant to improve his wardrobe. They stayed overnight in the hotel and took a leisurely return ride. Jessie said she'd be improving her wardrobe when they arrived in Kansas City and was excited because she knew how big the city was and it had much to offer in the way of clothing stores.

––––––

Earl finally had to depart for his training. Between his training and the time that he'd have to spend in Kansas City at his new office, he would be gone for a month. They had spent so much time together the past two weeks, most people would have been happy for some time apart, but that wasn't the case for Earl and Jessie.

As they stood together in the barn with Target saddled, Jessie wept, and Earl was torn by the imminent separation from his wife.

But he knew it was time to leave, so he finally mounted Target, and after walking him out of the barn, he set him to a trot to the end of the access road, turned and waved to Jessie before he rode north, then passed through Hopewell and headed to the nearest railroad depot at Clarksville another twenty-seven miles north.

———

He took the train to the training center and was warmly welcomed by the staff. He was the only student at the time, so he could compress the training to two weeks, which suited his overwhelming desire to return to Jessie.

After he had completed his accelerated training, he took the train to Kansas City where he met each of the assigned deputy marshals. Even though he was younger than all but three of them, there was no petty jealousy. His exploits were well-documented, and his affable manner of management was appreciated.

The biggest surprise when he was there was when he started the search for their new home. He thought it would be difficult to find a home in the fast-moving housing market in Kansas City with its rapidly growing population, but the previous marshal, upon retiring to his family home outside of New Orleans, had left instructions for the realtor to offer the house to his replacement first, and only if he refused the purchase could the agent sell it on the open market. He also said that the house would be sold to the new marshal for what he had paid for it, $950.

The amount was well less what the market would have brought, so the agent was disappointed when Earl bought the house with a draft on his new Kansas City bank account. The account still had a balance of almost seven thousand dollars after the purchase. They wouldn't have to buy any furniture either. But what really made the house special was that it had steam heat with radiators. The same boiler provided hot running water to the kitchen and the two bathrooms that even had water closets. He doubted if he'd be able to pry Jessie out of the tub, not that he wouldn't enjoy the attempt.

Jessie was always on his mind, and it was with eager anticipation that he boarded the last train for Clarksville and arrived in Texas fourteen hours later. He had packed minimally for the trip and had intentionally not sent a telegram to Jessie letting her know of his early departure. He hadn't even told her of his rapid completion of training in his letters to her because he wanted to surprise her.

When his train slowed as it arrived in Clarksville, he leapt from the train at the depot, trotted across the platform and jogged quickly to the livery where Target had enjoyed his three weeks of leisure. He was a man on a mission, and to him a much more enjoyable one than *The Mission*.

When he mounted Target, he could tell that the horse wanted to run, so Earl let him stretch his legs. The gelding ate up the miles, even though he had slowed Target down to a more pleasant medium trot after his initial surge. It was almost nine at night when he began the ride and he passed through Mount Pleasant at midnight. He and Target didn't slow down as his horse seemed to sense his eagerness, just not the reason for it.

He passed through Hopewell at three o'clock in the morning and just twenty minutes later, Target was turned into the access road of the family ranch.

Even though he was anxious to see his wife, he owed it to Target to see to his welfare, so after dismounting, Earl led him into the barn, removed his tack, then brushed him down and poured his feed bin full of oats then made sure the trough was full.

He then took a deep breath and wearing a smile that hadn't left his face since leaving Hopewell, he walked to the small house. Jessie had told him she'd be waiting for him there rather than her parents' home when he had gone to training because it was their home until they moved, and she belonged to him now and not her mother and father.

He stepped quietly onto the porch, slowly opened the door and closed it noiselessly. He sat down on the couch, removed his boots and jacket, then undressed, leaving his clothes in the front room before he slipped down the hallway. He turned into the bedroom and saw Jessie's sleeping face in the moonlight and almost melted before he carefully pulled up the quilt and slowly slid beneath the covers to join her.

As he lowered his head onto the pillow beside her face, Jessie's eyes suddenly popped open. He didn't know it, but she had been dreaming about him when he had slid in next to her, creating a moment of confusion until she felt his arms wrap around her and she saw his eyes lock onto hers.

Earl smiled and whispered, "You're the one, Jessie."

EPILOGUE

The next two weeks were busy as they prepared for departure. They had a freight company arrive to pack and ship some of the things they would be taking with them to Kansas City. They decided to take four horses with them. Earl took Target and the gray gelding he decided to call Steel. Jessie brought Butter and a brown mare she hadn't named yet.

There was a tearful departure with the two sets of parents but promises of future visits to their grandchildren.

They stopped in Hopewell before going to Clarksville and made their farewells to Pete and Barbara who could be always counted on to be in close proximity.

With their goodbyes finished, Earl and Jessie finally rode out of Hopewell. As they left their hometown, each turned in the saddle at the receding buildings and wondered if they would ever return.

———

When they arrived in Kansas City, Jessie was thrilled with the new house, and even though it had a full set of china, they mailed the card for the more meaningful set. The house was just a block from the marshal's office, so Earl didn't ride Target as often as he wished, but he did manage to sneak in two or three missions every year. His office was regarded as one of the best in the service, and Earl remained in charge of the office, despite offers of promotion.

———

Jessie's worries about not being able to have a child were dissolved when she joyfully revealed her pregnancy to Earl just three months after their wedding. She delivered their first child, a boy they named Nathan a year after they had arrived in Kansas City and their daughter, Sarah, was born a year later.

In 1880, after meeting with Earl and Jessie for six months and having copies of all the official documents, Barbara Procter, whose husband Pete had been selected to join Earl on his staff as a United States Deputy Marshal, wrote her book, **The Mission**, which she published as B.W. Procter at the recommendation of the publisher. The book became a best seller in the United States and England, although it took some stern letters from Barbara to her publisher in Britain to convince him that the book was not fiction. It was even selling well in Australia.

Both sets of parents fulfilled their promise and visited often to watch their grandchildren grow. Over the next decade as each of their parents passed on, Earl and Jessie decided to hold onto the farm and ranch but leased the properties to tenants until the children were old enough to decide for themselves what they wanted to do with the family legacies.

———

When Nathan and Sarah reached adulthood, Nathan and his bride Lillian moved to Hopewell and took possession of the ranch but Sarah and her new husband, John, stayed in Kansas City, so Earl and Jessie sold the farm and gave the money to Sarah.

It was on a visit to the ranch in October of 1921 when they were visiting their grandchildren, that Earl suffered a stroke. Jessie never left his side until he finally passed away on the last day of the month.

She was sitting on his bed and looking into his still warm, loving eyes and each of them knew he wasn't going to be with her much longer. Before he slid from life, he had looked deeply into those brown, tear-filled eyes with the purple streaks, seen the love behind them, then reached up with his shaking hand, then caressed her lined face with his fingertips and whispered one more time, "You are the one."

———

Earl's funeral was held in Hopewell two days later and was attended by many friends and relatives. He was lying peacefully in his casket on the very spot where he and Jessie had been married forty-seven years earlier.

All the praises and glowing words had been orated, the last hymn had been sung, and the final prayers had been said.

When the formal ceremony was finally over, the church remained full, but silent as Jessie left the front row pew, walked quietly to the casket and looked down at her husband's peaceful face.

She slowly removed her amethyst necklace that had never been taken off since the day Earl had hung it around her neck, laid it on his chest and touched his cheek saying, "Since I was ten, you were always the one."

Jessie passed away in her sleep that night.

HOPEWELL

1	Rock Creek	12/26/2016
2	North of Denton	01/02/2017
3	Fort Selden	01/07/2017
4	Scotts Bluff	01/14/2017
5	South of Denver	01/22/2017
6	Miles City	01/28/2017
7	Hopewell	02/04/2017
8	Nueva Luz	02/12/2017
9	The Witch of Dakota	02/19/2017
10	Baker City	03/13/2017
11	The Gun Smith	03/21/2017
12	Gus	03/24/2017
13	Wilmore	04/06/2017
14	Mister Thor	04/20/2017
15	Nora	04/26/2017
16	Max	05/09/2017
17	Hunting Pearl	05/14/2017
18	Bessie	05/25/2017
19	The Last Four	05/29/2017
20	Zack	06/12/2017
21	Finding Bucky	06/21/2017
22	The Debt	06/30/2017
23	The Scalawags	07/11/2017
24	The Stampede	07/20/2017
25	The Wake of the Bertrand	07/31/2017
26	Cole	08/09/2017
27	Luke	09/05/2017
28	The Eclipse	09/21/2017
29	A.J. Smith	10/03/2017
30	Slow John	11/05/2017
31	The Second Star	11/15/2017
32	Tate	12/03/2017
33	Virgil's Herd	12/14/2017
34	Marsh's Valley	01/01/2018
35	Alex Paine	01/18/2018
36	Ben Gray	02/05/2018

37	War Adams	03/05/2018
38	Mac's Cabin	03/21/2018
39	Will Scott	04/13/2018
40	Sheriff Joe	04/22/2018
41	Chance	05/17/2018
42	Doc Holt	06/17/2018
43	Ted Shepard	07/13/2018
44	Haven	07/30/2018
45	Sam's County	08/15/2018
46	Matt Dunne	09/10/2018
47	Conn Jackson	10/05/2018
48	Gabe Owens	10/27/2018
49	Abandoned	11/19/2018
50	Retribution	12/21/2018
51	Inevitable	02/04/2019
52	Scandal in Topeka	03/18/2019
53	Return to Hardeman County	04/10/2019
54	Deception	06/02/2019
55	The Silver Widows	06/27/2019
56	Hitch	08/21/2019
57	Dylan's Journey	09/10/2019
58	Bryn's War	11/06/2019
59	Huw's Legacy	11/30/2019
60	Lynn's Search	12/22/2019
61	Bethan's Choice	02/10/2020